ANOTHER DAY'S PAIN

ANOTHER DAY'S PAIN

A ROCKSBURG NOVEL

K. C. CONSTANTINE

THE MYSTERIOUS PRESS
NEW YORK

ANOTHER DAY'S PAIN

Mysterious Press
An Imprint of Penzler Publishers
58 Warren Street
New York, N.Y. 10007

First Mysterious Press edition

Interior design by Maria Fernandez

Library of Congress Control Number: 2023919089

Cloth ISBN: 978-1-61316-483-9
eBook ISBN: 978-1-61316-484-6

10 9 8 7 6 5 4 3 2 1

Printed in the United States of America
Distributed by W. W. Norton & Company

"If you ain't here now, you can forget there and then 'cause you ain't gonna get past this."

—Anonymous

JUNE 2003

"**A**re you who wants to 302 this person?

"Yes."

"And you're a police officer? Got some ID?"

Carlucci held out his shield and ID case.

"Carlucci, Ruggiero? Am I pronouncing it correctly?"

"Yes."

"Did you say she's your mother, or was that somebody else said that?"

"That was me."

"Your mother?"

"I just said that."

"And you're here to—"

"Start a 302 against her, yes. I am. She hit a police officer, in our kitchen, while I was standing right there. Hit him in the back of

1

the head with a cast iron frying pan. With the edge of my eight-inch pan, she fucking hits him in the head!"

"Did you arrest her?"

"What? No. The officer she hit, he was on the floor, his head . . . he was bleeding. Jesus. He wasn't just any police officer, he was my friend. I invited him in. We weren't inside more than a couple minutes, she comes in the kitchen, asks me who he is and what's he doing in her house, and he asked me where the glasses were, and I pointed to one on the drainboard, he took a step toward it, next thing I know she grabs the pan off the stove, turns around and—Jesus Christ, he went down like he was shot! And all I was thinking was get down there and make sure his head didn't move. Called for a bus, and I looked up at her and she was smiling. She was fucking smiling!"

Mrs. Carlucci piped up, "He's always swearing like that, he got no respect for me or nobody else, he just starts Jesus Christ this, Jesus Chris that, which I could understand maybe if he went to Mass every once in a while—not every Sunday like I do, but at least once a month, you know—"

"Don't you dare start on me about church. Don't you dare."

"But not him, no, just Christmas and Easter and weddings and funerals, that's all he goes to. Only got one suit, wears it every time he goes to something like that."

"Ma. Ma!"

"What?"

"Stop talking!"

"Oh that's good, why don't you say what you really wanna say, huh? You know, hey Ma, shut the fuck up. That's what he usually says, and watch what he's gonna say now, go ahead, say it, I dare you."

"Ma, I have never said those words to you, never in my life."

"See, I knew that's what he was gonna say, that's what he always says after he tells me shut the fuck up. Ha, ha, gotcha, Ruggiero. Gotcha a good one. Go ahead let me hear what you got to say now."

"Where the fuck's the bus Fran's on?"

"Where the fuck's the bus Fran's on?"

"Stop it!"

"Stop what?"

"Stop repeating what I say."

"Is that another of her behaviors?"

"Yeah. People used to tell me she was different when my dad was alive. Uh-uh, this is her, this is the way she's always been. Ask her she'll say it was my fault."

"It was! You just never wanna admit it was you distracted him."

"Which led to what?"

"This kid on a motorcycle, goddamn kid, he smashed into us, right into where my husband was sitting—he was driving. And this one here, he tries to say he was never there."

"As many times as I told you I wasn't—you still don't believe me. I was not there!"

"Well if you wasn't, hows come I'm a widow?"

JULY 2011

.

Carlucci was ignoring Mrs. Bernadette Caluso, even though her distended belly nudged his desk with every inhale. Three times in the last two months, he'd wiped her spit off his face. He was sure she intended to spray his face only once, he'd give her that. But the other two times? Well, he was sitting, he could wait better than she could. She was rocking from one foot to the other, no doubt trying to ease the pain in her knees from her weight.

"Hey, how long am I s'posed to stand here? I know you know I know your badge number. You're just sitting there, you ain't doing nothing."

"I'm thinking."

"You're thinking? Oh, that's a good one. You listen to me, Carlucci, whatever you think my Bobby was doing, he was with me the whole day, swear to God."

Carlucci's fingers gave him away. He was drumming the William Tell Overture on his mouse pad. Until Franny Perfetti told him the name of the music, he'd thought it was just the theme song for the Lone Ranger TV show he watched lying on his belly in the Caprarras' living room.

" Hey. Drummer boy. You listening to me?"

Carlucci nodded, but he wasn't. He was wondering if he could find out on the Internet exactly how the Lone Ranger reloaded his silver bullets, or how anybody reloaded ammo in those days of yesteryear, questions that never entered his mind when he was lying on the floor in the Caprarras' cramped living room, happily watching the Masked Man solve yet another prairie felony.

The last time he'd tried to talk to Balzic about reloading in the 1870s, he got nowhere. Balzic was more interested in telling him that what everybody thought they knew about the Texas Rangers was hype. The Rangers, Balzic said, were mostly hired guns, making Texas safe for white people. Everybody else, Indians, Mexicans, freed slaves, they just shot them. And lots of times, somebody was there with a camera.

"Long as you're looking things up," Balzic said, "dig a little into that Ranger famous for ambushing Bonnie and Clyde. His posse never identified themselves. Never said drop your guns, never said get outta the car with your hands up, never said they had an arrest warrant. Not one word. Just started shooting."

Carlucci wondered for a few moments why Balzic had gone off in that direction. All Carlucci wanted to know was if people could reload ammunition back then. He thought he'd made that clear. Hell, he hadn't even asked about the Lone Ranger's bullets being silver.

Instead, he said, "Hey, Mario, say hello to Ruthie for me, will you?"

Balzic cleared his throat, or tried to. After a long moment, he said, "Don't think that's a good idea."

"Huh? Saying hello to Ruthie's not a good idea? What's up with that?"

"Uh, a couple days ago, I asked Ruth, what's up with our girls them? I haven't heard from either one of my girls for a while now. Long story short, the older one, she started having some kinda thing with her husband, started talking to a clinical psychologist, counselor, something. Next thing Ruth knew, that one said she talked her sister into going in with her."

Carlucci tried to think if he'd ever heard Balzic talk about his daughters without saying their names. Wasn't sure. Thought it was weird, but let it go.

Balzic sighed. Looked at the wall behind Carlucci. "Thing is, turns out real quick they stopped talking about their husbands. Uh, started talking about us."

"Us? Which us, you and Ruthie?"

"No, us. You and me, that us."

"Huh? You gotta explain that, Mario, I'm not getting it."

"Well, I wasn't getting it either. Ruthie, finally, she said to me, you know you need to call your daughters. You don't need to hear this from me, you need to hear it from them."

Carlucci squinted at Balzic.

"Okay, you asked for it, here goes. Turns out my girls been holding a grudge against us. You and me, that's the us. For a long time. Turns out, talking to that counselor, the both of them found out what the other one's been thinking and feeling, and after all this time, they found out they were both thinking and feeling the same stuff."

"C'mon, Mario, quit stalling, this ain't like you, get to it."

"You ain't gonna like it—"

"Mario, man, c'mon."

"They think when they were young, about when you were a rookie, that all the love and respect they thought they should've been getting from me I was giving to you. Turns out I spent a lotta time talking about me and you, and about you by yourself. And they took that all in, stored it up, and far as they were concerned, you were the son I never had. Telling you, Rugs, I had no idea. Never did I think I was giving you more than I was giving them, but sure as God made wine, that's what they think now. And after all these years holding it in, never even talking about it with each other until they got into this therapist's office and, man, they are really, really pissed about this."

"Okay, Mario, okay, I get most of it. But there's one part I don't get. Two sisters? Growing up together? And never talked about any of this with each other until they got into that office? Years after the fact, hell, decades—they're gonna try to sell that? You and Ruthie, okay, you might've bought it, but all due respect, they're your daughters, I know, I know, and Ruthie's, too, but if they were sitting right here, in front of you and me, and tried to sell that to me? I'm not even gonna apologize, Mario, I'd look them straight in the eyes and I'd say, that's a crock. And you girls, you know it's a crock, and don't ever think you're gonna make me believe that's true. 'Cause it ain't."

Balzic shrugged, turned around, left without another word.

Carlucci stared at his friend's back as he walked away.

Mrs. Caluso's voice snapped Carlucci back into the now. Started telling Carlucci her Bobby was just two days shy of his eighteenth birthday.

"What? He's two days to what? His birthday? What's that have to do with him stealing the car?"

She started talking, just rambling, but Carlucci tuned her out. Her Bobby had spent almost as much time in juvenile detention in the last four years as he had in school. Carlucci had himself arrested Bobby twice, once after he'd tried to sell a case of WD-40 to a mechanic who was installing a new muffler on Carlucci's city-owned Chevy, while Carlucci was sitting not five yards away flipping through car magazines. When he asked Bobby what he thought he was doing, Bobby said he was trying to raise money to send the high school band to the Orange Bowl parade on New Year's Day.

Bobby stuck to that story in Family Court until the judge said his youngest son played trumpet in the band, and if the band was going anywhere over the Christmas to New Year's break his son would've mentioned it, "because I'd already told him we were all going skiing that week up Seven Springs."

"Well, maybe I got a little mixed up about which New Year's they was gonna go," Bobby said, "but I ain't mixed up about what he did to me. He entrappted me."

The judge said there was only one "t" in entrapped and then gave Bobby a pro forma lecture about blaming others for his own misdeeds. He ordered him to report to a Juvenile Probation Officer once a month for the next four months and to do exactly what the JPO told him to do. Bobby reported only twice, so the same judge issued a bench warrant for his arrest, and, hardly glancing at the pre-sentence report, ordered Bobby to serve four months in the county juvenile detention center.

The second time Carlucci arrested Bobby involved a tire he'd stolen from his Uncle Jimmy's wheel balancing and alignment shop. About twenty yards from his mother's house, Bobby accidentally rolled the tire over a crushed Pepsi bottle, which sent it bouncing into the marigolds in the front yard of their next-door neighbor, Mrs. Ambrose. She'd been pulling weeds when the tire wobbled past her. She thought Bobby bouncing the tire past her was a distraction so an accomplice could slip around to her back door and rob her. She whacked Bobby with her hand hoe, causing a nasty gash on the back of his thumb. His mother witnessed this from the bathroom on her second floor, where she was standing trying to wipe herself after having an attack of "loose bowels ."

That's what she'd told the first responder, rookie Patrolman Allan Lukosh, recently discharged back into civilian life after three years in the army, most of it with the military police in Germany. During his time there, he'd never had to calm two women, one middle aged and the other elderly, who sounded and looked like they wanted to kill each other. He called for backup.

Carlucci was getting ready to bite into a meatball hoagie when the dispatcher responded to Lukosh's call by asking if anybody was available to back him up. Carlucci's hoagie was getting soggier by the minute; he told the dispatcher he was on his way.

When he got on scene he couldn't hear Lukosh over the women shouting, so he led Lukosh aside. Lukosh said he knew he needed help when the women threatened to vomit on each other's grave—or crap on it, he wasn't sure which. He also wasn't sure how many times each one swore God would strike the other one dead before morning. Carlucci told Lukosh okay, he got it, then went and stood between the women and said he wasn't going to allow any killing that day, with or without God's help.

Mrs. Ambrose wanted Carlucci to arrest "these goddamn Gypsies trying to rob me." Mrs. Caluso wanted him to arrest Mrs. Ambrose for aggravated assault.

"Mother of God, if you'd get your cackeracks fixed, you could see we ain't Gypsies; we live next door."

"You don't even know how to say what's wrong with my eyes, so shut up, you. I know Gypsies when I see 'em."

Carlucci said if everybody would stop talking for a couple minutes, he wouldn't have to arrest either one of them, but then Mrs. Ambrose tried to spit on Bobby, blowing her top denture half out of her mouth. Then Mrs. Caluso picked up the tire and tried to heave it at Mrs. Ambrose. She missed by two feet, stumbled backward from the effort, fell on her hip, and immediately started screaming. She pulled her hand out from under her hip, held it up, screaming louder when she saw her little finger was bent backward toward her elbow and swelling fast.

The tire came to a stop against Mrs. Ambrose's downspout, snapping a bracket and popping it away from the house.

"Now look what youns did. Youns busted my gutter. Who's gonna pay for that?"

Carlucci told Lukosh to push the downspout back against the house, which he did easily, but as soon as he let go, the whole pipe clattered down in three pieces.

"Youns know how much them plumbers charge? Just to park their truck? I ain't paying for that."

"Think you're probably gonna want a roofer, not a plumber."

"You, police, you, you shut up."

Carlucci told Lukosh to write it up and send a copy to the city engineer. "Make sure she gets a copy," he said, nodding toward Mrs. Ambrose, "and try to make her understand the city'll pay for it, but don't give it more than five, six minutes, okay?"

Turning to Mrs. Caluso and Bobby, he said, "You and you, get in the back of my car and I don't wanna hear nothing outta either one of you."

He drove them to the Conemaugh Hospital ER, where, after they'd been treated, he had to listen to Mrs. Caluso say the city better pay their ER bill because Carlucci couldn't tell attempted murder from aggravated assault.

"Apples and oranges."

"What?"

"Whether the city pays your bill or not has nothing to do with whatever I write you up for."

"Oh no, wait, wait, the city gotta pay. I can't pay those bills 'cause the bastards at public welfare, they suspendered my Medicaid. They said I was cheating them. I don't know how to cheat them—I only finished ninth grade. And anyways, I don't even know who it was that turned me in."

"Doesn't matter who it was, you're still talking apples and oranges."

"What is it with you—apples and oranges? What they gotta do with anything?"

"I'm trying to tell you you're putting two things together that don't have anything to do with one another, that's all."

"Well why don't you just say that?"

"Next time it comes up, Mrs. Caluso, I will."

At the next city council meeting, Solicitor Tom McKelvey advised council to pay for Mrs. Ambrose's new gutter and down-spout and the Calusos' ER bill for her broken finger and her son's sutures and tetanus shot, but Councilman Egidio Figulli, acting as interim chairman of the Safety Committee during Mayor Angelo Bellotti's annual vacation, said the committee had not received an Unusual Incident Report and he wasn't going to approve paying any bills without seeing an UIR no matter what the solicitor said.

The next day, Patrolman Lukosh hesitantly approached Carlucci in the parking lot and wanted to know if he'd screwed up and if he did how could he make it right.

"You give a copy of your report to the city engineer like I told you? Send one to each woman? One to the chief? One to records? Back it up in your personal file?"

Lukosh nodded six times.

"Well so did I, so you got nothing to worry about."

"You sure nobody's pissed off about something I did?"

"What'd I just say?"

"I know what you said, but I'm, you know, I'm still trying to, uh, find my way around, find my way around here."

"Listen, man, I was born here, raised here, I still live in the house I was raised in. And except for the three years I was in the army, and the one year I worked at Kmart, the only thing I've ever done is be a cop right here. If anybody's pissed off at anybody, it's Councilman Figulli and I'm who he's pissed off at. Don't have nothing to do with you. He's been on me to retire for the last two, three years."

"And you don't want to retire?"

"Nah. And before you start believing the rumors, I'm gonna tell why I ain't gonna retire. My mother's in Mamont. Know what that is?"

Lukosh nodded. "I think."

"Don't think. It's a mental hospital 'bout fifteen miles south of Pittsburgh, and she's in the general pop there. Almost killed a cop, friend of mine—well, used to be. I started her out in Mental Health here, you know, on a 302 'cause of what she did to him. Then she kept getting more detention for I forget exactly what, and then she smacked somebody where she is now, got another thirty days. And then she hit somebody else, got six more months."

"Jesus."

"The guy she almost killed, the cop, he don't speak to me anymore, and I don't blame him, 'cause he ain't been right since. All he does is talk, constantly. Makes everybody crazy. Except when he sees me. Me, he don't talk to, he just stares at me. Breaks my heart. And the reason I keep working is I'm building my pension as big as I can get it because if they ever fuck up and let my mother out, I'm gonna need a pile of money to pay people to watch her. So that ought to take care of all the rumors you're gonna hear about me, and that's why I'm not gonna retire on the say-so of one big mouth councilman."

"Oh. Okay. Thanks for telling me."

———

After Bobby served his four months, he'd started joyriding in cars he claimed he was road testing for his uncle. His uncle scoffed that anybody would think he'd let Bobby road test a tricycle. In fact, Bobby's previous stay in juvenile detention was for crashing an '89 Ford into a maple tree in Westfield Township, concussing himself and totaling the car. A state trooper arrived at the scene, woke him up, and asked to see his license, owner's card, and liability insurance card. Bobby tried "to say somebody probably stole them while he was knocked out, 'cause nobody can hear nothing when you're out cold." Didn't take long for that logic to get around the courthouse.

The trooper ran the plates, and after hearing the trooper's testimony, the same Family Court judge sentenced Bobby to serve three to eight months and to pay restitution to the car owner and to his uncle. Bobby got partly off the hook because the car owner's insurance company won a judgment over Uncle Jimmy's insurance company. The judge then had a change of heart and thought it would be good for Uncle Jimmy to hire Bobby to sweep the shop floor, take the garbage out, and so on, become acquainted with the responsibilities of a job—as long as it didn't involve driving. Uncle Jimmy agreed because he thought it might shut Bobby's mother up for a couple weeks. Instead, Mrs. Caluso somehow twisted the idea that Bobby's wages were to settle Uncle Jimmy's loss to the other insurance company, and from that she concluded that her baby boy would be sweeping floors and dumping rubbish for the rest of his life.

"He's putting in so many hours at that goddamn garage he'll never get to go to college."

Carlucci stopped drumming.

"Probably be better if he finished high school first."

"Huh? Was that a wisecrack? What you just said?"

"No. Listen, your relative did not authorize him to take the car, and he saw him take that car, and when I happened to see the car, Bobby was at the Dairy Queen, leaning on the roof, talking to a coupla girls. You need to stop lying for this kid."

"He's my baby! I'm never gonna stop lying for him—and I'm not lying now, you're getting me all mixed up."

"Go home and think about what you just said, okay? You'll be notified when his hearing comes up—don't know why I'm talking, you know the drill. Meantime, juvey's full, so I'm gonna have to take him down the county."

"The county jail? You can't put him in there! Not with all those criminals!"

"Mrs. Caluso, you don't leave now I'm gonna take you with him. Go home, I'm not gonna tell you again."

"You Carlucci you, honest to God, you always had it in for him, you act like he's a killer or something."

"Nobody's acting like he's a killer, don't exaggerate. He's a thief. But a big reason he's a thief, Mrs. Caluso, is 'cause you never figured out sometimes you're supposed to say no."

"Oh oh, it's my fault now, huh? I taught him to steal."

"That's not what I said. I said you never told him no, so the kid's never had to figure out where he stops and the rest of the world starts—I don't know why I'm wasting time talking here."

Carlucci pulled Bobby up by his arm, turned him around, and cuffed him.

Twenty minutes later he was doing the paperwork with the duty district justice in Night Court in the Conemaugh County jail.

"This one looks familiar," DJ Tom Genova said.

Carlucci shrugged. "Been through the system a buncha times. Three for sure I know of. Done at least two out of the last four in juvey detention, probably some of it out of county."

"And still two days till you're eighteen? That definitely makes you a juvenile, but yet here you are, in big-boy jail."

"I think he ought to be segregated at least till his birthday since it's only a couple days off. I don't wanna have to answer for what might happen he gets in the general pop, do you? Smart mouth as he got, he could get killed in here."

Genova agreed and then he and Carlucci completed the paperwork. As a corrections officer started to lead Bobby away, Genova ordered the CO to segregate Bobby for at least seventy-two hours and to make a note in his duty log that Detective Carlucci, the arresting officer, was a witness to that order.

Bobby suddenly came alive when he heard the DJ's order to segregate him. "Hey, I ain't going in no solitary, aw no, nothing doing."

"You been watching too many movies," Genova said. "Every cell in here's a solitary. Haven't had to double anybody up for more than a week now. All the bad guys must be on vacation. Besides, until you make bail the last choice you had was whether or not to steal the car."

The CO started to lead Bobby away. Bobby stiffened his legs trying to dig in his heels. The CO was a head taller than Bobby, probably fifty pounds heavier, well skilled in take-alongs. He slipped his left arm under Bobby's right and took hold of his collar, stretching Bobby's arm upward, lifting him up on his toes.

By the time they reached the door out of the DJ's office, Bobby was hopping to keep pace with the CO, who said, "Two ways to do everything in here, and you just learned them both."

Carlucci shook his head just looking at the kid, made a note of when the arraignment ended, 20:32, nodded good night to DJ Genova, and left, picking up both his weapons from the gate guard's gun box.

Carlucci remembered all this because he no sooner turned the ignition key than the city dispatcher ordered him to report to the station. The dispatcher said nothing else, making Carlucci immediately suspicious.

"Go to channel three," Carlucci said.

"Negative. I repeat: 10-25 this station."

"I repeat: switch channels and put me through to the chief."

Long pause. "Negative. Chief says urgent you return."

What kind of bullshit is he gonna stick me with now?

Carlucci gave the dispatcher a 10-4 and said he was en route because he couldn't remember the 10-code for being en route. He hadn't worked patrol in a year. He was pissed off, as usual, at the city council for not hiring more bodies, pissed at all the married men with young kids in the department who thought a vacation wasn't a vacation unless it happened in August, pissed at Nowicki because for all five years Nowicki had been chief he still didn't seem to get that schools were closed in June and July as well as August, or that having children was no better reason for taking vacations in August than not having children was a reason for working double shifts to cover for all the patrolmen who annually spent two weeks in Disney World or Land, whatever the hell it's called.

Carlucci reminded himself to arrange a meet with William Raiford, the department's other detective, also unmarried, to see if there wasn't some way they could reach Nowicki's sense of fairness about this vacation crap, otherwise they were going to get stuck with double shifts every August until they retired or died, whichever came first.

Who else is out here tonight? What car am I in? Thirty-two? Who was in thirty-one? That rookie? The hell's his name? DeRenzi? DeRenzo? The hell's he doing now? Why didn't they call him? Aw fuck me, man, Nowicki, I know what you're doing!

Carlucci, driving angry fast, took about six minutes to get from the jail to the station. There, he slowed down so as not to squeal the tires pulling off the street, spent five minutes collecting his gear, strolled across the parking lot, and took the steps into the station as though they were covered with oil, ice, or mud. He eased the door open, tiptoed past the dispatcher who was talking to a nuisance Carlucci recognized and slipped past Nowicki's office door. Nowicki, his back to the door, was on the phone, rocking in his chair.

Sometimes, Carlucci thought, the little things go your way. The rest of the time on the job, life was just one shitty thing after another, interrupted once in a great while by something stupidly, freakishly, hellaciously dangerous.

At his desk, Carlucci pulled up the template for Unusual Incident Reports, filled in the blanks, sent one copy to his own file, sent another to records, printed one, which he carried into the chief's office, where he faked surprise at the sight of Nowicki in civvies, still talking on the phone.

"Oh, sorry, Chief, didn't know you were in here. Hope I'm not disturbing you."

"Call you back. Rugs, where the hell you been? You answered a call, must've been twenty minutes ago. Longer. You telling me you just got here?"

"No, sir, I would never try to tell you a lie like that. I've been filling out my UIR. Here's a copy, sir, for your very own personal file. I think I sent one to you, you know, electronically? But in case it didn't get here, I thought, you being you and me being me, I'd hand deliver one personally. Sir."

"Oh will you stop the sir bullshit."

"Be glad to stop the sir bullshit when it occurs to you that June and July are as much a part of summer as August. And when you convey that info to all the married patrolmen. The ones with the brats who will bust their precious little guts if they don't get to go to Dizzy World this same month every year. Sir."

"Rugs, how many years you been busting my balls about this?"

"Oh, I don't know, sir, how many years you been chief? Five? No, wait. I guess I didn't really start until the department promoted another detective to sergeant. Which is when both of us—who both happen to be single, that is unmarried without children—until we both got our detecting heads together and discovered we were pulling all this extra goddamn patrol duty every August. I guess that's when I really started busting your balls about it. Sir."

"Rugs, gimme a break, council's not gonna hire anybody until somebody retires—they don't have the money. How many ways you want me to say that?"

"Oh, wait. Who was that out there with me tonight? What's his name, DeRenzo? Who retired before he got hired?"

"DeRenzi. Special case. I'm not gonna talk about him."

"Why? 'Cause somehow he just happens to be related to Figulli? Jesus Christ. Think the whole department doesn't know that? Nowicki, man, I've been a good soldier here. Not once in the five years you been chief have I ever jumped over your head. Had your back the whole way. But I'm getting too old for this patrol crap. Six days last week, six days this week, and why'd you call me in now, huh? As if I don't know."

Nowicki coughed to clear his throat. "You're the only one can handle her, Rugs."

"I knew it, I fucking knew it! My ass, the only one—I made a mistake, okay? How long you gonna make me pay for that?"

"I'm not making you pay for anything—"

"Aw man, come on, stop it! She didn't have nothing to do with you or this department. Tell me I'm wrong, go ahead. And how long ago was that anyway? I thought she was straightened out, man, what the fuck? You cannot believe that I knew she was gonna flip out on the job."

"Rugs, no way I'm gonna send that kid DeRenzi up there, and I don't care what you believe—I'm not making you pay for nothing 'cause of her. But put yourself in my chair. You sat here. You gonna tell me you'd send a rookie up there? Knowing what you know about her and you?"

"Her and me, huh? Okay, okay, but I'm telling you, Wick, this is it. I'm not doing this patrol shit next year."

Carlucci went back to his desk, grabbed up his gear bag, glad at least that Nowicki hadn't used the word "girlfriend." Even if he had, it wouldn't have had anything to do with Carlucci's real girlfriend, Fran Perfetti, who just happened to be Nowicki's cousin.

Girlfriend was what almost every member of the department had taken to calling Virginia Carpilotti, the "manic-depressive with psychotic episodes." At least that was the diagnosis the last time she was committed involuntarily. The time before that, a different shrink said she was "paranoid schizophrenic with delusional behavior."

All Carlucci knew was she'd been driving them all nuts for almost two years now, especially him because he'd made the mistake of vouching for her when she applied for a laborer's job in the city recreation department. Then, after a week on the job, she said it was time for her to get a suntan. So, just like the guys, she took her shirt off.

When her boss said she couldn't do that, she started screaming about equal employee regulations and threw a shovel ful of dirt at him. It took two patrolmen and three EMTs to get her to Mental Health. And none found any pleasure in the process, despite some saying afterward how good she looked, you know, really good, for how old she was. Without a shirt. Or a bra.

As he passed the dispatcher's window, Carlucci leaned in and said, "Know who was after her the last time? The Indians. The Cleveland Indians."

—

Virginia Carpilotti called herself the Virgin whenever she complained about her husband's behavior in bed. Her complaints had nothing to do with ability, with "erectile dysfunction" or anything else remotely similar. She was furious because he flat refused to do anything with her that involved sex. Despite her complaints, she lived with him in a four-story house on Norwood Hill. Carlucci also lived on the Hill—only, he liked to thank the God of roads and streets, his home was on the opposite end of the Hill from her.

The streets were arranged so that on alternating terraces down the hill, all the houses on the north side had as many as twenty or more steps up from the street to their front doors, depending on whether they had a porch, while those on the south side fronted the street with their cellars built into the hillside. Over the decades, many of the owners on the south side had added decks to the rear of their first floors.

Tony Carpilotti repeatedly believed the Virgin's promises that if he took her back this time it would be different: this time she would stay in the cellar and sleep on the single bed he'd brought for her from his mother's house. This time she would use the kitchen only when the girls were in school and not try to horn in on their meals. This time she would not rearrange the furniture. This time she would not litter the backyard with pots, pans, pencils, pens, clay pots, blankets, towels, soap, and whatever else she found to throw, as she'd done every other time she'd flown into a rage over some offense, real or imagined, from him, the girls, or the neighbors. And this time, like all the other times, she promised she would take her meds, even though they made her fat and kept her from having orgasms, which she claimed had been personally guaranteed to her by God. Almost as an afterthought she promised this time she wouldn't, cross her heart and hope to die, barge into his bedroom at night to demand to know why he wouldn't make love to her.

Each time, for a few weeks or even a month, she did as promised, but then, as she would later tell whichever cops responded to the call from one of her daughters or a neighbor, the meds were making her gain weight again and she hated herself when she was fat because nobody loved her when she was fat. So, she threw the lithium down the toilet and doubled up on the Wellbutrin, which helped her shed weight but also, to her ex-husband's misery, made her horny. Hornier. And up she would come from the cellar in the middle of the night to crawl onto his sleeping body and pound on his chest and scream that any man in his right mind would give a week's pay to make love to her.

"Christ, I look better than most of those flabby-ass movie stars, Uma what's-her-name or that skinny bitch George Clooney's dating—even that one in the new Bond film, she didn't look half as good as me! Make love to me, goddammit, what's wrong with you?"

Because Tony had never been athletic or even slightly interested in developing his body, he had to lie under her and take the pounding and the insults until his daughters heard the ruckus and rushed in to pull her off. Usually, that's when she'd accuse one or both of taking her place in his bed and would grab the one closest to her by the throat and while that one was doing her best to pry Virginia's hands off her neck, the other would run downstairs and call 911.

———

"Virginia, you got half the Hill awake, turn Sinatra down, please."

"Ouuu, look who's here, it's Juicy Carlucci. What's the matter, Juicy? Scared to look at me and listen to Frankie at the same time? You oughta be. My husband catches you looking at me, he'll beat the shit outta you."

"Virginia, c'mon, he hasn't been your husband for what is it now, ten months? Last time I talked to him, that's what he told me."

"Aw Carlucci, forget all that crap, c'mon, look at me—I'm beautiful. Ask my husband how beautiful I am. And he's still my husband, I don't give a shit what all that paperwork says. He can pretend we ain't married all he wants, but for me it's what God put together, no goddamn judge is gonna pound his little wooden hammer and ruin it!"

"Virginia, turn it down, please. These old people, they have enough trouble sleeping. C'mon, that's not nice to do that to them."

"What'd these geezers ever do for me? Trash me, that's what. I walk past them, they spit, call me a whore! And what do you say? Huh? Be nice, Virginia, be nice—you come on up here, Carlucci, I'll be real nice to you."

Carlucci didn't move.

"All right, you fucker, if that's the way you're gonna be, call the firemen, tell the bastards to smash my front door in, like they did last time. You know that's the only way you're getting up here."

She was partly right. There were no stairs up to the porch from the yard. If Carlucci couldn't talk her into turning down the volume on her stereo, the only way up was on ladders, and the last time he persuaded the VFD to try that approach, she pushed the ladder away as soon as a fireman got two steps up on it. Then when they put their shoulders into keeping it rigid against the rail, she showered them with a pot of hot linguini. The firemen still hadn't forgiven Carlucci for that. They ended up going through the front door with axes. But it took three of them plus two EMTs to get her into the ambulance.

"Virginia, you stop taking the lithium again?"

"Whatta you think? That shit makes me fat! I ain't never getting fat again! I hate getting fat! I hate *me* when I get fat!"

"So you stopped taking it, right?"

"Here's a thought. How 'bout you take it, Carlucci, huh?" She spun around and disappeared into the house. Seconds later she was back. She leaned over the railing and rained pills on him.

"Aw come on, Virginia, why'd you do that?"

"They're all yours, Carlucci. Skinny as you are? Probably been trying to gain weight your whole life, huh? Tell the truth, c'mon. You know what? I hate all you skinny bastards. Don't run, don't lift weights, eat any goddamn thing you want, you never gain a pound. All you skinny pricks. If God don't send you all to hell, it's probably 'cause he's a skinny prick himself."

"You know how much those pills cost Tony? Those things are expensive, Virginia, c'mon."

"Then you take them. Fatten you right up—they're generics anyway, don't cost practically nothing."

"I don't wanna fatten up, Virginia. Happy just the way I am."

"Oh bullshit, nobody's happy just the way they are. Look at all them TV shows, nobody's satisfied with what they got. Make over your house, make over your body, don't like your chin, get an implant, don't like your cottage cheesy ass, get it sucked right outta there. Weigh two fifty? They can make you lose a hunnert pounds. You're lying, Carlucci. You ain't happy just the way you are, that's bullshit."

"No, Virginia, I don't want to *be* anything else. Some*place* else, yeah. Like right now."

"Oh you're as fulla shit as Tony, happy just the way he is. N'yeh, n'yeh, n'yeh—here's Tony, he comes home, first thing he grabs is a beer, next thing it's the remote, and that's him, that's his whole life right there. Asked him one night to take me dancing, you'd think it was the start of World War Three, the Russians are coming, or who-ever. Who we fighting now? Can't keep up with them goddamn guys in Washington! C'mon, Carlucci, who we fighting now, I forget."

"Maybe you should start reading the paper or watching the news, Virginia, give you something else to think about—instead of yourself all the time."

"Aw fuck you, read the paper, Jesus. All I ever got from reading the paper was a headache. Who's killing who, who's stealing how much, who's going out of business, who's getting laid off—that's supposed to take my mind offa me? Blaaaaah."

"C'mon, Virginia, please, don't make me call the firemen, okay? I know from the last time, Tony's homeowner's got a five hundred deductible on it, and if I have to call the firemen and you do what you did last time? He's gonna get stuck for a new door again. Virginia? I know you know that."

"And what? I'm supposed to give a shit what he gets stuck with? Ha, that's a good one."

"Virginia, c'mon, you're not stupid."

"Ouu, Carlucci, better watch out, that almost sounded like a compliment."

"Virginia, listen to me, okay? You keep sticking Tony with all your bills, what do you think's gonna happen? Sooner or later, he's gonna tap out, I don't know why he hasn't already, but he's going to, where's that gonna leave you? I know he's still paying the mortgage here, he told me he was. But you tap him out? So he can't make the payments? Then what?"

"Tony's been poor-mouthing since he was in ninth grade. He got it socked away, don't you think he don't. Buys the cheapest beer there is, that Old Milwaukee whatever."

Carlucci sighed, shook his head. "Virginia, where is he anyway? I need to talk to him."

"Good luck finding him. Took the girls right after supper, and away they went. You think they tell me where they're going? Probably some motel."

"Aw, Virginia, stop it—you make it sound like Tony's messing with those girls, and I know that ain't happening, not in a million years."

"Yeah, right, like you would know."

"I mean it, Virginia, don't say things like that, Tony doesn't deserve that."

"Like you give a shit what's really going on in my house."

"It's not your house anymore—if it ever was. It's Tony's. And I'm through talking. Turn that boom-box off and put some clothes on."

"Or what?"

"Or I'm calling the firemen."

"Hey, Carlucci?"

"What?"

"Here's what I think of you and the firemen."

Carlucci didn't know what was coming but something was, so he hustled to get under the cover of the deck. Seconds later he could hear liquid hitting the grass.

"That's from me to you, Carlucci. Fresh pee-pee, right outta my practically brand new pussy."

"Aw shit," he said, switching on his radio.

"No, Carlucci, not shit. Pee."

He ID'd himself to the 911 dispatcher and gave his location. "I need a fire truck. With portable ladders, you hear? Not the ladder truck, understand? Whatever you do, do not send the ladder truck up here. And no sirens either, there's enough noise up here already."

Ten minutes later, Fire Chief Eddie Sitko, holding an aluminum extension ladder over his head, came down the narrow passage between the houses. Alone.

"Where's the rest of them?"

"Rest of who? Soon as they heard the address, all of a sudden they all got the shits. Fucking pussies. I gotta tell you, Carlucci, those guys came last time? They're still pissed at you. That hot spaghetti, it's gonna be a while before they get over that. Okay, let's get to it."

"Whoa, wait a minute, whatta you mean, let's get to it? You know how many guys it took last time?"

"I heard, yeah. But see, if you remember, I wasn't here. That's why it took four."

"Uh-uh, not four. Five. Three of your guys and two EMTs."

"As usual, Carlucci, you ain't listening. None of them was me."

"Chief, I know you take real good care of yourself, all that running, all that lifting weights, but you're older than Mario Balzic—I know for a fact he's eighty-four. I was at his last birthday."

Sitko laid the ladder down and adjusted one of the leg levelers so it would stand straight on the severe slope.

"You comparing me to Balzic? Get outta here, I'm in better shape today than he was when he was forty. He never took care of himself. The way he ate? It's a fucking miracle he's still alive."

"Uh-huh. All right, then forget about him. This is about me now. Just you here? There's no way I'm going up there, just you and me, uh-uh."

"Who asked you? Just hold the fucking ladder. Can you do that much? Or do I gotta call my wife?"

Carlucci groaned, shook his head. "You ever seen this woman? I mean have you ever actually laid eyes on her?"

"Hey, Carlucci, what do I have to see her for, she's a split-tail, okay? Think you can get your dago brain around that? Quit yakking, hold the ladder. Wasted enough time already."

Sitko hoisted the ladder and slammed it against the deck railing. Carlucci shook his head, steadied the bottom as Sitko charged up the ladder. He was two steps from going over the railing when Virginia appeared with a burning candle in each hand. Without a word, she tilted the candles.

Sitko howled. Dogs all over the hill started barking. He shook his hands and let go of the ladder. Virginia growled, grunted, shoved the ladder, and Sitko and the ladder came crashing backward. The heel of one of Sitko's boots smacked Carlucci in the temple. He was out when he hit the ground.

When he came to, the ladder was angled across his legs, he was sprawled across Sitko's legs, Sitko was groaning and squirming to get out from under him. Virginia was laughing maniacally. Carlucci cursed, struggled, pulled his legs out from under the ladder, rolled to his right.

Set off Sitko howling again. "Get off! Carlucci, get off me! Crazy fucking cunt."

Virginia stopped laughing long enough to say, "Crazy fucking chief."

On the boom-box, Frank Sinatra was singing "That Old Black Magic."

29

"Oh, Virginia, you did it now," Carlucci said, looking up at her and rubbing his head. She'd taken the sheer nightie off and was once again dancing, this time mostly in one place, near the railing, a lit candle in each hand.

"Ouu, what'd I do, Juicy, huh? Did I do something? C'mon, tell me, what?"

"I'll tell you what you did," Sitko said. "You fucked with the wrong guy."

Groaning, rolling sideways, hissing, spitting, Sitko got to his knees. Started clawing wax off his hands. "I don't care how fucking crazy everybody says you are, you're gonna wish you never dumped that wax on me and you shoulda never fucking pushed that ladder."

"Hey, Mister Chiefy, I'm just a split-tail, remember?"

Carlucci's head was throbbing, he could feel a knot rising just above his right temple. At least it was on the outside.

Sitko was trying to stand up. His knees buckled. He grabbed his lower back with both hands. Glared up at Virginia, who was still dancing and laughing, but more quietly now.

"We ain't done yet, girlie. Not by a long fucking shot."

"Promises, promises," she cooed back at him, making circles with her hips, first in one direction, then the other.

"Virginia, you got any cold packs? Or ice?"

"Huh? What for?"

"I got whacked in the head, kicked, I don't know, maybe the ladder hit me."

"Say please."

"C'mon, Virginia, Jesus, quit screwing around."

"Say pretty please with a cherry on top."

"I'm starting to believe you. Fucking broad *is* nuts."

She upended newly melted wax on Sitko, who stumbled, turned away, caught most of it on his neck. Screamed again. Set off all the dogs again.

"You did it now, bitch!" Sitko snatched up the ladder and slammed it against the porch railing at a much less steep angle this time. He bounded up the ladder while Virginia scurried around, picking up more candles.

Carlucci wondered why she didn't just pop Sitko in the head with one of the candles. Some of them were a foot long, thick as a salami.

All those years of running and lifting weights had done something for Sitko, because eighty years old or not, he was up and over the railing just as she was turning around. Carlucci couldn't see but he did hear Virginia scream, heard her crashing down on her rump, scattering candles all over the deck.

"Jesus Christ, you broke my nose! You fucker, you broke my nose!"

Next thing Carlucci heard was Frank Sinatra's "Old Black Magic" cut off mid-note. Then he heard Sitko grunting, and the boombox crashing into the yard, pieces flying everywhere.

"Hey! If you ruined that CD, you bastard—"

"One more word outta you, bitch, and you're going over the railing."

"You bastard, you broke my nose, you broke my stereo, fuck you! Fuck you!"

"You asked for it, goddammit!"

"Chief? Yo, Chief? That's enough!"

Grunts, curses, punches, kicks roared through Carlucci's throbbing head. He ordered them to stop. They ignored him. He pleaded. They kept fighting. He drew his Beretta, fired three rounds into the dirt, and shouted, "Freeze, goddammit!"

Stunned by the gunshots, they stopped. Even the dogs got quiet. Seconds passed. Then Sitko howled again, louder than before, making Carlucci's temple pound.

Sitko crumpled to the deck.

"Virginia?" Carlucci called several times. When she didn't answer, and despite his every instinct to the contrary, he scrambled up the ladder and over the railing.

Sitko, knees drawn up to his chest, rolled from side to side on his back, moaning, whimpering, holding both hands over his crotch.

"Jesus, Virginia, what'd you do to him?"

"I grabbed his balls *and I twisted*, that's what I did," she said, squeezing and twisting the air with her right hand until it was a fist and shaking it at Carlucci. Suddenly she bent over and began searching for something on the deck floor.

"Virginia, freeze, you hear me? Freeze!"

"It's around here somewhere, I know it is."

"Last time, Virginia, freeze!"

"Oh freeze this," she said, shaking her butt at him. "Musta left it in the kitchen."

She straightened up, started to run past Carlucci. He turned his Beretta sideways and slapped her forehead with it as she rushed by. Her knees buckled. She started to go down. He caught her right arm and eased her down. Smacking her with his pistol was bad enough. *Her head hit the deck, Jesus, how much trouble do I want?*

He rolled her onto her stomach, pulled both hands behind her, and cuffed her. Then he ran through the house to his car. Opened the passenger door. Unzipped his kit. Rooted around until he found a bunch of plastic ties.

Back out on the porch, Virginia was trying to sit up. Carlucci knew he didn't have much time. If he didn't use the plastic ties to hook her ankles to the handcuffs, he was in for it. No way was he a match for her. She sighed heavily and fell onto her back again. Carlucci rolled her over, hooked the chain of plastic ties to the handcuffs and then to her ankles.

When he straightened up, he was sweating, breathing hard, but Virginia was hog-tied—not to the point where she'd have trouble breathing, but just enough to where she couldn't hurt herself or anybody else. The front of her head was swelling, fast. Blood was gushing from her nose.

He reached for his radio. Shit. Wasn't on his belt. Must've dropped it when Sitko came flying back. Instead of trying to find it in the bad light below, he hustled out to the street, used his car radio to call for two ambulances. With luck, each would have crews of two EMTs, enough bodies to get Virginia to Mental Health and Sitko to the ER.

With an afghan he'd grabbed off the living room couch, Carlucci got back on the deck, found Sitko still on his back, knees drawn up, eyes squeezed shut, holding his crotch, cursing Virginia, ball busters, and nut squeezers everywhere. Carlucci draped the afghan over Virginia, who immediately started wriggling to shake it off.

"Get this offa me—get if off! You got this offa the couch!"

"Okay, okay, hold up, Jesus."

"Everything in there—this is what you bring? Tony got this outta my mother's house on purpose, it's all wool. Fucker knows wool makes me itch. Get it off me, Carlucci! Off!"

"Virginia, you keep scooching around like that, you're gonna get splinters in your, uh, chest."

"Listen to you. Chest. Can't even say tits. How 'bout boobs, Carlucci, can ya even say boobs, huh?"

"You knew what I meant."

"God, you're such a wuss, you're worse'n Tony—get this thing offa me, goddammit!"

"Whatever it is, Carlucci, you leave it right where it is—hope it fucking itches her to death."

———

It was 2:30 A.M. when Carlucci finally got home. His knees were shaking as he climbed the steps up to his front porch. Inside, he dropped his kit beside the front door, and sank onto the couch to strip off his backup gun and ankle holster. He eased backward until his head touched the top of the couch. He knew his ridiculously long and thoroughly crappy night was going to get longer and crappier because he had reached the point where the excitement of everything that happened on Virginia Carpilotti's porch was bouncing off his physical exhaustion like a hot wire; it was going to be hours before he could sleep.

He kicked off his shoes, shoved them aside, padded into the kitchen. Warm milk was what he needed. Sliced turkey breast. Tryptophan. Lots of it.

On his way to the fridge, he saw three messages on his machine. He poked the play button. The first must have been a wrong number, just a pause and a click. The second started and he heard a welcome voice saying, "I don't care when you get in, call me." The next call, recorded two hours later, after midnight, was the same.

He lifted the phone, touched the only non-work-related number on his speed dial. He opened the fridge, filled a two-cup measuring pitcher with milk and grabbed the package of sliced turkey out of the deli drawer. Before he could get the milk into the microwave, Franny Perfetti picked up, sounding very wide awake.

"This you, Rugs?"

"Bad day? Bad night? Or both?"

"I'll tell you mine if you tell me yours."

"Two words. Virginia Carpilotti."

"Oh God you just had a go-round with her—like two weeks ago?"

"Gone around with her so many times, can't keep track. You know, the thing I wonder about her—no, no, you first. I don't wanna think about her anymore."

"I know what you mean," she said, speaking slowly.

Carlucci thought there was something wrong with how she sounded, like maybe she'd been to a dentist? Nah.

"Got a newbie tonight," she said. "Total denial. Pissed off at everybody, the judge, the group, me, just yelling at everybody, about everything. God, I don't know how anybody can just keep yelling like that. Any time anybody said anything, she'd jump in with how stupid that was, how stupid the whole thing was, and we were all a bunch of stupid assholes, and she kept it up the whole session. I was ready to strangle her. Didn't get one damn thing accomplished. Maybe one thing, her venting—if that's an accomplishment."

"Might've been," Carlucci said, rolling up a couple slices of turkey and holding them in his mouth while he set the milk in the microwave and the timer for fifty seconds.

He bit off some turkey and chewed for a moment. After he swallowed, he said, "Must be something else."

"Huh? Something else? Me?"

"Yeah. Every time you get a newbie they're either feeling way sorry for themselves or they're pissed or they're just locked in, right? I mean, isn't that the usual, one of the three? Or all three?"

"Yeah. I guess."

"You guess? C'mon. Must be something else. A doper belly aching loudly, that wouldn't be a two-message night, you know, call me no matter when."

Long pause.

"Yo, Fran? Franny? I know you're still there, I can hear you breathing, what's up?"

"Okay, okay, with ten minutes to go, I finally just told her enough's enough, she needed to sit down so the rest of us could, I don't know what I said, regroup, something really smart like that. And she got in my face . . . started em-effing me and next thing I knew I was on the floor and my head, Jesus. Found out later she punched me—honest to God never saw it coming. Somebody told me I closed my eyes, probably me trying to get centered, or stay centered, or something I don't know what, soon as I did, she hit me. Couple guys had her on the floor when I finally came to."

"Aw shit, Franny, I'm sorry—d'you call the cops?"

"The cops? No. Why?"

"Why? Franny, you were assaulted. Aggravated. We talked about this, coupla times, c'mon."

"Rugs, calling the cops was the furthest thing from my mind. Anyway, you're the cops."

"C'mon, Fran, I told you this was gonna happen eventually. All these years you been doing this, you been real lucky. And never before? Did it ever happen and you didn't tell me?"

"No, it never did."

"Well, Fran, it was bound to, and I told you when it happens you gotta call the cops. Let us handle it, that's what we get paid for."

"Rugs, don't you remember what I told you would happen if I called the cops? Don't trust Perfetti—something happens, she calls the cops, I'd never be able to run a group again."

"Franny, c'mon. You forgetting who signs your checks?"

"Am I forgetting who signs—hey, Rugs, you're awful close—"

"C'mon, Fran, County Adult Probation and Parole, that's who you work for. And that doper violated her parole, she needs to get in front of a judge, who needs to put her ass in a cell. Where it belongs."

"Rugs, this is not what I need to hear right now."

"Fran, listen, just let me say some things, okay?"

"No, Rugs, no! I know what you're gonna say, and I don't want you to say those things—oh, I shouldn't've told you, I knew it."

"What're you talking about, course you shoulda told me."

"No, you're taking it all wrong."

"Franny, wait a minute, forget how I'm taking it, tell me something. You okay?"

"No. My head hurts—I mean my cheek."

"So that's why you were talking like you were at the dentist's. You go to the ER?"

"No. Jeez, why?"

"'Cause you lost consciousness? 'Cause you might maybe have a concussion?"

"I'm fine, I'm okay."

"Just said your head hurts."

"I meant my cheek, not my head."

"Well which is it? And did you get cut?"

"It's my cheek and, no, I didn't get cut."

"I wish you would've gone to the ER—how 'bout we go up there right now? I'm still dressed, just gotta put my shoes on."

"Oh, Rugs, don't make this a bigger deal than it is, okay? Just listen, please."

"Hey, Franny, you leave two messages to call you no matter when I get in, and now you don't want me to make a bigger deal?"

"I don't. And I shouldn't've said it that way. On your machine."

"Okay, okay, I know about guys being hard-heads, trying to fix it, solve the problem, when all women want is for guys to listen, I heard Reseta say that, but, damn, this is not some little thing here, Fran. This is a felony, which is a heavy-duty parole violation. You can't let her get away with this."

"Rugs, stop it, will you? Jeez. Hey, mom's ringing her bell, I gotta go."

"Aw no, c'mon, Fran, don't hang up, I won't try to fix anything, I promise. You don't wanna go to the ER, we won't go."

She hung up before he could promise he'd just listen for as long as she wanted to talk, no more trying to solve what she didn't think were problems, but that he knew were, whether she wanted to hear that or not. She was going to hear it from somebody—as soon as her boss did. In the courthouse? End of the first coffee break everybody would've heard about it.

Why didn't I just shut up and listen? Reseta told me I don't know how many times. I gotta quit being a cop with her. What's the point of going to a therapist if I'm not gonna listen to him. Every time we go in there he tells me. And I'm sitting there going, yeah, yeah, I know, I know. But when I see something coming she doesn't, it just gets me to stand there and dummy up, just to avoid a hassle. That's like waking up in the morning and saying, yeah, today I'm gonna get stupid, really fucking stupid—on purpose.

And then, aw shit there's, Ma. Haven't heard anything in almost a week. God, hate to think . . . I gotta go see her. Can't keep putting it off. Christ. And screwed up with Fran. When am I gonna learn to shut my mouth? Yo, Rugs? Anybody home in there? Listen. L-I-S-T-E-N, do you fucking get it? She's a big girl, been doing a big girl's job for a lotta years now, never got popped before, why couldn't you just listen? Why . . . couldn't . . . you . . . just . . . listen? I'll tell you why, 'cause you're Answer Man, that's why . . . faster than a speeding conclusion . . . more powerful than a courthouse rumor . . . able to leap tall hesitations in a single bound . . . yes sir, that's me, Answer Man! Ha! Where'd that come from? Oh, yeah, yeah, I remember now. Comic books. Superman. Reading them in the basement of Jackie Morano's house.

Carlucci woke up shaking. Huge cubes of fuzzy white dice, higher than he was tall, bouncing ominously at him, in wobbly slow motion. Someone ordering him to stop them, build a wall out of them, but for every one he stopped, two bounced past him, one on either side. He was frantic he would never be able to build the wall, the commander behind him was urging him to go faster, move quicker, stop more dice, build the wall before they got out.

The commander didn't say who they were, but they were inside and if Carlucci didn't build the wall they were gonna come out screaming, yeah, oh yeah, then he'd be sorry. Sorry? So sorry he'd wish he was on patrol full time . . .

He swung his legs off the bed, held his head with both hands. *Dice . . . build a wall outta fuzzy white dice . . . Jesus Christ, that's a new one . . . I know what Reseta's gonna say in our next session . . . same thing he says about all the rest. "Can't stop the bad stuff, Rugs, much as you think you ought to be able to. All you can do is set your own table, cook, put the food on the plates, taste it, you know, really taste what you cooked, wash the dishes, man, that's it. It ain't rocket science." Yeah, it ain't, right . . . but that don't make it easy.*

Alarm clock showed five thirty. And in about an hour and a half, he was going to get his stones crushed big time, all because His Royal Fire Chiefness Eddie Sitko thought Virginia Carpilotti was just another split-tail a real fireman could handle with one hand tied to his leg.

In the ER last night, after Sitko got where he could stand fairly straight and wasn't holding his crotch anymore, he started on Carlucci like it was Carlucci who'd grabbed his balls and twisted. Sitko was making no sense. Carlucci knew he was just ranting. Sitko was famous for it. Anybody who'd ever been around Sitko for more than fifteen minutes said they never knew anybody who liked to talk as much and as loud as he did. Or cursed as much.

Sitko also liked blaming people. In his world things didn't go wrong by themselves. If something went wrong, somebody had to let it go wrong, or make it go wrong. If a fire started in a house because of bad wiring, then it was either the electrician's fault because he didn't know what he was doing, or it was the residents' fault because they were too dumb to change the batteries in their smoke detectors.

"Maintenance," Sitko said every time somebody quit talking long enough for him to jump in, "that's what keeps the goddamn world going the right direction. You can't sit around on your fat fucking asses and hope nothing's gonna break. Even the dumbest shitbird knows eventually everything deteriorates, degrades, just plain fucking wears out. Replace it! Repair it! Get off your lazy ass and do it! Why do you think our department is ranked as high as it is? I'll tell you why. 'Cause we fucking maintain our equipment, that's why."

And while he was stomping around the ER, he started speechifying how he had a good mind to go to the next council meeting and give them an earful about Carlucci's "dago incompetence, because you should've been more specific about what I was getting into up on that deck."

"How many ways you want me to say it? I told you how many guys it took last time—"

"Aw shit, all you dagos exaggerate—"

"Exaggerate? Yeah? Don't tell me I didn't give it to you straight! All you wanted to talk about was how you weren't there the last time, that's why it took all your guys plus the EMTs."

"You should've told me you were giving me the real scoop, not just some dago bullshit."

"And if I'd've said it was the real scoop, would you have paid attention? And anyway, you know what? I'm getting sick of all this dago this and dago that. Knock it off."

"Or what, you skinny little wop?" Sitko got in front of Carlucci and drew himself up to his full height. He was a head taller than

Carlucci probably thirty muscled pounds heavier. Eighty years old, but still.

Carlucci felt sour heat rising in his throat, the pulses in front of his ears ramping up. If he didn't get out of there soon, he knew he might do something he'd really be sorry for. Bad enough he already had to explain putting three in Virginia Carpilotti's dirt. City ordinance prohibited discharging a firearm in the city. A violation required an explanation to city council—no exceptions for cops.

Plus, when Virginia Carpilotti regained full consciousness after Carlucci had slapped her with his Beretta, she started screaming she wanted Sitko and Carlucci arrested for assault, and after they were found guilty in court, she was going to sue their asses off, all of them, Sitko, Carlucci, the police department, the fire department, the whole goddamn city!

Fortunately for everybody in the ER, the doc in charge had injected some haloperidol into her about two minutes after the EMTs wheeled her in. He also supervised placing her in four-point restraints after the EMTs had removed the restraints they'd put on the gurney, so screaming was all Virginia could do, less and less coherently as the haloperidol kicked in.

Carlucci finally just walked away from Sitko, leaving him crowing about how it had taken five hundred crack Italian marksmen to shoot Mussolini twice, a joke that was moldy when wise asses used to tell it to Carlucci's father and uncles.

He went back to the station and filled out a UIR with as few details as he thought could fly past Nowicki, fully intending to add the rest in the morning.

Now here it was, not six hours into the morning, and he had compounded the mess with Carpilotti and Sitko by trying to solve Fran Perfetti's problem when all she'd wanted was an empathetic ear.

Carlucci smelled himself and shuffled into the shower. Fifteen minutes later, clean and shaved, he drank three cups of coffee and ate two pieces of toast with a kind of margarine Mario Balzic had insisted would help him keep his cholesterol down. After Carlucci's last physical, his good cholesterol was down and his bad cholesterol, triglycerides, and blood pressure were all up, proving once again that being skinny in itself was no guarantee against clogged pipes. His doctor prescribed Lipitor and exercise. Balzic told Carlucci all the ways he could make rolled oats taste like pasta and also gave him a couple small tubs of margarine that he'd been telling him would jack up the effects of the oats and Lipitor.

"But you gotta start walking, Rugs. Exercise, man, pain in the ass, but you gotta do it."

"Yeah, that's what the doc said. Just don't tell me I gotta run."

"Nah, walking's enough. Every other day, thirty minutes, that's what I do. Twenty minutes is probably enough for you. Split it up, do five minutes at a time."

Despite Carlucci's best intentions, finding the time to fit exercise walking into his life was a problem, especially now, in August, when he was filling in for the married patrolmen with kids who apparently couldn't live another year unless they made their annual pilgrimage to Disney World. Fuck Walt Disney. Fuck Mickey Mouse. And fuck Nowicki. Every year, same bullshit.

"Last three weeks of the year, Rugs, saving them just for you," Nowicki said. "This year, that's the twelfth through the thirty-first," *blah, blah, blah. And every year I fall for it. So who's the numb nuts here?*

Carlucci scooped up his kit and headed out to the unmarked Chevy. Normally he wouldn't report until 10 A.M. but if he was going to have to justify firing his Beretta, he wanted that done as quick as possible.

Two of Rocksburg's city councilmen were retired, but they could usually be found hanging around the city administrator's office, the electric shop, or the streets department. The mayor came in every morning at around seven to check up on things before he left at nine to run his insurance business. Since the mayor was chairman of the Safety Committee and the two councilmen who hung around city hall every morning made up the rest of it, Carlucci figured he might as well get in and get it done. The only thing he wasn't sure of was whether the mayor was back from his vacation because the mayor could usually be counted on to keep Councilman Egidio Figulli from flying too far off his handle.

First thing Carlucci had to do was stop in Virginia Carpilotti's backyard to find his radio. He was sure he'd dropped it there when Sitko kicked him in the head. The knot just in front of his right temple was about the size of half a walnut shell. It had started to swell almost immediately after he'd been kicked. Even though he'd held a plastic sandwich bag filled with ice on it for fifteen minutes after talking to Fran Perfetti, the knot didn't look or feel any smaller. In the ER everybody had been too busy with Carpilotti and Sitko to pay much attention to him. Wasn't anybody's fault. He didn't feel ignored. He hadn't asked anyone to check him out.

In Virginia Carpilotti's backyard, he learned he had another problem: no radio. Her backyard was maybe twenty-four feet wide and no more than thirty feet deep from the foundation to the fence separating her yard from the house below. He gave himself ten minutes to cover every square foot of it after the first walk-around revealed nothing but pieces of the boom box Sitko had thrown off her deck.

After he'd given up the search, he thought, *Let's add this up: Eddie Sitko is thinking of going to the next public council meeting to tell them what a screwup I am; I put three in the dirt here, and the Safety Committee is gonna want to know why; Virginia Carpilotti has eight sutures in her head where I whacked her, and when she gets back to whatever level of sanity she's on, she's gonna start screaming for somebody to do a number on me for excessive force and aggravated assault; and if all that isn't enough, now I gotta tell the Safety Committee I lost one of their brand-new $229 radios.*

Well, Sitko can piss and moan whatever he wants, I don't work for him. Besides, Virginia Carpilotti starts screaming excessive force, Sitko has no choice, he's gonna be on my side no matter how incompetent he says I am. My only problem with that is, Nowicki's gonna wanna know why I didn't hit her with pepper spray. It would've been a lot less of a hassle to have somebody wash her eyes out than sew her head up. And Nowicki, of course, will be right. Problem is a couple weeks ago, when I was scuffling with a kid who had smacked his mother with the shower door, I lost the pepper spray.

The Safety Committee was waiting in the parking lot when Carlucci arrived. He was relieved to see the mayor was back.

"Good morning, Sergeant," Mayor Angelo Bellotti said. "I'm sure you know why we wanna talk to you."

"Can't say I'm surprised."

"I can understand why anybody would want to fire their weapon to get Eddie Sitko's attention. There have been times I wish had a gun when he starts making speeches."

"Wait a second, Angelo," councilman Figulli said, "you know the rules. Cop shoots his gun, we ain't supposed to start sympathizing with him, not just 'cause he couldn't get Sitko to shut up."

"Egidio, I know what we're supposed to do. But I also know this Carpilotti woman, all the trouble she's been causing, giving everybody a hard time, so all I'm saying is if those two were up on the porch like he says and he couldn't get them to stop fighting, I can understand why he had to do something drastic."

"Yeah, yeah, but when I woke up this morning, I got I don't know how many calls about what all the shooting was about last night. People on the Hill up there, they wanna know what the hell's going on."

"I'm trying to find out, Egidio, if you'll just stop talking and let me."

"Wait a minute? We holding a hearing? Here? In the parking lot? Who's recording this? You? I ain't. Are you, Radio?"

"Does it look like I am?" John "Radio" Radoycich said.

"Just settle down, Egidio," the mayor said, "I didn't say anything about holding a hearing, I'm just trying to find out whether we should or not."

"Oh what? Like this is practice? And we decide we're gonna have a hearing, he shows up with an FOP lawyer and knows all the questions we're gonna ask 'cause you already asked them? Why don't you just hand him a script and we'll call it a rehearsal?"

"Egidio, for Chrissake, shut up for two minutes and let Angelo find out what he wants to find out so we can see where we are."

"Thank you, Joe, very much," said the mayor. "Now, Sergeant, I'm wondering why, after you finally went up on the porch, or deck or wherever, your first instinct was to, as you put it in your incident report, give this woman a slap with your pistol instead of giving her a shot of pepper spray?"

"Yeah, well, normally, that's what I would've done, but see, I was on the ground when I fired my weapon. They were up on the porch."

"I'm confused," Radio said. "Is that when she grabbed him by the nuts? While you were still on the ground?"

"Yeah. But I didn't know that till I got up on the porch."

"So what that says there, Angelo," Radio said, "he heard him scream, and that's when he went up the ladder, right?"

"Right," Carlucci said, before the mayor could answer.

"And what? He's on his back, holding his crotch and rolling around, is that it?"

"Yeah, and then Virginia, she starts looking around for something on the porch, she's bent over, and then she straightens up and starts to run past me and I, uh, I knew there was no way I was gonna get into a physical thing with her—Jesus, I'd be in the hospital right now—so I just turned my piece sideways, flat like, and gave her a slap as she went by."

"So why didn't you hit her with your pepper thingy?"

"Uh, 'cause, uh, I didn't have it. When I had to settle that kid down? The one that decided to attack his mother with the shower door? Coupla weeks ago maybe? Uh, that's when I lost it."

"A couple weeks?" Figulli said. "And you didn't get a new one? How'd you lose it?"

"I'm not sure. Just remember getting called as backup for that kid was beating up his mother—"

"I thought that was mandatory, that pepper spray? Ain't you required to have that on you at all times? When you're on patrol?"

"Yeah. I am. It is."

The three of them stared at him.

"I was gonna requisition a new one, just hadn't got around to it yet."

"Coulda bought it yourself," Figulli said. "Didn't have to screw around waiting for the city to buy you one. Only cost like, twelve, thirteen bucks the size you guys carry."

"The other thing is, and I don't know how this happened either, must've been when Virginia pushed the ladder, and Sitko kicked me in the head. Uh, that's the only time I could figure it. Uh, I lost my radio."

"You lost your radio?" Figulli said. "Those things are brand new. Two hundred twenty-nine bucks we paid for them. Apiece. How could you lose your radio?"

"You get whacked in the head, you don't have real good recall what was going on right before that, uh, happened, know what I'm saying?" *Jesus Christ, did I just say that?*

"First you lose your pepper thingy, then you lose your radio? Good thing your ass is bolted to your belly button, Carlucci, or maybe you'd lose that, too."

"All right, all right, that's enough, Egidio. The detective here's been a fine officer for many years, nobody needs to be getting sarcastic."

"I was making a joke. Whatsamatter? He can't take a joke?"

Carlucci shrugged. "I wasn't complaining." But he wanted to. He wanted to take out his Beretta and slap Figulli in the head, give him a cut that required at least eight sutures, then maybe Figulli and Virginia Carpilotti could start a support group. Sutures Anonymous.

"Detective?"

"Huh? Sorry, I was thinking of something."

"Try to pay attention here, Carlucci. It ain't outta the possibility you could wind up suspended, losing two pieces of equipment you're supposed to have on you at all times."

"Okay, hold on now, wait a second, let's not start talking suspension here, I mean, things happen."

"Yeah? Shoots his gun? Three times yet? Loses his spray hicky? And his radio? C'mon, I don't think a week or even a two-week suspension—I'm not making threats here, I'm just saying—for what he did? Two weeks off without pay, that wouldn't be outta line, that's all I'm saying."

"Oh for Christ sake, Figulli, why you always gotta be making such a big deal?"

"Hey, shooting a gun in the city, that is a big deal, and that's why we're gonna hold this hearing. On that. I, for one, wanna know why any cop thinks it's all fine and dandy to shoot off his gun."

"That's what I'm trying to find out, Egidio."

"Well right now I think you should stop trying, I think we should take this inside, put it on the agenda for the next meeting, set up a formal hearing date like regulations say we're supposed to. Call witnesses, know what I mean? Record the meeting, do it right. If that's me making a big deal, then that's what I'm making."

"All right, okay, I don't wanna argue about this. You guys set it up. I gotta go to work. Looks like you're gonna have to call your delegate, Detective. And your lawyer."

Carlucci shrugged, shook his head, as he started walking toward the station just ahead of Figulli and Radio. He reached back and held the door open.

"Think maybe it's time you start thinking about putting in for your pension, Carlucci."

"You been thinking that for how long now? Two years? Three?"

"Yeah. I think any cop starts shooting his gun, loses his pepper thingy—spray—and his radio, he should start thinking maybe he's getting a little slow on the uptake."

Carlucci turned in to the station's records room while the two councilmen headed for the stairs to council chambers.

Figulli stopped at the stairway and hollered, "I mean it, Carlucci. Time for you to start thinking about that."

"Thinking about what?" Nowicki said, blocking Carlucci's path.

"Nothing," Carlucci said, trying to slip around Nowicki, who put his arm across the doorway.

"Don't tell me nothing, he's been on my ass since I got here this morning—about you up in Norwood last night. You fire your weapon?"

"Nowicki, c'mon man, you know as well as I do what happened."

"You fire your weapon or not? Gimme an answer. 'Cause if you did, that's a little detail you neglected to mention on your UIR."

"You know I did, why you asking me?"

"'Cause Figulli got his nose open for an investigation, according to regulations."

"Jesus, he's already working on it. Him and Radio. That's where they're going. Put it on the agenda for the next meeting."

"You gonna file another UIR?"

Carlucci shot him a gimme-a-break look.

"I'm serious, Rugs, 'cause the one you handed me last night, that ain't doing it."

"That's, uh, sorta why I'm here now—if you'd just get outta the way so I could get to it."

"Just gimme a one-two-three, will ya? What happened?"

"You want it? Here it is. Last night my ass was dragging and you had yourself a big yuk thinking I should respond to the Virgin, and when I called for the firemen, the only one who showed up was Chief My Dick Is Bigger Than Everybody's, talking about how his guys all got the runs when they heard whose address it was, and I tried to tell him how many guys it took to get her in the ambulance the last time she flipped out, but he thought that just was me doing some dago exaggerating. He puts the ladder up there, she dumps hot wax on his hands, pushes the ladder, something hits me in the head, I go out. I wake up, Sitko's screaming, he wantsa kill her, she hits him with some more hot wax, he goes up and over the railing, hits her with I don't know what, knocks her on her ass, she's screaming he broke her nose, she gets up, they start fighting, both of them cussing each other, my head's throbbing, they wouldn't stop, so I put three in the dirt. That stops them for maybe five seconds. Then Sitko, he starts screaming, she's screaming, I go up, I don't know what I'm gonna do when I get up there, but I figured if I don't do something, wound up as she was? As they both was? Someone's gonna do something really crazy. I get up there, Sitko's on his back, he's holding his crotch, groaning, moaning, and her, she's naked, and she's bent over looking for something, I don't know what, but she straightens up, starts moving past me real fast, I don't have time to think, I just give her a quick slap with my piece, right across her forehead. She goes down, I cuff her, and hog tie her, then I called Mutual Aid. Two ambulances. After that, it was just a matter of getting her and Sitko to the ER—where he busted my balls for way too long, dago this, dago that, the prick. Now, okay with you if I go write it up?"

"Yeah, right," Nowicki said over his shoulder as he went back into his office, "' I wanna go over it with you, make sure you don't give them a bullet to shoot you with—you know, like right now? This time of year? If they're gonna do it, in other words, they gotta do it on their own, I'm gonna make sure you don't help them."

"Well thank you very much for your over-fucking-whelming vote of confidence."

"All I'm saying is we go over it together, that's all, we make sure you don't give them something. Anything. Trying to help you out here, Rugs, I owe you."

"Owe me? And this is how you're gonna pay me? I'm not gonna get the three weeks at the end of December now? Those weeks you promised? No thank you, I think I know how to write up a UIR. Been doing it for forty years, never needed your help before."

"Just trying to give you another pair of eyes, what're you getting so pissy about?"

"What am I getting pissy about? If it wasn't for you, I wouldn't have to be thinking about any of this."

"Who else was I supposed to send up there? That rookie?"

"You. You were here. You coulda gone. Every now and then, your predecessor used to respond to a call, I know you know that."

"Don't be bringing Balzic into this. He was always in it up to his armpits, c'mon. Hey, Rugs, you know I loved the guy, but no way I'm gonna put myself in the jackpots he used to get into. Spent half his life fighting with council, the other half fighting with Sitko. And all 'cause he couldn't keep his ass in the chair—wouldn't.

That's all he had to do: stay here, mind the department's business, wouldn't've had one-tenth the grief he had."

Carlucci wanted to say that avoiding grief might be enough to get Nowicki through the night, but other people, every once in a while, they might try to find something better to hang on to, though right then he couldn't say what that might be. Besides, as deep as he was in it with the Safety Committee maybe he should be a little slower to brush Nowicki off.

Before he could say anything else the dispatcher hollered that he had a call. "It's about your mother."

Aw shit. Now what? He pointed at Nowicki's phone and said, "All right?"

Nowicki nodded and stepped around Carlucci into the hall.

"Carlucci here, who's this?"

"It's Ethel Thigpen, Detective? Your mother's social worker?"

Like he could forget whose thankless job it was at Mamont State Hospital to try to prepare his mother, along with twenty-some other women in her group, to reenter real life. Thankless? More like hopeless. At least he was hoping it was hopeless. No way his mother was ever coming back to real life, not emotionally. Physically now, that was another question, one the state's budget writers were mulling over right now.

"Hi, Miss Thigpen, what'd she do this time?"

"I'm sorry to have to tell you, Detective. She assaulted another patient. Shoved her with a food tray. Knocked the woman down. Broke her wrist."

"Damn."

"And this one's not goin' to go away real easy for you."

"I'm afraid to ask. Why not?"

"Her son's real upset and he's supposed to be pretty big in the Democrat Party in Allegheny County."

"Okay, give it to me."

"He wants to talk to you. And if you don't talk to him, he says he's goin' go to the papers and the TV stations, poke us all in the eye with a stick."

"So he's blackmailing me? For what? I'm fifty miles from there."

"I don't know, Detective. He's stomping around here saying you better come talk to him, that's all I know."

"I'm working. And I'm already in, uh, a thing here. Is he there now?"

"Yes, he is. He was on his way in for a visit, pulled in like maybe ten minutes after it happened."

"Which was when?"

"About forty-five minutes ago."

"Miss Thigpen, this don't make any sense. I wasn't there, if he's got a stone gripe with anybody, it's with you guys."

"Tried to tell him that, he doesn't wanna hear it."

"Why ain't he with his mother anyway? Broken wrist, you guys sent her to a hospital, right? Don't answer that, I know you did. What's this guy's game? Don't make sense."

"Well—and this is just my guess now—I think he's why she's in here. I think he's probably feeling a whole lotta guilt 'cause he had her committed and now she got hurt, and so he's trying to take it out on the other woman's son, know what I'm saying? Little projection going on."

"Miss Thigpen, you know more about this stuff than I do, but . . . where's my mother now? You got her restrained? Don't answer that, I know you do. Is she all right?"

"She's all right. But of course she's back in the Binger Building. Last time I heard she was in two-point restraints and sleeping off the haloperidol. And just like the last time, remember? She won't get outta there till her treatment team reviews the incident, decides when she can regain some of her privileges, just like before."

Carlucci remembered. All too well. In the first month of his mother's commitment, she attacked one of the hospital's maintenance workers, insisting he was putting thoughts in her head when he was mowing the lawn.

Afterward, she said, "He's out there cutting the damn grass every day, he puts a thought in each one of those pieces of grass, and I walk around on them and they get stuck on the bottom of my slippers and then when I wipe them off, they just shoot right up through my fingers. Usually I stop them when they get up to my elbows, but yesterday a couple slipped through, and all night long I had these nightmares about him beating me with a frying pan. So what else was I gonna do? Had to be stopped."

Great, he had thought. *Now she's dreaming somebody's beating her with my pan. Never gonna admit it was her who hit Fischetti with my goddamn pan.*

The second time, after Ethel Thigpen asked her why she hadn't made her bed, Mrs. Carlucci said if Miss Thigpen wanted the bed made, she could make it herself because she's who wanted it made. Mrs. Carlucci said she wasn't going near that bed. When Ethel turned around to motion for an aide to assist her, Mrs. Carlucci punched her in the back and blamed it on one of the monsters under the bed.

"Everybody knows monsters hate bossy people."

"No monster did that, that was you."

"Sure it was me, but the monsters told me to do it, they're sick and tired of how you're always bossing me around. I wouldn't've done it on my own."

That time, Mrs. Carlucci had to "visit" the Binger Building for a month before she was allowed to return to her group. Since then—until this latest incident—she'd been relatively calm and cooperative.

"Miss Thigpen, I don't care who that guy is or who he thinks he is, I can't come in there now. I, uh, I did something not real smart last night and it's gonna take me a couple days at least to get it straightened out, you know? So, long as you guys got my mother restrained, I'm not gonna come in there and argue with some guy talking through his, uh, his hat. Thanks very much for calling me, but I have to go now."

He told her he'd call when he had more time and then hung up before she could say anything else. He quickly hustled into the dispatcher's cubicle and said, "No more calls for me today about my mother, okay? If they wanna leave a message, fine. Otherwise, I'm on the job and you don't know where I am."

When Nowicki tried to find out what was up, Carlucci asked him, "You want the UIR from last night? If you do, then you gotta let me get to it. All I'm gonna say is it's about my mother. Same as last time. Last two times—no, last three times."

That said, Carlucci went to his desk, locked his weapons in the gun drawer, opened his computer to his personal files, took the time to do a more thorough job filling in the blanks on the UIR template, saved a copy for himself, sent a copy to records, and put a hard copy in Nowicki's in-basket. Nowicki wasn't in his office.

Now where the hell'd he go? Always around when you don't want him . . . Jesus . . . maybe it is time to put in for the pension. But it ain't gonna be because Figulli hangs a suspension around my neck. Not for putting three in the dirt. Or for losing a radio either. It's a wonder he didn't say I gotta pay for the bullets. For sure he's gonna make me pay for the radio. What the fuck, maybe I should. I did lose it. Can't figure out why it wasn't in her yard. I called for the firemen on it. But I called the EMTs on the car radio, so where'd it go?

As soon as he thought he could get out before Nowicki came back from wherever he was, Carlucci drove to Tony Carpilotti's house on Norwood Hill, and spent fifteen minutes blocking out the backyard and covering every square yard of it, just like he'd done this morning. With no better result.

Think, Carlucci. Go back over it. Where'd you have it when you were holding the ladder for Sitko? Where I always keep it. Back right pocket. Then she dumps the wax on him and shoves the ladder. Him and the ladder come straight back, I go out, and when I come to he's hollering at me to get off him. C'mon, man, close your eyes, go back there, visualize it. Ladder's on top of me, I'm on my back on top of him, he's on his back. Ladder's across my right leg, angling off to the right, he's hollering about his back's broken—talk about exaggerating. I shove the ladder off me, roll off his leg, and then he really starts hollering, get off, get off my leg. Why was he hollering then? Had to be 'cause the radio was digging into his leg. So right in there, before I roll off, I still have it. So what happened then? He stands up, his knees buckle, he grabs his back, then he grabs the ladder and up he goes. And I didn't touch the ladder again till I went up.

"Hey, Rugs, is that you?" came Tony Carpilotti's sleepy voice. He was in his underwear looking down over the railing. "What're you doing here?"

"Looking for my radio. Lost it last night. Has to be here, I didn't go anywhere else."

"Wait a second." Tony disappeared into the house. Moments later he was back. "This what you're looking for?" He dropped it into Carlucci's hands.

"Oh man, where'd you find it? I've been up here twice looking for it."

"Josie found it. Right about where you're standing."

"Hey, man, thank her for me, really. Saved me a big hassle."

"Speaking of hassles, where's Virginia? As if I don't know."

Carlucci nodded.

"I figured." He put his elbows on the railing. "I don't know what I'm gonna do about her, Rugs, I mean it, man. I'm outta ideas, my lawyer's outta ideas, plus every idea he gets costs me money. She's driving me crazy, driving the girls crazy. They're so afraid she's gonna be here, they don't even wanna come home anymore. Josie can't eat, Tina can't stop eating. Josie lost twenty pounds in the last three months. And Tina, Jeez, she gained everything Josie lost, plus about ten more, I'm not kidding. I mean, feels like we're at the end of the line here.

"The shrink up at Mental Health, he says I should move. I says, move where? What do I do with my mother? Or Virginia's mother? I'm doing their shopping, the girls are cleaning their houses, I'm taking care of their yards, putting out their garbage, I'm supposed to just up and move? Even if I had the money—which I don't—I can't just leave them here, Jesus, not with her to take care of them.

Shit, she hasn't talked to my mother in ten years. Don't even talk to her own mother."

"Jesus, I'm sorry Tony. I wish I had an answer."

"I mean, you know, the girls, God bless them, they help out every way they can, but, hey, Josie's a senior this year, she wants to go to school for dental hygienics or something. That's gonna cost money. Where am I gonna get it? I haven't worked in eight months; who's gonna loan it to me? And if they do, how'm I gonna pay it back? My Blue Cross ran out three months ago. The kids got whattayacallit from the state, but that's only good till they turn eighteen, then we're all shit outta luck.

"Then, then there's the credit card companies, I'm telling you, those motherfuckers, every other week, they're sending Josie credit card apps, here, here, sign up, buy whatever you need for college. She works at the fucking Dairy Queen for Chrissake. She's lucky she gets twenty hours a week. Those bastards, those fucking credit-card companies, they piss me off, man, hooking kids like 'at, might as well be pushing dope.

"Virginia comes, flipping through our mail. Finds one of those credit card apps, fills it out, tells all these fucking lies, card comes back—she's here waiting for it, and then off she goes, man. Goes to the stores, signs Josie's name—the shit she buys you cannot believe. Last month, truck from some furniture outfit pulls up, got a new bedroom suite on there. I says hey, man, what the fuck, you ain't unloading that here, take it back. Driver calls the store, hands me the phone, she got one of them deals where you don't make no payments for eighteen months, no interest, nothing. I says there's only one problem. The person you sold it to, that ain't Josephine Carpilotti. That's my schizo ex-wife you sold it to and she stole that credit card app outta our mailbox. So she goes, well we checked with the credit card company, and it was a legitimate card. I says checked how? You swiped it and nothing blew up, that's how you checked it. Then she starts telling me the law says they ain't allowed to ask for another form of ID. And that's just the latest.

"Christ, Rugs, last March, she shows up here, she's driving a Ford pickup. A 2008. At that time, she was outta Mental Health for, like, maybe three weeks. She told the dealer she had a job, they believed her. Loan company never made one fucking call to find out whether she could even make one payment on that thing. Can you believe that shit? She didn't care, she had it for four months before they repo'ed it. I try to say something to her, she says, 'Hey, dummy, I had a free truck for four months, how much you paying for that heap you drive?' I says, 'Virginia, that ain't the point, the bills come to this address!' She says—get this—I'm just pissed off 'cause she knows how to beat the system and I don't. I says, 'Virginia, what system you think you're beating? Every fifteen, eighteen months you doing time in Mental Health. One of these days, they ain't gonna turn you loose.' She just laughs."

"Got any prospects, Tony?"

"For a job? Oh yeah, absolutely. Soon as business picks up they're all gonna call me, I'll be rolling in it."

"Seriously."

"Seriously? I could be a greeter at Walmart. Don't know what they pay. Ain't shit, that's all I know. They'd guarantee me thirty hours a week. I says do I get a discount in the grocery store? This guy, he gives me this look, like what're you, some kinda jagoff? I told him my fucking bill at the Giant Eagle comes to more than half what you guys are offering, never mind my mortgage, utilities, phone bill, gas, oil for the car. I told him, I says, 'At the end of the year, I would owe more than you guys paid me.' Meantime, I says, 'You say you're gonna pay me for thirty hours. How many hours you gonna work me off the clock?' He says, 'Oh that ain't true, we don't work nobody off the clock.' I says, 'Not true, huh? You think 'cause I don't have a job, I forgot how to read? You guys got fucking sued more than any company in America last year for breaking labor laws, among which was working people off the clock.' Know what he does? He laughs, the prick. I says, 'You think that's funny? That's slavery, motherfucker.' He gets all huffy, he says, 'I won't permit you to use that kind of language with me.' I says, 'Here, you jagoff, permit this.'" Tony grabbed his crotch.

"Wish I could tell you something good, Tony. All I can tell you is same thing I been telling you—go see Jimmy Reseta—about Virginia, I mean. Get her to talk to him or talk to him yourself. He can't prescribe drugs, and everybody I talked to about her? They all say she needs something from a drugstore, don't say what, but something for sure."

"Yeah, right, sure, they prescribe them, but they never say who's gonna make her take them. She takes them for a couple months after they turn her loose. Every time, same thing, soon as she starts feeling good, down the toilet they go. Then the shit wheel starts turning all over again."

"He might be able to tell you, you know, how to protect yourselves."

"What's he charge?"

"Don't worry about that, I'll talk to him."

"I don't want no fucking charity, Rugs."

"Tony, couple minutes ago you're asking me for advice. I tell you about somebody who could give you advice—this guy, the advice he would give you, that'd be worth hearing, it's not like listening to me."

"Fuckit, I ain't no charity case. Not yet."

"It wouldn't be charity, Tony. Jesus, man, I think he could really help you out."

"If you don't have to pay, the fuck you call it?"

"Tony, man, you're being a stone-head."

"Hey, Rugs? You been really good about all this, uh, all this crap with her. You've taken a lotta shit from her—and about her, and I really appreciate it. But I can't stand a nagger, man. So I'm going inside, get cleaned up. Thanks for talking to me."

"I'm not nagging you, Tony, c'mon, listen, I'll leave his name and number in your mailbox."

"Okay, okay, Jesus, I'll give him a call. Man, you're fucking relentless. Oh wait. Can you make it look like a credit card app? Virginia, you know, she might take it."

———

Next day, Carlucci called off sick; he was damned if he was going to take a vacation day in order to hear face-to-face from staff in Mamont what his mother had done. Already knew what she'd done. He wasn't sure why he was going. Maybe to pick a fight with this hotshit Democrat from Allegheny County whose mother his mother shoved with a fucking food tray. Real good finding weapons in food prep. He called the station, to leave a message for Nowicki.

"Before I put you through to the chief, someone called the station looking for you."

"Don't put me through, I just wanna leave a message. Who was it?"

"They didn't leave a message."

"Then why the fuck are we talking about this? Just tell the Chief I called off sick."

"Connecting you now."

"Jesus Christ!"

———

"You ain't sick, Rugs, you're going to see your mother."

"Believe me, I'm sick."

"Oh yeah? Who wrote your med-excuse, huh? You never go to the doctor, Rugs, I know you don't. Anyway, after you see her, you're gonna be sick no doubt. But not before."

"You want me to take a vacation day? Okay, I'll take it. You happy now? I'm not gonna argue just 'cause you feel like busting my balls."

"Up to you. But I'd stay gone all day if I was you."

"Why?"

"'Cause when I got here this morning, Figulli, he was asking me for that UIR—not the one you rewrote yesterday. He wanted the original."

"Who told him there was an original?"

"He wouldn't say—but it wasn't me. So that'll be another one you owe me."

"It wasn't you, but it'll be another one I owe you? For what?"

"For telling him he had bad information."

"See? That's why I couldn't stay chief."

"What's that mean?"

"Means you got the leadership-by-blackmail part down." Carlucci hung up before Nowicki could come back at him.

It was less than fifty miles from Rocksburg to Mamont State Hospital, but the only route Carlucci knew was through the southern suburbs of Pittsburgh, and it seemed like every traffic light turned red just as he was approaching it. It took him almost an hour and a half. Plenty of time to think. Plenty of time to notice a dark blue car that seemed to be going the same direction. Had it been there since leaving Rocksburg?

Jesus Christ, now he was acting paranoid.

By the time he drove onto hospital grounds, he really was sick in his stomach.

A vacation day for this. Fucking Nowicki.

Do I actually have to see her? I mean, it's my choice, ain't it? Nobody can make me see her. Ethel Thigpen, nice as she is, for sure she's never been anything but nice with me, for sure she knows what's going on, so she's not going to tell me I have to see her. She can't. She can't do that. But if I don't see her, if I could make it out of here without actually being in the same room with her, what would stop me from doing that? I know what a lotta people would say, yeah. Nothing but plain old Italian Catholic guilt.

Right. Like I'm back in school with Sister Mary Michael, Hitler's daughter. Who am I kidding? If I'm gonna do anything here today, it's gonna be me working on Ms. Thigpen . . . thinking up some way to tell her she never lets her get out of here. God forbid she ever convinces somebody they should turn her loose. Her. Way to go, Carlucci. Can't even say who her is, can you? Fucking coward, it's your mother, can you say that? Yeah, I have to. Why can't I say my mother?

Just saying that caused acid to gusher up his throat; the next thing he was jamming on the brakes, wrestling with his seat belt and the door, leaning out, throwing up.

What am I doing? Trying to dodge Bellotti, Figulli, Radio? That's nothing; just more bureaucratic bullshit. Part of the job. But coming here? Where she's knocking people down with trays? Breaking bones? Jesus, Mary, and Joseph—man, why am I thinking that? C'mon, man, you gotta stop talking religious shit.

He put the Chevy in gear again and drove the 15-mile-per-hour speed limit over the long, winding, two-lane macadam road, laughing at himself for even thinking that driving slow would do more than postpone the inevitable as long as possible. What a joke. Supposed to laugh at jokes, right?

He finally reached the Hixon Building parking lot and pulled into a visitor slot. Still queasy, he opened the trunk and put both his weapons in it, then tried to draw himself up out of the slouch he was feeling from his pelvis to his neck. Almost succeeded by the time he reached the desk where he had to sign for a visitor pass.

The graying, paunchy security guard asked for two forms of ID, with photos.

"Two? What's going on? Every other time my ID was all it took."

The guard looked left and right. "New security chief," he whispered. "Apparently wants to make sure no bad boys slip by me, you know, blow up our radar station."

Carlucci tried to smile. Didn't. Couldn't. You got to try to smile? He kept trying as he took out his shield case and operator's license.

"You a detective? Where?"

"Not bragging about it. Rocksburg."

"Hell, I was always bragging about it. If I didn't, nobody else would."

"Yeah? Where?"

"Pittsburgh. Thirty years. Last sixteen gold shield. Ten of those major crimes. Made a couple good pinches in my day. Finally I said the hell with it, convinced the wife to move up to her old man's cabin up the Allegheny Forest, which he left her, free and clear. Oh man, fished off the dock, grilled them up on a real spiffy Weber grill, watched the sunset, started on a six-pack of Iron City Lite, had the world by the ass . . . for a while. So I thought."

"What happened?"

"We were there about four months, wife looked at me one morning, said she was going nuts. Nobody to talk to, nearest neighbors weren't the friendliest people in the world, all the night noises give her the creeps, she says she's moving back to the city, I could come or I could stay. I thought she was joking, didn't even give her the consideration of an answer. She wasn't. Two days later, I went down the dock right about dawn, come back up for lunch, she's gone. All her clothes, cell phone, everything, including the truck, which was not hers to take. All she left me was the grill, my clothes, my fishing rigs. Turns out I didn't know her half as good as I thought."

Carlucci found this story fascinating because the longer the guard talked, the longer he could delay the reason he'd come.

"Ever hear from her?"

"Got nothing to say to me. Took me damn near a week to find her—find her hell. Stumbled on her actually. Talked to her brother's wife, lives right where Shadyside bumps up against East

Liberty. All she'd tell me was my wife was trying to make a life for herself, wouldn't say where she was. So, I was hungry, heard they had a good deli in that, uh, new grocery there, went in to get lunch, and there she was, stacking up Romano cheese. Tried to talk to her, she said, 'Some detective you are. Crime right under your nose, you don't have a clue.' Had no come back."

"How long ago was that?"

"Two years, two months, one week, two days. But who's counting?"

"Still trying to get her back?"

"Call her every day, send her flowers once a week. All I get is her answering machine, won't take delivery on the flowers."

"Sounds like it's a lot more than unfriendly neighbors, creepy night noises."

"You think, huh?"

"Aw, hey, I didn't mean anything by that, really, I was just, you know, running my mouth."

"It's all right, don't worry about it. Say the same stuff to myself every day. So, uh, who're you here to see, Detective, uh, Carlucci is it?"

"My mother—no not really her, uh, her social worker. Ethel Thigpen."

"Okay, trade me a signature for a pass, I'll give her a call—she expecting you?"

Carlucci nodded and waited until the guard hung up and asked him if he knew where Conference Room 2 was. Guard told him. He nodded again, and, with a lame wave, shuffled off.

Carlucci found Ethel Thigpen alone in the conference room, stuffing notebooks, clipboard, and pens into a tattered tote bag with a picture of a blue jay on it. She brightened when she saw Carlucci standing in the doorway.

"Hi, Detective. Hi y'all doing this fine day? You as glad as I am the humidity took a day off? Hoo, man, I was about to die yesterday. Hottest day of the summer, don't you know my AC up and quit on me? I was so mad I couldn't spit. C'mon in, c'mon, have a seat, I'll be right with you, soon's I get packed up here."

Carlucci took a seat and waited, wondering how this woman could work here and be cheerful, always smiling, looking like every day was at the beach instead of being in charge of twenty-some women with who knew how serious their mental problems were.

"You know, I can't really tell you any more today than I told you on the phone yesterday."

"She still over in Binger?"

"Oh yeah, CVO for at least a week, probably longer, depends how fast she comes back to ADL."

Carlucci knew from all his previous visits what those letters stood for: Constant Visual Observation and Attention to Daily Living.

"What about the other woman? What's the word on her?"

"Oh, I'm guessing she's gonna be in the hospital for at least another day, maybe two. Depends how soon they think she can start rehabbing. You know how that goes."

"So what about her son? He around today?"

"Haven't seen him, Detective. Doesn't mean he isn't here. Sounds like old Rooster Claghorn to me, but I'm not from Allegheny County, so I don't know what kinda big deal he is. Or if he is. Some of the staff around here, ones from Pittsburgh and the burbs? Say he's some kinda mover and shaker—whatever that means."

"So in other words, his nose is still open for me, right?"

"Last time I talked to him, yes. Tried to tell him he wasn't making noooo sense, you know, politely, but still. Wanting to pick nits with you? Like I said on the phone, sounds like a whole lot of projection going on."

"Projection? Is that like misdirection?"

"Say what?"

"You know, what magicians do. Give you all the razzle-dazzle with the left hand while they're hiding whatever with their right. The pols too. Don't want you to know where they're hiding, what they're stealing, so they invent some crisis. Always working misdirection. So obvious about it, makes you wonder."

"Oh, I remember the one butchered our budget. Can't tell you how much federal money we don't have any more. And God knows what Medicaid's gonna look like when he and the rest of his praise-the-Lord-and-pass-the-ammunition bunch gets through with that. Call themselves Christians. Not a one of them can even spell charity. Bible used to say faith, hope, and charity. Then somebody changed it to faith, hope, and love, and for a long time there, I thought that was a good thing, you know, 'cause everybody needs love. The older I get, the more I ask myself if that's really as good as I used to think it was."

Rugs thought, *Start talking, man. Keep talking long enough, you might be able to skate right outta here, won't even have to talk to . . . you know. Her.*

"Yeah," he began, "I used to think charity was a good thing, till I got involved in this one huge mess where I work, and I found out most of the people who do charity, they just do it to dodge taxes. Get all dressed up and have a dance and a fancy meal, get their pictures in the paper, give their money to whatever they like, and the rest of us gotta pay for what they don't like."

"Oh, do you think? I don't know, maybe sometimes they're really helping people."

"Yeah? Well, far as I know, the only reason there's any charitable foundations is so rich people can hide their money. 'Cause believe me, what they have to give away each year to keep their tax-exempt status is nothing compared to the taxes they'd have to pay if somebody, you know, actually had the guts to repeal that part of the Internal Revenue Code."

"Detective, you, uh, you sure you know what you're talking about?"

"Tell you what, Ms. Thigpen. You ever get some free time? Go online, go to Certified Public Accountants. Just pick one out, one close to where you live, set up a meet, tell them you got a whole lotta money and you're trying to hang onto as much as the law allows. Tell them you heard about something called Section 501(c)(3) of the IRS Code, and you don't wanna do anything illegal, you know? But you're skeptical about what this somebody told you, and you wanna have it explained to you."

"Oh I couldn't do that, my voice'd give me away. I'm a terrible liar."

"You don't have to lie. Tell them you'll pay for a consult, then just listen to what they have to say."

"And how much is that consult gonna cost?"

Carlucci shrugged. "Shop around till you find one just starting up, you know, hurting for business. Then bargain with them."

"Detective, you really think I need to know this? Or you just trying to keep me talking here, so you can put off seeing your mother long as you can? And don't shrug. Talk to me."

Carlucci dropped his arms between his legs.

"I know your mother's given you a real rough road to go, but don't you think, you know, maybe it's time you tried to forgive her? She really doesn't know what she's doing. And not forgiving her, that's not hurting her. But it's eating you up. I could be wrong now, I'm not saying I'm right, but, hey, what do you think?"

"Ms. Thigpen, you're a kind person, and I'm sure you're good at your job, and I know you're trying to help me. But I'm gonna be straight with you now—not that I've ever not been straight with you before, but . . . you know what I'm trying to say, don't you?"

"Well, before I say anything I find it best to let people say what they wanna say."

"C'mon, Ms. Thigpen. Don't make me say it. I feel guilty enough."

"Say it, Detective. Just say it. I think you get it out here, where we can both look at it, it won't be anywhere near as bad as you think."

"Oh, man, it's terrible."

"No it isn't. Just say it. C'mon."

Carlucci hung his head and rubbed his hands. "I know you're supposed to be trying to get these women ready to go back . . . you know, back where they came from."

"Uh-huh. And?"

"Oh, man, do I have to—you gonna make me say it?"

"Yes I am."

Carlucci took a deep breath, then blew it out, covered his eyes. "Ms. Thigpen, you can't . . . you gotta stop trying . . . where she's concerned."

"Who?"

"Aw, c'mon please, you know who, don't make me do this."

She gently pulled his hands away from his eyes. He let her. But as soon as she did, he shut his eyes.

"Detective, you can open your eyes, there's nobody here's gonna hurt you. God knows not me. I would never hurt you. You know why? 'Cause nobody needs to, 'cause you do a better job of it than anybody else ever could. Stop punishing yourself, that's what I'm telling you. And the best way to do that? Admit what you're punishing yourself for. So just go ahead and say it."

"I can't. Just thinking it makes my stomach turn."

"Yes, you can," she said gently. She took his left hand in both of hers. "Detective? You listen to me now. I'm goin' tell you something. God ain't got time to worry 'bout whether your mother's here, or back home with you. God got a whole lot more important things to be worrying about. So you can quit using your good old Italian Catholic guilt, you hear me?"

"I never said I was Catholic. Stopped going to Mass long time ago. Weddings and funerals, that's it."

"Who said anything about goin' to Mass? You think I think you have to go to Mass in order to feel guilty? With the name you got? Ruggiero Carlucci? You goin' tell me nuns didn't have you in grade school?"

He shook his head and started laughing and crying at once. "Worse than that. All twelve years. Used to play the drums on my knuckles."

"So see? You think 'cause you're thinking it you're doing it. And you know better. I know you have never, ever arrested anybody for thinking about doing something wrong, now have you?"

"No. 'Course not."

"But when it comes to you know who, you have arrested yourself, tried yourself, convicted yourself, and don't tell me you haven't sentenced yourself."

Carlucci couldn't look at her. He choked back a sob.

She patted his hand and said, "Detective, you need some relief. Believe me, you need to say what you're thinking, you need to get it outta you. It's all tied up in knots way inside you. How many times have you said this to people—bad people, people who've done terrible things? You know you've told them they would feel better if they just told you what they'd done—and those people have actually done something. Not you. You haven't done anything—you're just thinking it."

"Ms. Thigpen, I'm not gonna tell you all the crappy stuff I've done . . . all I'm asking . . . all I want . . . where she's concerned . . . just don't do your job, that's all."

"Where *who's* concerned?"

"You know who."

"Say it. C'mon. All the way out. Stop holding it in."

Carlucci buried his face in his hands, sobbed, croaked, "My mother."

"There," she said, putting her arm around his shoulder. "There, there."

On his way to the Binger Building, Carlucci stopped in the visitor's restroom to splash cold water on his face. Ethel Thigpen warned him against seeing his mother because she was in two-point restraints, confined to the bed by a strap around each wrist.

"And they're not goin' let you be alone with her. Somebody from her treatment team goin' be with you the whole time. And if they ain't available, you can be sure an aide will be. You all right with that? 'Cause if you ain't you shouldn't go."

"I'm all right. Least I was the last time she was there."

"Yeah, I know, I know. Okay, go on over, I'll tell them you're coming and who you want to see. And, Detective? You're a brave man."

"Brave? I'm shaking in my shoes"

She patted his face and said, "You're a brave man. You think you're not, but you are."

Inside the Binger building, an aide was waiting for him. Aides never seemed to do much, but two of them were always around, sometimes three, and Carlucci learned early on to respect the almost nonchalant way they interacted with patients.

This aide was a light-skinned Black man in his mid forties, with freckles and red hair, who continually scanned the room while talking to Carlucci.

"Here to see Mrs. Carlucci?"

Carlucci nodded.

"Ethel tell you what you goin' see?"

Carlucci nodded again.

"Seen her like this before?"

"Yes, I have."

"Just making sure," the aide said, motioning with his head for Carlucci to follow him.

"Never seen you before," Carlucci said.

"Worked 'leven to seven for nineteen years. Thought I got a life two weeks ago."

"How long'd you say you worked that shift?"

"Nineteen years this month. Been daylight for two weeks and had more fights with my wife in the last week than I did the whole previous nineteen years. Found out she kicks, she found out I snore. Married seventeen years and never slept in the same bed at the same time, and already she talkin' how we should maybe see a marriage counselor. I say we don't needa see no marriage counselor, I just needa go back on 'leven to seven. Getting ready to, too. Here we are. Need anything, I'll be right outside. And somebody from her treatment team will be, uh, should be coming, soon."

Carlucci took a deep breath, blew it all out, then stepped inside the narrow room, hardly big enough for a single bed and a washstand. His mother was on top of the sheets, apparently asleep.

He tiptoed up the side of the bed to where the restraints were. "Ma?"

"'Bout time," she said, her eyes snapping open. "Wondering when you was gonna show up. Forget I'm alive? Probably wish I was dead, huh, doncha?"

"No, Ma, didn't forget you're alive and I don't wish you were dead."

"Well, what I remember, smart guy, is you're the one put me in here. In this jail."

"Wasn't me, Ma. A hearing master did that."

"That's what you say. I know better."

"Okay, Ma, whatever. How long you, uh, think you're gonna be, uh . . ."

"Tied up? Just little words, Ruggiero. Don't know how to say them?"

"I was gonna say restrained."

"Ouuu, re-straaaaained. That's different. When you're re-straaaained the straps ain't from the bargain basement. They're from the top floor."

"C'mon, Ma."

"C'mon what? I'm in here now 'cause some crazy person told me I was gonna go straight to hell, and the reason she was even talking to me in the first place is 'cause some judge put me in here 'cause you told him—I can't remember how long ago it was—you said I hit some so-called friend of yours with a pan."

"Ma, we been over this I don't know how many times. I never testified at your hearing. I didn't say one word. The cop you hit? He's who's did most of the talking—you're lucky he didn't die. He got screws holding his skull together, and I don't know what all's wrong with him. He don't talk to me anymore."

"Oh, poor you, he don't talk to you anymore, poor Ruggiero. One less friend than you used to have—hey! Look at me! I'm in here with crazy people! Tied to a bed! Can't even go to the toilet like a normal person!"

"C'mon, Ma, cut it out, Jeez."

"That's your answer for everything, ain't it? 'C'mon, Ma, cut it out.'"

"Ma, just tell me something, okay?"

"I ain't telling you nothing!"

"Ma? Did you knock that lady down?"

"Lady? What stupido said she's a lady? She's one of them Jesus freaks. Every time you see her it's the same thing: c'mon, pray with me, put your hands up, wave them all around, sing some goofy Jesus song, that's all she does. Makes me sick. I told her, I said you stay away from me, I mean it. I warned her plenty a times. Did that stop her? Nooooo. Started telling me if I didn't accept Jesus I was going to hell. I told her I was Catholic, I don't have nothing to do with your kinda Jesus. Wouldn't stop, kept it up, you're going to hell, you're going to hell. She got right up in my face, wouldn't get outta my way, so I shoved her. Next thing I know, I'm waking up in here—on a 'visit.' That's what they call it when they stick you in this place, you're on a visit."

"So you did knock her down?"

"I shoved her, I just told you. With my tray. She fell down, I didn't knock her down."

"So shoving her with your tray caused her to fall down?"

"Oh stop playing detective with me—ain't you done enough? You trying to put me in here for life without parole, ain'tcha? You hope I never get outta here, doncha? Admit it, c'mon."

"Ma, Jesus, stop it, please."

"Oh, yeah, that's nice. What're you doing now? Praying or swearing? Maybe what's-her-face shoulda been your mother, maybe you'd like her better. Youns two could pray together."

She raised her head up and shouted, "Hey you, Red! I'm talking to you."

The aide stepped quickly into the room, despite Carlucci's trying to wave him off.

"Something I can do for you, Mrs. Carlucci?"

"My son wantsa trade me in for that goofy lady's always praying, you know the one I mean? The one everybody says I knocked down—which I didn't—and supposedly she busted her shoulder or wrist or elbow or something. See if you can take care of the paperwork, all right? Trade me for her—for him." She pointed with her chin at Rugs.

"Don't think I can make that happen, Mrs. Carlucci."

"And stop calling me that! I don't want nothing to do with him no more." She shot a wicked face at her son. "If he's gonna keep calling himself Ruggiero Carlucci, from now on I'm gonna be, uh, lemme see. Oh yeah. Mrs. Aspi Spumante."

"I believe it's Asti."

"Asti, aspi—you trying to tell me you're Italian now, I guess. Look at him, Ruggiero. Ever seen a red hair on someone like him before? I never did. Look at all them freckles. How'd you get that red hair and all them freckles?"

"Well, I'll tell you, Mrs. Spumante," the aide said, lowering his voice and looking over both shoulders. "But this has to be our little secret, hear? You can't go around telling everybody."

"Yeah, yeah, yeah. So how's come your head's red?"

"My parents, see? They started the Church of the Holy Sunrise. Everything in our house, it was all the color of a sunrise. You had to get up every morning with the sunrise and bow down to the east, and the only thing you could eat was food that was either red or orange or pink. Watermelon, cantaloupe, strawberries, raspberries, oranges, peaches, tangerines, apricots, tomatoes, salmon, beef. But the beef had to be raw. Wasn't allowed to cook it, no sir. And you couldn't eat no pork, no chicken, no green peppers, cabbage, lettuce, celery, nothing like that. And pretty soon, you ate all that stuff long enough? All the babies started popping out looking like strawberries. Just like me."

"Aw get outta here, you're so fulla shit."

"Hey, you axed me. I told you." He winked at Rugs as he turned away.

"Everybody here's a smart-ass—or they're cuckoo. When you gonna get me outta here?"

"I told you, Ma, told you I don't know how many times—I don't have anything to say about that."

"Well did you get me a lawyer yet?"

"The next hearing you have, whenever that is, I guarantee you'll have a lawyer."

"He better be better than that last one. That one didn't even go to lawyer school. He used to book numbers for Muscotti."

"No, Ma, no, that was his father used to book for Muscotti. The son—who represented you—believe me, he went to law school."

"That's what you say—what're you doing here anyway? You fishing around trying to find out where I hid my money?"

"Ma, why you always saying that? You don't have any money."

"That's 'cause you ain't found it yet. Ha, ain't going to neither, I hid it too good. Never find it in a hunnert years."

"Believe me, Ma, I'm not looking for it."

"You think I'm gonna slip up, doncha? You think one day you're gonna come in after they give me one of them shots and I won't be able to keep my mouth shut. Well, joke's on you, Mister Big-Shot Detective. I know how to make my head go all empty. I learned that when I was eleven, before I was even a teenager. No matter what anybody says, if I don't wanna say nothing I don't. You know why, huh?"

"Why, Ma?"

"'Cause once you learn how to make your head empty, you'll never tell anybody anything you don't want to. All my secrets, they're where nobody can get at 'em. You might as well go now, 'cause I'm gonna make my head empty right now. There won't be no point you trying to find out anything else from me, Mister Big-Shot Detective."

"Okay, Ma, okay, whatever you say. Anything you need? Or want?"

"I want outta here, that's what I want! But I ain't telling you what I need. Ohhhhhh no, nothing doing, you find out what I need, then you got me. I ain't falling for that one. Go on, get outta here, go home, you don't belong here. This place, this is just for us."

"Right, Ma. Okay. I'm going. You need anything, tell Ms. Thigpen. She'll call me."

"Ms. Thigpen," she said, turning her head toward the edge of the bed and trying to spit. Only the sound came out of her mouth, no saliva. "She's another looney, always walking around with a buncha papers, talking how she works here, always asking questions, writing the answers down, trying to make you think—she don't work here. Thinks she got me fooled, ha. Double-ha. I know a phony when I see one. She's crazier than all the rest, all the time laughing and singing."

Carlucci wanted hard to say good bye, but as much as he wanted to leave he was trapped between guilt over whether to try to kiss her on the forehead or just pat her hand before he left. If he hesitated when he got close, if his body language tipped her off that he was bending over to kiss her, she'd spit at him, or if he got too close to her feet, she'd kick him. Better just slip out, quick wave at the door, fake a smile, hustle back to work.

"Get me some cannolis."

"What? Now? You want me to get cannolis? Ma, I don't know my way around here, where any bakery is."

"You're a detective, you can't find a bakery? Who's the smart guys hired you? And make sure they don't make them with cottage cheese neither. Make sure they use ricotta. Taste them, don't take their word for it, you hear?"

Carlucci couldn't lie that he would because he knew he wouldn't. Head down, he sidled out the door.

As Carlucci passed Red the orderly whispered, "That's the drugs talking, man. She's your momma and all that, but she don't know what she's saying."

"You think it's drugs, huh?" Carlucci said, not breaking stride. "Believe me, she knows goddamn well what she's saying."

On his way to the parking lot and his car, he talked quietly to himself. *Knows what's she's saying. Knows everything she's doing. Knows exactly how to get what she wants. Never took no for an answer. Not even from Dad. She had him like she knew the combination to the safe, and he didn't even know there was a safe.*

———

Back in the parking lot he noticed what seemed to be the same car as earlier.

But who would care what I'm doing enough to follow me? They must be laughing at my terrible fucking life that this is how I spend a vacation day. Visiting Mamont State Hospital. Jesus, I deserve to be in there myself, seeing an old car like any other and thinking it must be about me. Yup, paranoia, that's the first sign of going nuts if there's any.

On 51 South, he went round and round about her—*Would she get out? Could she get out? Where would she go? What am I thinking? Nobody would put up with her. This is on me, and I'd need at least two people. Who am I gonna get? Can't get Mrs. Viola or Mrs. Comita again. Mrs. Viola's living with her sister in Florida, and Mrs. Comita, last time I saw her, she had her arm in a sling. Said she tripped going up her steps, broke her arm, and the docs said they couldn't help—her bones were like Swiss cheese. So where's that leave . . . us? Us? Her and me, that us? Yeah, right where we were before she broke Fischetti's head. She can't get out. She can't. She gets out, Jesus, it's over. I'm done.*

Guilt grabbed his gut. Acid seeped up his throat.

Should've let Bellotti put her name on the list for the county home when he still liked me for chief. Nah. She'd've never gone for that. Soon as she saw where we were going, she'd've started pounding my head, grabbing the wheel, doing some kinda crazy shit. Killed us both. Or worse. Put us in wheelchairs.

He said, "Stop." He'd read about that in a book Franny had given him. She said if anybody needed to read it, he did. Reseta piled on, said it was one of the best self-help books written in the last twenty-five, thirty years.

"But you gotta do the exercises, Rugs," Reseta said. "You can't just read it and say, oh, that's good, I'll do that, sure, next time. Uh-uh. You gotta get yourself a notebook and you gotta write it all down, every one of the exercises, man, especially the ones you think couldn't possibly apply to you. Trust me. Every exercise in there applies to you."

The hell was the name of that book? How'd I forget that? Jesus, just read it a couple months ago. First time I read that stop thing, I thought how the hell could just saying stop get you to stop thinking the same goofy thing over and over? But it did. Surprised the hell outta me.

Feeling Good, that's what it was. Soon as Fran saw him with it, she got all excited.

"I've been telling you for months now, Rugs, you're depressed! You keep saying no, uh-uh, not me."

"You think I'm depressed? What, you think I'm gonna eat my gun? I ain't gonna do that. I wouldn't do that in a million years. Might not be the sharpest tack in the rug, but I've been holding down my corner just as good as anybody else."

"You, Rugs, you just don't have any—I know you hate this word, but it's the truth—"

"Aw you're not gonna say that again, Franny, c'mon, where's it written down life's supposed to be fun? Huh?"

"I never said life's *supposed* to be fun, Rugs. I said you're *allowed* to have some fun. Everything can't be all gloom and doom. Sometimes the sun shines, it's not always raining. And even when it's raining, sometimes the sun's shining. If it didn't we wouldn't have rainbows. And don't tell me I don't have *your* mother. I have *my own* mother. Remember?"

Franny's mother was living on their first floor, sleeping in what had been their dining room. Franny borrowed a home-improvement loan against the house to have a handicapped-equipped bathroom built on the back porch on the outside wall of the kitchen. Mrs. Perfetti had recoiled at even a hint of going to the county home, or to any assisted-living home. She begged Franny, even got on her knees once, clawed at Franny's legs. "Please, God, let me die first."

When Franny told him what her mother said, Rugs just turned his palms up and shrugged. What could he say? Decades ago, long before they met, they'd begun to care for their mothers, and

gradually, in all the days, weeks, months, years of unspoken con-
cessions, the care was assumed, as binding as if it had been drawn
up by lawyers. Now, Rugs was praying to nothing he believed in
to keep his mother in Mamont, and Franny was being ground
down by working days for the county and nights for her mother,
no weekends or holidays off. Most days she was able to console
herself that there were millions of children all over the world
doing the same for their parents. Sometimes that consolation was
thin as a tissue. She admitted to Reseta that more and more often
lately she slipped away to her room, closed the door to shut out
the signal of her mother's hand bell. Then, moments later, guilt
drove her to see to her mother's need and then the guilt doubled
after she heard herself saying, "Sorry, Mom, I didn't hear it, I was
in the bathroom."

A horn blowing repeatedly snapped Rugs back to the present,
as a pickup truck edged closer to him from the left lane.

Jesus Christ. What's with the fucking cars today?

Glancing at the driver he saw a face red with fury shouting
something he couldn't make out. He lifted his foot off the gas and
dropped back, but the pickup slowed and swerved into his lane,
the driver gesturing with his right hand, middle finger thrusting
upward repeatedly and then pointing to his right.

The pickup pulled into a gas station, the driver clearly expecting
Rugs to follow.

"Jagoff. Like I'm gonna let you get in my face." He hit the gas.
The speed limit on that stretch of Route 51 was 45; in seconds he
was doing 65. At that speed if he got lucky and caught a couple
lights, he could forget the pickup. Last thing he needed was to
get on the wrong side of a road rager. He checked his mirrors for

a while, saw no sign of the pickup, slowed to the flow of traffic, and resumed thinking about what he'd do if the treatment staff at Mamont decided his mother could "manage normal life" again.

She hadn't "managed normal life" since her husband had died a week after he'd taken a hit on the driver's side door by a kid on a motorcycle while on their way to the grocery store. Who was he trying to kid? She was like that long before that happened.

He enlisted in June '72, two days after graduating from Central Catholic High School. His mother had plans for him, none of which she'd ever talked to him about before his graduation. After the ceremony was over, when he was ecstatic that he was finally free of the tyranny of the Sisters of Mercy, instead of allowing him to go to the one party he'd been invited to, his mother practically dragged him out of the car and then into the house where she revealed her plan for him to enroll at the community college to learn to be a chef.

"A chef? When did you ever hear me say that's what I wanna be? Only thing I know how to cook is rolled oats."

"That's why you got to go to college. They teach you everything you need to know. In two years you'll be working at one of the big hotels in downtown Pittsburgh. I got the brochures right here, look at them."

"I don't wanna look at them. You don't know how happy I am I don't have to go to school next year."

"Well, you are going to school next year, Mister Big-Shot thinks he can survive in today's world without college."

"Ma, why'd you wait till now to tell me this? Could've talked to me about this anytime. Why now?"

"Sister Mary Michael, I don't know how many times she told me, she said you need direction, you need somebody pushing you, or you'll never amount to nothing, and you don't need to be told about anything in advance 'cause the way you think that'll just give you the chance to skip out on it."

"Sister Mary Michael is Hitler's daughter—"

She slapped him. Hard. "You watch your mouth about Sister!"

"Ma," Rugs said, holding his left cheek, "Sister M and M had it in for me the first week I was in tenth grade. Some idiot threw a cherry bomb down one of the toilets, blew it off the floor, water went all over the place, she said 'cause I had a hall pass when it went off, it had to be me."

"Could you prove you didn't do it?"

"Could I prove I didn't do it? Ma, you ever see me with a firecracker? Huh? Ever?"

"Just 'cause I didn't see you don't mean you don't go shooting them things off. What do I know what you do when you're not home?"

"Aw, Ma, Jeezou, I don't mess with them things."

"Oh, right, yeah, like I should believe you and not Sister."

"I'm not gonna do that, Ma. I'm not gonna be what you think I should be 'cause you been listening to her. That woman, she made my life miserable for four years."

"She ain't a woman, she's a Sister of Mercy, what's wrong with you?"

"Yeah, that's what she says, but if she ever showed anybody any mercy, you couldn't prove it by me—or any of the other guys. Speaking of which, I got invited to Jackie Morano's party and I'm going."

"Oh no you're not! You're gonna sit right there and read those brochures. Took me half an hour in the community college just finding that department, but I found it and I got them all by myself. I knew you wouldn't go get them."

"Well, I'm sorry you did that, Ma, but if you'da asked me I woulda told you, don't waste your time, I'm not gonna do it. I'll tell you what I am gonna do. I'm gonna change clothes and I'm going to Jackie's party. And day after tomorrow, I'm gonna enlist in the army."

"What? You're gonna enlist in the what? Are you crazy? There's a war going on! In Viet-some place—I don't know where it is—whatta you thinking?"

That memory was as raw as most of the others. His mother screaming about something she wasn't going to put up with, blaming it on something passed down from his father's side of the family. Blamed his father's family for everything she didn't like about him. As far as she was concerned, he'd always really been his father's son. Never been any son of hers.

Traffic had come to a stop. Somebody was pounding on his window. For a second, he thought it was his mother stomping around the first floor, shouting that she was putting her foot down.

On his left were the wild eyes of the driver of the pickup.

"You almost put me into a bus, you fucking asshole! Get outta the car!"

Jesus Christ, my mother's not enough? Got this jagoff—so stupid he don't know what a Municipal plate means?

Carlucci cracked the window and shouted, "Go back and take a look at my plate."

"Fuck your plate! Get out!"

Carlucci squirmed around, found his ID case and gold shield, and smacked it against the window.

"Fuck d' you find that? Some parking lot?"

Doesn't know the plate, thinks I found the shield, jagoff gives me no choice. Carlucci reached for his Beretta. He grabbed hard plastic, a pinch of cloth. His stomach went queasy. Jesus fuck! They're in the trunk! Put them there at Mamont—oh man. Why am I doing shit like this? Really dumb shit?

Wild man continued to pound on the window. Carlucci put his portable red light on the dash and turned it on, as well as all the other lights on the Chevy: the grille lights so they lit red and blue alternately and the tail lights so they'd go strobic red and white. Picked up his mike and switched on the speakers behind the grill.

"I'm a police officer, step away from my vehicle, put your hands behind your head. Do it now!"

Wild man's face turned a pasty white. He put his hands on his head, but took only a half step back.

A long line of traffic curved to the left about fifty yards behind them. Drivers who hadn't heard the PA or couldn't see his lights started laying on their horns. Carlucci didn't care about them but the next move was his because if he didn't do something now some idiot beyond the curve might throw a tantrum—like this numb nuts.

Carlucci popped his seat belt, opened the door far enough to slip out of the car with his right hand behind him, hoping wild man would think he was holding a gun because once out of the car Carlucci saw how large wild man was.

Carlucci said, "I'm gonna move off this road, and you fucking well told better be right behind me. You try to leave, I'm gonna start shooting, tires first, you second, you hear me?"

When wild man got into his truck and followed him off the road, Carlucci thought, *What the fuck? If this idiot had any brains, he would've pulled away as soon as traffic started moving, which it had—and here he is, walking fast, walking mad.* With the power of the PA behind him, Carlucci said again, "Get on your knees, put your forehead on the panel above the wheel—the front wheel! You got three seconds. I won't kill you but I will put one in your knee. One thousand one . . . one thousand—"

Wild man sank to his knees and scooched forward until he was about a foot from the front fender. Lost his balance. Fell against it head first. Carlucci struggled to get out, got his handcuffs and wild man's left hand down, then his right, locked the cuffs. At least he hadn't put his cuffs in the trunk, he hadn't been that far out of it. Done that, he'd really be in a jackpot.

Maybe Figulli was right, maybe he should retire. Even as a rookie, he'd never forgotten where his weapons were. Forgetting them now? Fucking Christ.

"You can breathe, but you move anything I will shoot you," Carlucci said, hustling to the trunk of the Chevy, hoping he'd popped it with the inside latch. Please show me I didn't forget. He touched the trunk. It was springy. *Jesus Christ I did something right!*

Keeping his eyes on wild man, he felt around and found his Beretta, holstered it, then found the Smith & Wesson snub nose and slipped it into his jacket pocket. Couldn't put wild man into the back seat without hooking him up to a leg restraint, but that was in his duty bag on the front seat. Shit, had no choice, get him in the back seat first, close the door, then get the leg strap, keep telling him not to move. Worked so far. How's he gonna know whether I'd shoot him?

Carlucci hurried back to wild man's left shoulder. "What's your name?"

"Oh man, listen, please, okay? I was just acting, that's all. I'm taking acting classes, there's a pretty good chance I could maybe get a part in a movie they're shooting right here in Pittsburgh, gonna start shooting two weeks from now, I was just doing a little improv, honest."

"Last time I'm gonna ask—what's your name?"

"Really, Officer, is this necessary? I mean, you know, soon's I call my teacher, he'll straighten this all out, I'm serious."

"Okay, John Doe, you got a wallet? With ID? I'm gonna search you now. Am I gonna find anything sharp on you—knife, razor, needle? I get cut or stuck? And I get some terrible disease? And die? My friends will hunt you down, and I guarantee you they will give you some pain, you understand me? So what's it gonna be?"

"No no no, I don't have no needles, I ain't no junkie, man, no. No blades either, no knife, razors neither, honest."

"So you were just gonna beat on me with your hands and feet, is that it?" Carlucci said, systematically going through wild man's pockets.

"I'm telling you, Officer, I was just rehearsing, honest, man, just doing a little improv. You know what that is? That's where you don't have a script, you just wing it."

In wild man's left back pocket, Carlucci found a misshapen wallet bulging with pictures and credit and debit cards. Wild man's face did not match the picture on the operator's license. Worse, no owner's card, no liability insurance card.

"Oh, hey, Officer, I almost forgot. That's not my wallet. I found that last night. At the school. In the parking lot when I was, uh, when I was looking for, uh, for my wallet."

"Uh-huh. So naturally, your license and the owner's card and insurance card, they're all in your wallet, right? Which you lost last night. And you just happened to find this wallet. So when I run the plates on this truck, this Francis A. Martin? His name's gonna be on the cards? 'Cause you don't look anything like him. Or maybe you're all disguised. Maybe another part of your acting class, I guess, make up maybe, huh?"

"Man, I can explain that. You let me get in my truck, you can follow me to my apartment, and I'll find you everything you need to prove who I am. Even call my professor, let you talk to her, she'll tell you."

"Couple seconds ago, it was a him. C'mon, John Doe, get up. You're going in the back seat till Pittsburgh PD gets here."

"Aw, man, don't . . . don't do that, please? Don't call Pittsburgh, okay, please?"

"Why? Got a little history with them, do you? I'll bet you do. Watch your head."

Carlucci closed the back door, opened the front door, hit the button locking all doors. Then went around to the passenger side. And there remembered—Jesus Christ—he'd just locked all the doors. Had to go back to the driver side and hoped to somebody up somewhere he remembered to take the key out of the ignition. He shook his head. Whatever. I'm not praying. I'm not praying goddammit. I am not gonna pray, bust the window with my goddamn Beretta first.

He reached into his right front pocket. Found the keys! Remembered! Opened the driver door. Opened all the doors. Got a leg restraint out of his bag. Hustled back around to John Doe, wrapped the strap around John Doe's thighs, closed the door on the other end of the strap, locked all the doors again.

Then he called 911, got transferred to a dispatcher from Pittsburgh PD, identified himself, requested assistance, asked them to run the plate on the pickup. Then he moved the pickup in front of his car. Went back to his car, slumped behind the wheel and immediately started deep breathing: four in, hold it for four, blow it out for four. Again. Got into a rhythm. Slowly began to come down.

Carlucci checked out John Doe in his mirror. He was crying. The prick was crying. Real tears.

"How you make yourself cry like that? More improv? I'm impressed."

"Hey, man, I know I was outta line, but you gotta cut me a break here. That there's my brother-in-law's truck. He doesn't know I got it. I had to get to this job interview, man, I been outta work for like two months now, and I knew he wouldn't loan it to me."

Carlucci stared at him. "Man, you are something. Don't get what a municipal plate means and just now you confessed to grand theft auto. What's next? There paper out on you?"

"What? No, no paper. Huh? What kinda paper?"

"What kinda paper? What kind you think? Outstanding warrants."

For a long moment wild man appeared to freeze. Then he started bouncing. Rocking the car. Carlucci sighed and got out. Stay in here with this jagoff my head's gonna break. Where the fuck's Pittsburgh PD?

Five minutes later, he heard the siren, then saw the lights, started waving and yelling. The black-and-white pulled in behind his Chevy. A black cop emerged, late forties, thighs wider than Carlucci's belly, clearly short of temper about something.

Carlucci nodded, introduced himself, showed his ID and shield.

"I'm gonna tell you right now, Detective, I got exactly one hour and forty-four minutes to get to my little girl's wedding. You better not be handing me no hairball."

"I'll try not to, but—"

"Wait a minute. That truck up there? This about that truck?"

Carlucci nodded.

"I know that truck." He bent over and peered into the back seat, then jerked on the back door, still locked. "Awwww man, you again!"

"Open it up! I'm goin' kill him, swear to God, I'm goin' kill this motherfucker. Jaggers, motherfucker, I tol' you never come in my precinct again, didn't I tell you that?"

To Carlucci he snarled, "C'mon, man, pop the lock, pop it, goddammit!"

Carlucci popped the locks and stood back out of the way.

"Jaggers, get yo' ass out here." The cop reached in, caught the leg restraint in his left hand and pulled hard. Jaggers snapped over onto his right side, protesting that he wasn't Jaggers. The city cop jerked Jaggers out onto the gravel. Coming out, Jaggers hit his head on the door frame. He started howling and whimpering, but the city cop wasn't having any of it.

"Asshole. If I have to pick you up, I'm goin' kick you in yo ass so hard next time you shit you goin' have to wipe yo nose! Now giddup!"

Carlucci cleared his throat and said, "Uh, is this all necessary?"

"Hey! You called for assistance, you got me. I was you, I'd be on my way, and I wouldn't waste two seconds worrying about what is and what ain't necessary."

"Just asking," Carlucci said.

City cop's eyes froze into slits. Carlucci held up his palms, shook his head, skittered behind and around the city cop to get into his car. First break in traffic, he spun up gravel pulling into the flow, thinking of all the ways today he'd lost focus. *And why? Do I have to ask? You think maybe it's so I wouldn't have to think about her?*

———

Back at the parking lot behind Rocksburg station, Carlucci pulled into the slot reserved for detectives. He slipped inside the station, hoping to avoid any member of council's Safety Committee that might still be hanging around. Couldn't tell with these guys; they were all poster boys for idle hands working for the devil. Well, not the mayor: he still had his insurance business. But Radoycich or Figulli? Those two got their jollies just hanging around. Johnny Radio, left to himself, wasn't too bad, but Figulli always had his nose in somebody's business. Always crowing he knows how to do whatever faster, better, and naturally at lower cost to the city. Sometimes he did, had to give him that. But sometimes what he did wound up costing the city in ways money couldn't measure.

Like vouching for his niece. Figulli talked council into hiring her as a meter maid. Rumors flew he expected that after a year or so on the job she would automatically move up to a patrolman's slot when one opened. She was always chirping about her degree in criminal justice from the community college, how she'd passed all her weapons and physical tests. Which might have been true, probably was, but the one test she flunked every day was attitude. Never seemed to grasp the concepts of breakfasts, coffee breaks, and lunches, as applied to people who bought lunch from the breakfast and lunch shops within blocks of the courthouse. First week on the job, she figured if she hung around those shops, she could write a whole bunch of violations and wouldn't have to walk far to do it. End of her second week, every deli owner within three blocks of the courthouse was in the city hall parking lots with home-made posters about whoever hired the idiot meter maid ticketing their regulars. Two of them had portable bullhorns.

Mayor Bellotti managed to get her aside and explained to her, yes, she'd been hired to enforce meter violations, but she had to use some common sense. People have only so much time to eat lunch and what was she doing? She was ambushing drivers who were picking up their take out.

"What I'm hearing," the mayor said, "is soon as you're on the job, you leave the station, you head right for the delis. You need to spread out, you know, be someplace else at that time of the day."

"Uh, huh, but we're only a couple blocks from the courthouse."

"Exactly my point. Instead of walking north when you leave the station, from now on you walk south. Away from those delis."

"How far south?"

"Well how about to the city line? Where it meets South Rocksburg."

"I didn't even know there was meters down there. Or a South Rocksburg."

"Well not everybody knows, there is a sign, not very big, but now you know, so you go till the meters run out, then you cut east and you hit those side streets where there's permit parking, then you cut west, and you go back and forth like that, see? That should keep you going, say, till around one o'clock, then, of course, that's when you would be working your way back to the courthouse."

"My uncle warned me to watch out about showing favoritism."

"Well, of course, yes, Egidio's right, treat everybody the same, but what I'm telling you is, and I hope you understand me now, you just show no favoritism in the opposite way from where you've been going, you know, when your watch begins."

A week later, the mayor was accosted by Marlene Derzepelski, a diabetic from South Rocksburg whose left leg had been amputated just above her knee. She and her scooter were well known to Rocksburg PD, and as she pulled to into his path, she was waving a ticket at him, howling about who told the meter maid battery-powered wheelchairs had to have a motor vehicle license.

"What're you talking about?"

"This," she said, thrusting the ticket at him. "I come over the city line yesterday 'cause I'm going to the post office like I been doing every day for the last four years, ever since I got this scooter. This goofy meter maid, she's standing there, she goes, 'You come over the line I'm gonna arrest ya.' I go, 'For what?' She goes, 'It don't look like you got a license to drive on the street.' I go, 'Who's driving on the street, I'm on the sidewalk, like I'm s'posed to. You think this is a motorcycle? This is a scooter-wheelchair, you don't need no driver's license for this.' She goes, 'Oh yes you do,' and she writes me this ticket says I owe seventy-five bucks! I'm on Social Security Disability, where am I s'posed to get that kinda money?"

The mayor took the ticket, tore it in half without looking at it, shoved it in his inside coat pocket. "Don't worry about it. She's new, just a little too overly conscientious, know what I mean?"

"Well, somebody needs to straighten her out, I don't need no car license. I got all the permits I need. And I renew every year just like I'm s'posed to."

The mayor met again with the overly conscientious meter maid—this time with her uncle present—and by the end of the conversation everybody seemed to be on the same page.

So no one was more surprised than the mayor, not even Figulli, when two days later on the editorial page of the *Rocksburg Gazette* there appeared a letter from Mary Francis Ippolitto, the meter-maid's grandmother and Egidio Figulli's sister's mother-in-law, referring to "the fine sense of justice among today's public-spirited young people."

"It's a shame," the letter said, "that the older people in city government can't be as conscientious in the administration of justice as these young people who are merely doing the jobs they were hired for."

Next morning, the mayor arrived at City Hall ten minutes earlier than usual, slapping a rolled-up *Gazette* against his thigh.

"Hey, Egidio," he said, waving the paper at Figulli after he got out of his car. "The hell's going on here? You see this?"

Figulli threw up his hands. "Jesus, I just got here. What're you talking about?"

"This letter in the *Gazette*. This niece of yours, she know she got five and a half months to go on probation? During which time she can be fired without cause?"

Figulli took the paper and read the letter, which the mayor had circled with a red pen. "Oh, this ain't right," he said.

"Really? It ain't, huh? Two weeks on the job, it's one thing after another with her. She thinks this is how city employees express their grievances? Letters to the editor?"

"No, that ain't what I meant. My sister's mother-in-law couldn't've written this. First place, she's practically blind, she can't see good enough to write nothing. Second place, even when she could see, no way she could spell conscientious. Hell, I can barely pronounce it."

"So you saying the kid wrote it?"

"Well right now I don't know who wrote it, but lemme talk to my sister."

When Figulli came back to work after lunch, his face was blotchy and his breathing shallow. He poked the *Gazette* and dropped it on the mayor's desk.

"You ain't gonna believe this. I just found out my sister's been writing this kid's papers since she was in grade school. I go, 'You mean to tell me it was you wrote this letter?' She goes, 'Well not exactly, we sorta been working together ever since she got an F in ninth grade.' I go, 'How the hell'd you think this girl was supposed to learn anything if you was writing her papers for her?' 'Well,' she goes, 'I didn't want her to get another F.' I go, 'That don't answer my question.' She goes, 'Well, Egidio, you wasn't so smart yourself.' 'Maybe I wasn't, but I got all those bad grades on my own, there wasn't no relative helping me.'

" 'Well, there you are, she goes, you turned out pretty good, big shot in the city and everything.' I go, 'That ain't the point; your daughter ain't doing her job right and I'm who talked council into hiring her and now both of youns, youns're making me and the mayor look like a coupla jackasses.' She gives me this shrug; 'The girl's just trying to do her job right.' I go, 'The hell she is. You should've let this girl flunk on her own.' 'Oh,' she goes, 'nobody flunks in school nowadays, teachers don't wanna hurt their self-esteem.' "

"Oh yeah?" the mayor said. "What about my self-esteem? What about yours, Egidio? You ask me, this is classic she's pissing on us, telling us it's raining. You go find this little relative of yours and you fire her. She wants to know why, you tell her we don't have to tell her why, goodbye, period, end of story. And, Egidio, you got any more nieces like this one, tell them check out the private sector first."

All Carlucci had to do to lower his emotions after a ruckus with Figulli was just remember the niece—as long as his face was straight when Figulli happened to look at him. Harder to do now that Figulli seemed to have it out for him.

The Monday morning after Figulli strongly suggested Carlucci reconsider his retirement plans, he found a notice in his in-basket that said in two weeks "Council's Safety Committee would convene an inquiry into the reason why Det. Sgt. Ruggiero Carlucci fired his sidearm on Norwood Hill on the night of August 6, 2011. Carlucci is hereby ordered to appear with his representative from FOP Chapter 107 and an attorney of his own choosing."

Carlucci appeared with Panagios Valkanas, Esq., known around town as "Mo," a nickname he loathed and failed for years to drive out of currency.

He nodded at the mayor and the rest of the council as he sat down. Carlucci couldn't help but notice the smug look Figulli shot back.

Jesus Christ, of course Figulli is taking this inquiry as an opening salvo in his war to get me to retire. What else does he have up his sleeve? How far would he go?

Just as Mayor Bellotti was calling the inquiry to order, Chief Nowicki burst into the room and said, "We got a situation. Rugs, I need you right now!"

"What kinda situation?" Figulli said.

"Some guy on Popper Street just shot his roommate and now he's shooting at cars on the street—I need everybody we got."

"How you know he shot his roommate?"

"His roommate is who made the call—don't have time to explain, c'mon, Rugs."

Carlucci trotted out behind Nowicki.

"You got a shotgun in your car?"

"'Course I do."

"Then get going!" Nowicki said. "I gotta go get one."

"Wait a minute—where am I going?"

"Four-fifty-one Popper. Supposed to be shooting out of the second floor. Park in the alley behind it. I'll be right there, soon's I get a shotgun and ten-ninety-nine everybody."

Ten-ninety-nine, Carlucci thought. "What're you calling everybody here for? Don't you want them going there?"

"Can't remember the ten-number for that," Nowicki said, running into the station.

Carlucci tried to remember if there was a ten-number for calling everybody to a report of shots fired. He couldn't. *Sometimes, no shit, it's a miracle we get anything right.*

He stopped moving for a moment to think where Popper Street was. Then he remembered it ran parallel to Main, State, and Harrington, and between Harold and Willow on the west end. He was pretty sure the 400 block was between Stanley and Sycamore going north and remembered there was a cluster of three- and four-story apartment buildings rented mostly to students in Conemaugh County Community College or Western Vo-Tech School. Community college students were mostly county residents, but Vo-Tech students came from all over southwestern Pennsylvania.

With lights and siren, Carlucci drove through intersections as fast as he dared, pulled into the alley behind the 400 block of Popper, jumped out, opened the trunk, shrugged into his vest, flinching every time he heard a shot from either a shotgun or a center-fire rifle. Short silence, followed by many cracks of a semi auto rimfire. His last grab was for the shotgun.

A male was shouting, cursing. Carlucci looked up, saw only the fire escapes and back porches of three floors of apartments. Tried to understand the shouter but heard just fear and panic. Nobody visible. He listened for a moment. Only sound he heard was the noise he was making loading his shotgun. Pushed the slide forward, clicked the safety on with his thumb.

He caught a glimpse of a face ducking back on a second-floor porch. Brought the shotgun to his cheek and aimed up, then backed away to the other side of the alley, shouted, "Hey! Police! Tell me what you know!"

No response. Heard more rimfire cracks, definitely coming from the front of this building. Shouted up again. Again no response. Looked at the cellar wall of the building, garage doors side by side the length of the building.

Heard five more cracks in quick succession, then somebody yelling again.

Ran across the alley and tried every one of the garage doors. All locked.

Shouted up again, sure he had seen somebody up there on either the floor directly above him or the one above that.

Again no response.

"Hey, if you can hear me, I'm the police! You look, you'll see I'm the police, I need to know what's going on!"

"I don't know what's going on."

"What floor you on?"

"Second."

"What floor's the shooter on?"

"I don't know."

"Is he on your floor?"

"I don't know."

"You alone?"

"Yes."

"Can you look out in the hall?"

"Yeah. But I ain't going to."

"You have a cell phone?"

"Yeah."

"You got a number for anybody in this building?"

"A couple."

"Call them."

"Why?"

"Why—Jesus! Ask them if they know what floor he's on, what room he's in, if anybody's with him, anybody's hurt, anything they can tell you will help me. Right now the only thing I know is somebody's shooting."

"What if they don't know anything?"

"Can't know till you call them—got more than one number?"

"Yeah. I know three."

"Then start calling them, all right?"

For nearly a minute Carlucci heard no shots. Then the voice above said, "Nobody's answering."

"You call all three numbers?"

"Yeah. No."

"How many'd you call?"

"Two . . . one."

Carlucci coughed up some saliva and spit.

"Listen, what's your name?"

"Sylvester. Syl."

"Okay, Syl, I'm Rugs. I know you're scared. So am I. But right now all I know is somebody on the front of this building is shooting. He's got at least two guns, one of them's a shotgun or a center-fire rifle and the other one's probably a semi-auto .22. I really need to know where he is and how many guns he's got, understand? Hold up—can I get into this building from down here?"

"Uh-uh, you gotta have a key."

"You have a key?"

"No."

"Know anybody who does?"

"Yeah. But I ain't gonna ask them now."

Shit. "Okay, okay, then call those other two numbers!"

Carlucci scanned the rest of the porches to see if anybody else had come out. Then he heard a car turning into the alley, saw it was a civilian who was definitely wrong place, wrong time. He stepped into the middle of the alley, held his shotgun overhead, and started waving for the driver to back out.

Instead, the driver started forward. Carlucci leveled the shotgun at him.

The driver stopped, his window went down, he leaned out, said, "Hey. I live here. What's going on?"

Carlucci moved toward him. "You live here? What floor? What room?"

"Right up from where that car's at." He pointed at Carlucci's car.

"Listen to me, somebody's shooting in the front of this building. Whoever it is shot his roommate, who called 911, and that's all we know. Since I got here, I've heard at least ten shots, most of them from a .22. But the first couple I heard were loud, either a shotgun or a center-fire rifle. Any idea who that is? Or what room he's in?"

"Aw jeez oh man, that's Kipple. Yeah, gotta be. There's a couple guys in there got guns, but he's the one scares me."

"Why?"

"'Cause he's all the time acting like he got everything all under control. Top of which, he just did, uh, three months, whatta you call it? Aw—oh! Interning with some police department around here."

"Interning with some PD around here—you know this guy for sure?"

"Yeah, yeah, I know him, but I'm telling you he scares me. Wants to be a cop. Anybody shooting in there, it's him."

"Where's he live, what floor, what room?"

"Second floor. Two doors down from me. I'm in 201, he's in 205. Aw man."

"What?"

"My cat's in there—he hates cats, always talking how everybody oughta shoot them anytime they want. Oh, man, he hurts my cat—better not hurt my cat."

"When you were pulling in here, were you going into one of these garages?"

"Yeah. Yes. Why?"

"Why do you think—I have to get up there."

"Huh? You gonna try to get up there? Really?"

"Whatta you mean really—what'd I just say? But I can't unless you let me in, tell me how the place is laid out, where your room is."

"Well okay, yeah, but what if it's not him? I'm just guessing, I could be I'm wrong."

"Listen, doesn't matter if it's not him, okay? It's somebody, and whoever it is, he gotta be stopped."

"I don't know—you sure you're a cop?"

"Hey, just open the door, okay? And when we get inside you need to draw me a floor plan."

"Yeah. But how do I know you ain't the guy shooting?"

"What? Open the fucking door!"

The driver shook his head.

"Listen up, kid: I'm ordering you now, open that door!"

The kid eased his car carefully around Carlucci just as Nowicki skidded to a stop in the other end of the alley. Nowicki scrambled out of his car with two bandoleers of shotgun shells crossing his chest. Reached inside his back seat, struggled with the bandoleers, brought out two shotguns. He started to trot toward Carlucci, who was walking behind the kid who drove to the next-to-last garage door. Carlucci waved to Nowicki to hold up.

"This kid thinks he knows the shooter and where he lives. He's gonna let me in—he better let us in."

"His name Kipple?"

"That's what he said—how'd you know that?"

"It's his roommate called 911. Said he took one in the chest."

"And he told you his name? Anything else?"

"Said he did three months interning with Level Valley PD."

Carlucci shook his head. "That's what this kid said. You talk to anybody from there?"

"Course I did, whatta you think? Chief's coming. Says it can't be him, 'cause the Kipple he knows, says he wished he had a kid just like him."

Carlucci shook his head. "Oh yeah, I believe that, right—the door's open, let's go."

Carlucci went in first, looking all around, but didn't see anybody.

"Aw for Chrissake."

"What? What?"

"That kid, asshole—took off while we were talking. Jesus Christ."

"Now what?" Nowicki said.

"Gotta be stairs here somewhere. Jesus, the landlord really went all out for the lights—there's the steps," Carlucci said, pointing with his thumb behind him. "Gimme one of those bandoliers."

"Hold it, hold it—not making a move till that Level Valley chief gets here. I want all the intel we can get."

A loud shot from above. Then another.

"Hear that?"

"'I ain't deaf! But we need intel, man, can't just go busting on up there."

"Speaking of intel, everybody can't be on vacation. You got your radio, call them."

"Where's yours?"

"Why did I need a radio in front of the Safety Committee?"

"Supposed to have it with you all the time—"

"What the fuck, you goin' all Figulli on me? Now? You set a vacation schedule that had more than one month in it—like the one we're in now? I wouldn't be in a uniform, would I?"

"Really think this is the time—?"

"What else I got to do? You don't wanna go upstairs, you wanna wait on this chief from, uh, wherever. Next thing you're gonna say is you should call SWERT."

"Now that you mention it, I think that's exactly what I should do."

"Aw for Chrissake, Wick, if you haven't called them yet, it'll be ten minutes before they even get here. Then they gotta set up—how long for that?"

"What? Who used to tell me heroes get killed—was that you? What, you have a fight with my cousin?"

Carlucci's mind flashed back to his last talk with Fran Perfetti and the ugly taste it left in his mouth. "Leave her outta this."

"Jesus Christ, you *did* have a fight with her. So what? So now you wanna kill somebody? What the fuck, Rugs, you ain't gonna get killed on my watch, nothing doing, you stay right here beside me till that chief gets here."

"You gonna call anybody to see who's out front? Or if they're out front? Said you need all the intel you can get but we don't know who's out front of this building."

Nowicki pulled his radio out of its holster. "All units copy, I need your 10-20s ASAP."

"Raiford here, I copy. I'm in the attic of a house across from the shooter, not directly across, because this is a real narrow house, so it sort of looks like I'm a quarter of a lot short of being directly across from where he is. But I only just caught a glimpse of him. Raiford out."

"Uh, DeRenzi here. I'm on, uh, the north side of the 300 block of Popper. I can't see anybody, but I hear every shot. Don't see no other of our mobiles. He keeps shooting at cars, hitting the back fenders, like he's trying to set a gas tank on fire. I see some of the holes real plain. They're big. Like maybe shotgun slugs. I should say out now, right?"

Nowicki shook his head, waited a moment, then said, "Anybody else wanna give me their 10-20?"

No response.

"There you go, Wick. Veteran detective sergeant in the attic across the street and a rookie patrolman in a car, out front and you and me. You know, I'm starting to like this doofus who picked now to shoot up the street. Gonna save me a whole lotta time—"

"Rugs, don't start with me about that, I'm trying to think."

"Think away. Need help, I'm right here."

"What'd I say—I'm trying to think goddammit!"

A loud shot from above, then two more. Then silence.

Then someone was coming slowly down the steps behind them, someone trying to choke back sobs. Nowicki and Carlucci turned, scooted behind Carlucci's car, leveled their shotguns at the sound. It was the kid who'd let them in. He was holding something in his arms.

"He killed my cat. Look. He shot her . . . shot her head off," the kid said, holding the limp body of a tiger-striped cat. They came out from behind the car, looked at the kid, then at the cat, most of its head shot away.

"That bastard, he said he was gonna do it—and he did it! Look what he did!" He sat down on the bottom step, put the cat up to his face, sobbed into its ribs. "This cat never even killed a bird . . . don't have claws . . . why'd he do this? Said only queers and old ladies had cats . . . I ain't queer and I ain't an old lady—look at my cat!"

Nowicki and Carlucci looked at each other, shook their heads.

Carlucci said, "Sorry about your cat. Had a dog once. My mother gave it away. Might as well've shot it. Think I know how you feel."

"You wanna kill her? 'Cause I wanna kill him! Shoot his head off!"

Carlucci thought about the times he wished his mother was, not dead necessarily, just not living with him. He snapped back to now.

"When you got up there, did you see him? Was he in the room where you said he'd be—205, was that it?"

"Yeah. He came out when I opened the door and he saw me and he had his gun up to his shoulder and he said, 'Find your cat yet?' Then he started laughing, the prick. Then he went back inside his room and I went inside . . . look for my cat . . . look what he did! I had this cat since I was nine . . . ten years I had her and he does this—oh God kill him! Kill him please!"

Well, we might have to, Carlucci thought, *but not for killing a cat. Might have to 'cause maybe Kipple killed the guy he shot . . . I doubt he knows how much killing people fucks with you. Takes your mind out, feeds it to the demon dogs growling in your head.*

In one second Carlucci was back in 'Nam . . . slogging in the middle of a shallow ditch, boots sucking at every step, bullets zipping by . . . somebody grunting, *Jesus, that guy's arm, is that Tufton? Tuf, Tuf, you okay?. . .* somebody screaming, *Get down, get down, get down!* He dropped, water gushed up his nose, *Jesus fuck,* spitting, sputtering . . . *come all the way over here and I'm gonna drown? Don't even get a shot? Not one shot? At anybody?*

"Rugs! Hey!"

"What?"

"You here?"

"What're you yelling for, I'm standing right here."

"Lost you, man, you got that look."

"What look?"

"The one says you ain't here. Get your ass back here, man, now! I need you."

"I'm right here, what the fuck?"

"Okay, okay—you hear what he said—what's your name?"

"William, uh, Cyril. Mark. William Timoshenka."

"Which is it now, Cyril or William or Mark?"

"It's Cyril Mark. My parents the only ones call me that. I'm just William."

"William, huh? You hear him, Rugs? What he said about where the shooter was?"

"I'm standing right here."

"You were tuning me out, man—all right, never mind. So you heard he's still in his room. That's two-oh-five, right, William? So how far's that from the steps you just came down?"

"I don't know, three rooms from the stairs."

"Well how big's your room? How wide?"

"I don't know, ten feet? I don't know!"

"All these rooms the same?"

"No, no," Carlucci said. "They used to be four-room apartments. Real small. Claustrophobic. Then when this tech school opened up this outfit from Pittsburgh came in, about ten, twelve years ago, bought them all up, turned them all into two rooms each."

"How do you remember that?"

"How do I remember that? How you remember anything?"

"No, I mean, why do you remember that?"

"Now you wanna know why I remember it?"

"Why do you remember that in particular—you respond to something here? I'm just trying to find out how this building's laid out, Rugs, okay?"

"Mostly I remember that all the plumbing's at one end, there's one big shower and a big bathroom, right, kid? William? Is that right?"

"Yeah. All down the other end."

"Opposite from here?"

"Yes. Right."

"So, Wick, what's the plan? You got one, right?"

Nowicki chewed his lower lip, said nothing.

"You're still thinking SWERT; I can see your wheels turning."

"Hey, when you need those guys, you need them."

"If I had the rifles they have, the ammo, the time, I could shoot just as good as any one of them."

"Man, Rugs, you got one gigundous hair up your ass today."

A loud shot from above. Then two more. Then another, but not as loud.

"Think you better call out front, sounds like somebody else returning fire."

"Huh? All units, copy. Raiford? You copy? Over."

"Raiford here, I copy."

"What's going on?"

"Think our rookie just went John Wayne on us."

"What? Where is he? DeRenzi, you copy? You shooting? Is that you? DeRenzi? DeRenzi! You copy? Goddammit, DeRenzi, ten-twenty ! You copy?"

"I copy. I had a shot at him. I took it."

"What? You had a shot and you took it?"

111

"Yeah, I went two blocks back, and I went across the street, and I stayed close to the buildings, and I came up like almost right under the window where he's at. Saw the barrel come out, I shot at it."

"You shot up? At the barrel?"

"Yeah."

"You forget the rule says you gotta be sure what's behind your target? You think where that bullet's gonna come down? Huh?"

No response.

"Didn't think so. You listen up! You get your ass back where you were, and don't move unless I tell you, you hear me? And no more shooting up! Out."

"Uh, ten-four to that. Yes, sir. Out. Sir."

"Fucking Christ," Nowicki said.

Carlucci couldn't resist. "That's what happens you let the rest of the department go to Dizzyworld."

"Knock it off, Rugs, I'm telling you, knock it the fuck off!"

"So, all right then, Wick-man, what's your plan?"

"Why you such a wise-ass today? You beefing with Franny again?"

"Told you before, don't have nothing to do with her. How many bodies we got? Besides us? How many did twelve to eight yesterday? How many did eight to four? Two each, right? And they're all home now—for Chrissake call them! They're no good to us sleeping. None of them's gonna forget to look what's behind their target. Send that rookie home."

William Timoshenka stood up and walked toward them with the body of his cat stretched out in front of him. "What about my cat? You guys gonna do anything about my cat? Or you just gonna stand there and yell at each other?"

"We're talking here, that's all," Carlucci said.

"Well you gonna do anything about my cat? Give me one of those guns I'll do it myself." He burst into tears.

"William, be better if you sat back down for a while."

Before Nowicki could say anything else, they heard somebody calling out behind them.

"Chief Nowicki, you in there? Chief Newsome out here, Level Valley PD. Spoke to you earlier on the phone."

"In here. Just inside the door, come on in."

Chief Newsome peeked around the doorframe of the garage. He held out his ID case and gold shield. "Mind if I see yours?"

"No," Nowicki said, walking toward the open door, showing his own shield and ID.

The chief, a round man with an even rounder belly, wore a white shirt with a gold star on the collars and a white cap with gold scrambled eggs on the black bill. He stepped around the door frame and extended his hand. "We met last year at the county chiefs meeting. You may not remember, I gave a little talk on our athletic program—out there in the Valley."

"No, I don't remember. This is Detective Sergeant Carlucci, Rugs for short. And the gentleman with him lives up on the second floor two doors from the shooter. William Timoshenka. Shooter killed his cat."

"And you're absolutely certain the shooter is Ronald Kipple?"

"William, is that his name? Ronald?"

"Yeah, that's him. The fucker."

"I can't believe this. That's just not the fella I been working with for the last three months."

Two loud shots in quick succession.

"That him?"

"That's him."

"I have to call this boy, I can't believe this."

"Well you got his number, call him."

"Yes I do, let me get on it here."

Newsome poked the numbers on his flip phone.

"Ron? Chief Newsome here. Is this Ronald Kipple? Ronald Reagan Kipple? . . . just finished an internship with the Level Valley PD? A three-month internship? It is? Well, son, what's going on—is that you shooting up there? . . . It is? Well what's brought this on, son? This is not like you at all, I mean, you're the last person in the world I would think be acting this way. . . . So it is you. Well yes, I'll take your word for that, but now—wait a minute here—hold it, son, you're talking way too fast, slow down. . . . That's better, yes, that's fine, so now what's this about? . . .You've been drinking? . . . Been drinking all night? Why're you doing that, son? I never knew you to drink even one beer. . . . You just got pissed off? Well, what is it pissed you off, that's what I'm trying to get you to tell me—Ron? Ron?

"Hung up."

"Probably just dropped the phone," Nowicki said. "Call him back, don't quit."

Newsome waited a moment, then called again. He put the phone to his mouth and shook his head. "I'm just having a hell of a time getting my mind around this. . . . Ron? Me again. What happened we got cut off. . . . Dropped it, huh? Well, that's what I thought. But now listen, son, I think I know you well enough and I think you know me, you know you can confide in me, tell me what this is about before somebody gets hurt. . . . Oh. Somebody is hurt? . . .You shot him? . . .You! Around ten o'clock this morning,

09 57 hours. . . .You made a note of that? . . .Well I don't doubt you did, son, I'm sure you been keeping an accurate record, I wasn't doubting you, not at all, no sir. . . ."

Carlucci whispered to Nowicki, "Keep him talking. Don't let him hang up. William? You come with me, c'mon, don't say anything, just follow me."

"Wait a second, what're you gonna do?"

"Oh for Chrissake, what do you think? Just keep fat-stuff talking, don't let him quit, no matter what. C'mon, William, put your cat down, let's go."

"Not going anywhere 'less you give me a gun."

"All right, all right, we get upstairs and you show me where his room is I'll give you a gun, okay? Now let's go."

"Promise."

"I promise I'll give you a gun."

"Hey," Chief Newsome said, "where you two going?"

"Just gonna do a little recon, that's all. No big deal, just keep your boy talking. We'll be right back."

"Oh no, nothing doing, I'm not gonna be a party to this, you go up there and shoot that boy while I'm talking to him, that'll be on my conscience the rest of my life. You gonna do recon, you leave your weapons here, you don't need weapons to do recon."

Carlucci looked at Nowicki, and they both looked at Newsome.

"Leave my weapons here? You really a cop?"

"Am I really a—of course—that's insulting. Chief Nowicki, you need to discipline this man."

Nowicki cleared his throat. "Uh, Chief, that's not gonna happen. Sergeant Carlucci's been in this department longer than I have, got two pages of commendations and, uh, actually, he was the chief here before I was, so that's not gonna happen. If I was you, I'd just keep your guy talking."

"I will not," Chief Newsome said, poking at his phone.

Carlucci laughed and shook his head. "Goddamn. Wick, I'm telling you, man, the last three weeks, it's been one freak show after another. Okay, I'm going up. And, Chief whatever your name is, when I get up there, that jagoff's waiting for me at the top of the stairs 'cause you gave him a heads-up? You need to think about this mess from my point of view instead of his, okay? 'Cause I don't wanna kill him, but I don't wanna get killed either, you got me? Come on, William, you coming or not?"

"Not if you don't promise to give me a gun."

"Already promised you that, remember? Right when we get upstairs." *Then all I'd have to worry about is you tripping on the steps and putting one in my back . . . promise to give you a gun, Jesus Christ.*

"Hey, whoa! You're not going up there without a radio!"

"Okay, okay, get me one. And don't forget how many radios are out there in the alley. You call those guys were on eight to four yesterday? They coming in?"

"Canoza's in front of a judge, support hearing. Esper's wife said he's fishing out Twin Lakes. I'm calling Park Police now, see if they got somebody out there can message him. And, Rugs, I mean it, man, you stay put, I'm watching you."

"Yeah, right, I can see you're watching me."

Chief Newsome shook his head. "The way you people talk to one another, it's no wonder you have a discipline problem here."

"Uh, Chief, how many people in your department?"

"What's that have to do with anything?"

"It's a number, that's all I'm asking. Twenty, thirty, what?"

"Four."

"Four?" Carlucci said. "Jesus Christ, man, we got twenty-eight, and by population and geography we're supposed to have at least thirty-six. So unless you can provide something smart about what we should be doing here, keep your, uh, observations to yourself."

"Young man, you watch how you talk to me. I'm not your chief."

"*Young man*? I joined this department when I was twenty-two, I been on the job for thirty-five years. What do you say, old man, how old're you?"

Chief Newsome cleared his throat. "You certainly don't look fifty-seven."

"Oh I look it, and fuck knows I feel it."

"Esper's coming," Nowicki said. "Park Police had a unit there, found him right away. Said he'll be here in fifteen."

Five loud shots from above, in quick succession.

Nowicki clicked open his mic. "Raiford, what's going down?"

"Raiford here. So, so."

"Anybody hit?"

"Negative. Still shooting cars, still hollering nonsense."

"Sent anything your way yet?"

"Negative. Haven't given him any reason to think I'm here. And the rookie hasn't moved since you told him. Raiford out."

"Your man reported things were so-so? That's his professional report?"

"So-so, same old, same old," Nowicki said. "Means nothing's changed. So, Rugs, been meaning to ask you—how long you been talking to Reseta?"

"What? We're in the middle of this shit and you wanna how long—what're you doing, Wick? Fuck you doing? You call SWERT?"

"No, I did not."

"You didn't, huh? The fuck—why you lying to me?"

"Hey!" Timoshenka shouted, thrusting his cat's body at Nowicki. "Anybody gonna do anything about my cat?"

Carlucci put his hand on Timoshenka's shoulder, who twisted violently away and said, "Don't touch me! You're not gonna do anything about my cat, don't touch me!"

"William, listen up," Nowicki said. "I'm just trying to get us calmed down enough so we don't make a mistake."

"Glad you said that, Wick. Now I know. But I think we're calm enough."

"Wait! Don't do anything," Chief Newsome said, "I want to talk to him again."

"So talk to him, who's stopping you?"

"Well you're getting ready to go up there! And if you go up while I'm talking to him, he's gonna think I'm in on it—part of your trap!"

"Oh man, you're worried how it's gonna look to the DA, right? More than you're worried about stopping him, right? You sure you're a cop?"

"Think what you want, but please don't go up there till I talk to him, that's all I'm asking."

Carlucci shrugged. "What about you, Wick? C'mon, give me your radio and go get one outta get your car."

"Not a good idea."

"What's not good about it?"

"Not good 'cause you're all over the place today."

"Wick, how long was I in 'Nam? Eleven months, and half that time—we were on patrol, like every third or fourth day. I was lucky as hell, no doubt, but it wasn't all luck—I learned how to stay alive, 'cause every day, people were fucking trying to kill me on purpose!"

"That was forty years ago."

"Think I forgot everything? How long we gonna screw around with this guy? Probably already a murderer. Whyn't you check on the vic? "

Nowicki called the hospital. After a very short conversation, he said, "Vic's DOA."

"Well, there you go, it's official. So go or no go?"

Nowicki sighed and said, "Up to you, Rugs. You volunteering, fine with me, I'm not ordering."

Carlucci held out his hand for Nowicki's radio. After he shoved it into his right hip pocket, he said, "Be back when I'm back."

"For Chrissake, don't get killed, I don't wanna have to tell my cousin, okay?"

Carlucci made sure he had a round in the chamber of his pistol and one in the chamber of his shotgun. "Anybody dies up there, it ain't gonna be me."

He turned to Timoshenka and said, "Your room's 201, his is 205, right? Who's in 203?"

"Nobody. Guy used to be in there moved in with his girl."

"Okay. Now how's the place laid out?"

"It's just two rooms, that's all, same as mine, so's everybody's."

"Is there a door between them?'

"No."

"But when you went up and he came out in the hall and asked you if you found your cat, any doors open, either to the hall or inside?"

"I was thinking about my cat!"

"Okay, okay. So what I'm asking you now is, think hard, close your eyes, think about when you were up there. You hear any doors, opening or closing?"

"I don't have to think. My cat, okay? That's all I was thinking about."

"Okay. Okay, William, one more thing. Are there carpets up there, in your rooms, in the hall?"

"Yeah. Real ugly green. Looks like puke."

"All I wanna know is if I'm gonna make noise walking with my shoes on, understand?"

"Well all the floors squeak, if that's what you wanna know."

"Okay, that's good to know. Thanks. Here I go."

When he reached the first-floor landing, he saw blood going up the stairs, glanced back and saw blood going down as well. Who was bleeding? The cat? Does it matter?

He shook himself to hear if anything rattled. His keys. Only noise was from his clothes. On the second-floor landing, he checked his breathing and pulse. Pulse for fifteen seconds was twenty-two. Breaths steady at five plus for the same time. Both up. Only surprise would be if they weren't. Took ten deep breaths, filling his diaphragm slowly and emptying it just as slowly. Considering where he was and what he was getting ready to do, he felt close to calm. Maybe too close ?

He avoided stepping on the blood as he opened the door by pushing against the jamb before turning the knob. Started pulling it back toward him, heard the hint of a squeak. Stopped pulling. Listened. No sound from the other side of the door. Pulled again. Definite squeak. Stopped again. Listened. No sound. Then three loud shots. Between them the unmistakable sound of the slide on a pump shotgun. Quickly, quietly opened the door open and tiptoed four steps to get inside Timoshenka's room, 201.

Two more shots. The shooter was either at the front window in 205 or very close to it. Felt sure the shooter had just emptied his shotgun. Carlucci's Mossberg held four in the tube and one in the chamber. Unless the shooter had a newer police shotgun, state game law allowed no more than five shells in a pump—*oh shit, man, come on, think this kid paid attention to game laws? Anybody's laws?*

So where the fuck did all this blood come from? Why do I care—man, get your ass here now! Carlucci held his breath trying to hear if the shooter was going for another gun or reloading the one he'd just emptied. Couldn't tell. Peeked into the hall, saw nothing, tiptoed to 203. Tried the door, pushing on it, then turned the knob like he'd had done at the door at the top of the stairs, but the 203 door was locked. Listened hard trying to identify noises coming out of 205.

Okay, man, what now? In the hall next to the shooter's apartment, the only cover you got is your vest.

Slow down, man, slow down—except when you move, be quick . . . how quick . . . quicker than him . . . he's late teens, early twenties, and you're fifty-fucking-seven, man! Wanna be fifty-eight? Better be quicker than him. . . .

Tiptoed to the door of 205. Peeked in, saw no one, took the step that put him squarely in the frame of the door. Blood trail led straight from the door to the feet—there he is! There's the motherfucker! Shotgun pointed at the ceiling, resting on his right shoulder, between two beds, Jesus, blood all over the bed on his right. He's singing, the motherfucker is singing! The singing's crazy, but not as crazy as the motherfucker's size: over six feet, large arms, T-shirt, no sleeves, cut off jeans, ten-inch boots, no socks.

"Freeze! Police! Drop the gun! Get on the floor!"

"What? Huh?"

"Freeze! Got a 12-gauge middle of your back!"

"Aw, fuck, shoot me, fuck I care? World's biggest loser, that's what I am."

"Last time! Drop the gun! Get on the floor!"

"Which mouse are you? Mickey Mouse or Mighty Mouse? Please, Jesus Christ, at least be Mighty Mouse."

"Counting to three. Not on the floor by three I'm gonna shoot!"

"Roommate steals my girl . . . she picked him over me! And here's Mighty Mouse . . . if that don't top it all."

"One!"

He swung the shotgun forward off his shoulder and dropped it on the bloody bed. Eased down to his knees, scooched back until he was far enough away from the wall to lie face down. Put his hands behind his back. "Go 'head, Mighty Mouse, cuff me. What the fuck, it's what I deserve."

Wait! Why's he so quick to get down? So quick to get his hands behind him? Carlucci edged ahead, moved closer, eased his shotgun onto the other bed, fuck it, jerked his cuffs out of their holster, dropped to his right knee on Kipple's hip. Kipple? Ronald Reagan Kipple? Before he could get the cuffs on and locked, Kipple bucked his hips up and slammed his right elbow into Carlucci's right shoulder. Wildly off-balance, Carlucci scrambled for a hold, anywhere. Grabbed Kipple's shirt collar. Kipple convulsed again, pumped his right elbow back. First two pumps hit air. Third one got Carlucci's neck. Next one got his shoulder. Again.

Carlucci's eyes blinked when his neck got slammed. Squeezed cloth as hard as he could. Knew if he let go of Kipple's shirt or lost his balance it was over: prick smelled drunk, already murdered somebody—even if he didn't know it. Carlucci reached for his Beretta but still had his cuffs in his right hand. Didn't know whether to hold the cuffs if there was a chance to get them on Kipple or toss them behind him so Kipple couldn't use them on him. He tossed them backward through the open door. Grabbed at the retention strap on his holster. Kipple jerked again, swung his elbow. Carlucci let go of Kipple's collar, made a claw with his fingers, raked it over Kipple's eye, missed, jammed his forehead into Kipple's neck. Kipple's head recoiled away. Carlucci tried again to rake his eyeball. Couldn't. Tried to get his thumb and middle finger on Kipple's carotid. No way.

Kipple buried his chin in his own neck, shook furiously, rolled, pinned Carlucci under him. Kipple raised his right leg, slammed his right heel onto Carlucci's right shin. Carlucci screamed. Wrested his leg inches to the right. Kipple raised his right foot again, kicked it down again. Missed. Then missed again. Kipple moved his aim, drove his heel down onto Carlucci's shin. Carlucci his bottom lip and screamed louder.

Kipple bucked hard again. Carlucci tried again to claw Kipple's eye. Kipple tried to bite Carlucci's hand. Carlucci pulled his hand away, made a fist, tried to punch Kipple's eye with his thumb knuckle, hit Kipple's cheek with the first punch, his eyebrow with second. Saw Kipple's right leg going up again, jerked his right leg beside Kipple's left leg. When Kipple's leg started down Carlucci thrust his leg to the right. Kipple's heel barely grazed Carlucci's shin. Kipple lurch ed hard to his right, rolling Carlucci over onto his Beretta and holster.

Carlucci bucked hard, trying to get off his pistol. It was cutting into him between the top of his hip and his last rib.

Kipple singing, "Whatchu gonna do Mighty Mouse, whatchu gonna do when they come for you?"

Prick was singing theme music for a goddamn TV show—*Cops*!

Carlucci heaved his hips up again, somehow freed his right hand, reached for Kipple's face, scraping furiously at Kipple's eyes. Kipple arched upward and backward and got his right arm over Carlucci's right arm, trapping Carlucci's right arm against his ribs. Carlucci fought to claw Kipple's left eye with his left hand. Felt only cheek. Kipple smashed his right heel into Carlucci's shin again.

Pain exploded up and down his leg. Carlucci howled.

Kipple laughed. "Whatchu goin' do when they come for you, bad boys, bad boys. . . ." He rolled farther to his right. Carlucci's Beretta stabbed deeper above his right hip. Kipple rolled, grinding his hips downward.

"How you like that, Mighty Mouse? Like that, huh?"

Carlucci's Beretta had become two knives, slicing deeper with Kipple's each roll.

Carlucci smelled blood. Whose? His?

Carlucci clung to Kipple's face with his left hand, to his belly flesh with his right thumb and index finger, barely a pinch. Kipple still had Carlucci's right forearm trapped. Carlucci, using everything he had to hold Kipple down against him, sensed he had only seconds until Kipple's weight and strength beat him.

Carlucci knew if he lost here and now for even a second, he would die. He couldn't lose it . . . wouldn't let it himself lose it. *Prick's aiming for death anyway . . . lose it now, I'm dead. . . . Fuck you, prick, ain't gonna die, fuck you, might die, maybe yeah . . . but not 'cause you killed me . . . ain't gonna let you kill me.*

He dug his fingers in, squeezing hard. Kipple tried to arch up and away, but his neck, where it curved into his right shoulder, mooshed into Carlucci's face. Carlucci opened his mouth as wide as he could and bit. Hard. Kipple screamed. Carlucci dug and bit with everything he had in him. Then kicked his heel backward onto Kipple's shin. Again. Biting. Clawing. Deeper. Harder.

Kipple reared up, rolled to his right. Carlucci hung on. Kipple scrambled to his feet as though Carlucci weighed nothing, scooched backward fast, slammed Carlucci's back into the wall. Air burst out of Carlucci, like death coming for him. Lost his grip, gulped for air, slumped to the floor. Kipple stumbled three steps away. Turned around. Reached to where Carlucci had bit him. Held up his hand. Looked at the blood smeared over it.

"Look at you, you skinny bastard." Kipple looked from his hand to Carlucci and back at his hand. "I could take you easy . . . you fucker . . . my arm's going numb . . . what the fuck?"

Carlucci, gasping, snarling, "You ain't getting me, you ain't getting me, not now, not now!"

Kipple reached across his body for the shotgun on the bloody bed with his right hand. His hand touched the gun but didn't grasp it. He reached out with his left hand, picked the gun up, turned it over, tried to aim it with his left hand, but the barrel drooped.

Carlucci fumbled with the retainer strap on his holster. Kipple's shotgun waving, Kipple struggling to control it. Didn't. Couldn't.

Carlucci jerked the Beretta out of his holster. Jesus! Finally! Tried to shout freeze, but it sounded like slush melting toward a storm drain.

"Freeze or I'll shoot," Carlucci said, words sounding like that slush melting even faster.

"Freeze yourself, Mighty Mousefucker!" Kipple mimicked Carlucci in falsetto. Pulled the trigger of the shotgun. It clicked!

Through teary, cloudy, blurry vision Carlucci aimed low, fired twice.

The first hit Kipple's left hip, the second his left quad. He folded from the waist, collapsed, stiff legged, to the floor, groaning.

"You little fucker, you . . . you little piss ant."

"Freeze," Carlucci said. Didn't know why. It was so frothy, so weak, so lacking command.

"Fuck you, piss ant. Fuck your mother, fuck Julie Meyers . . . especially fuck her . . . and fuck my roommate, fuck that motherfucker."

"He's dead."

"Good! Good! Don't know how he made it outta here, shot him . . . got him . . . right in the middle of his scrawny fucking chest."

"Made it out long enough to ID you."

"Oh goody, fucking goody for him . . . asshole . . . what she saw in him . . . ohhhhh, Jesus Christ!"

"Hurt? Does it hurt?" Carlucci struggled to get to his knees and then to his feet. "I'm glad it hurts. I made it hurt—know why? 'Cause you don't give a rat's ass where you shoot. You don't care who you hurt. People don't care who they hurt? Should've never been born."

"Rugs, you copy? Rugs? Do you copy? Rugs?"

It took Carlucci a long moment to locate the radio, going, as he was, back and forth from looking for the sound and watching Kipple trying to control the shotgun. He was still holding it, but Carlucci knew it was empty. He spotted the radio on the floor beside Kipple's right ankle.

"I'm gonna reach for the radio by your foot. You move, I'll shoot you again."

"Fuck you, if I thought you could shoot, I would move!"

Despite the pain burning in waves from the lower middle of his back to pins and needles in his feet, Carlucci moved as fast as he could. Grabbed the radio. Once in hand, he put all his weight onto his right foot and stepped on Kipple's left ankle twisting it outward. Kipple screamed.

"Rugs! Rugs! What was that? You copy?"

"Quit yelling at me, I ain't deaf! That's him, that's a little payback for all the names this perp—this twerp was calling me."

"You okay? Over."

"No I ain't okay! He beat the hell outta me, but he needs EMS quick or he might bleed out. I bit him once and I shot him him twice, but I don't see nothing spurting. Wasn't trying to hit vitals, but might've . . . Carlucci out."

"Ten-four on the EMS. Over."

"Goddammit, Wick, I'm beat to shit and back, stop giving me that *over* shit, I don't wanna talk no more!"

"Whoa! Who's screaming? Over."

"I'm standing on his ankle . . . leg I shot him in. No more overs!"

Carlucci switched off the radio and tossed it on the bed next to his shotgun. He reached down and grabbed the barrel of Kipple's shotgun. He bounced on Kipple's ankle and said, "Let go! Let go, goddammit!"

Kipple screamed, "Get off! Oh God, get off!"

"I'll get off when you let go!"

"There! I let it go, get off!"

Carlucci pulled the shotgun free and stepped away as quickly as he could move. Electricity burned down the back of both legs. He shoved his Beretta under his belt and worked the slide on Kipple's shotgun. No shell ejected. Worked it again, same result, threw it on the bed beside his.

"And you were gonna be a cop, huh? Want to show people how tough you are, why didn't you join the fucking army, they would've found a war for you. Paid you too, yeah."

"Fuck the army. Fuck you—where's EMS at?"

Carlucci heard footsteps. Nowicki burst into the apartment, pistol drawn.

"Jesus, Rugs, you look awful."

"Think I was making it up?"

"Uh, no, but . . . hey, go in the other room, Rugs, man, Jesus, sit down before you fall down."

"Keep your eyes on this son of a bitch. Every time I thought he was done, he wasn't."

Moments later came the sounds of the sirens winding down as ambulances pulled into the alley below.

Carlucci shuffled into the other room, sank slowly onto a lop sided couch, sucking in air, spitting it out, growling from the pain in his back, his side, his legs, his feet.

He fogged in and out of consciousness, felt himself strapped onto a gurney, carried down steps. More fogging, in and out, waking up briefly in Conemaugh Hospital ER . . . did he ever feel this tired . . . ever? His right leg quivered. Then his left. Then both. Every slight shift of his body, the knives, now duller, sawed into the flesh above his right hip. Nurses talked to him, then docs, one said something about blood loss, Carlucci didn't know who they were talking about.

"Can't let you . . . murder somebody . . . already did . . . wasn't me . . . it wasn't me!"

"Sir? You need something? Who're you talking—aw you're okay, just, just let yourself go."

"Who's okay? Go away . . . leave me the fuck alone . . . I'll be okay?"

———

". . . what haunts us is shit we stuff in our own minds . . . tell ourselves crap, gonna believe crap, gonna do crap . . . sleep is a process . . . best thing I ever learned from him . . ."

"Who's he talking about?" Nowicki said.

"Might be Jim Reseta," Franny said. "Sounds like some of the stuff they used to talk about."

"How long you been here?"

"Not long. Twenty minutes, maybe."

". . . didn't know how to relax . . . fell into bed 'cause I was tired? . . . don't work . . ."

"He's gonna just go on like that, I don't think there's much point me sticking around."

"He wakes up, I'll tell him you were here."

"What'd the docs say, anything? Or they just gonna keep on keeping him quiet for a while? They say how long that might be?"

"Haven't talked to one today. Haven't seen one since I've been here."

"So you don't know any more today than you knew yesterday?" She shook her head.

". . . full-body scan . . . focus . . . tense it, relax it . . . Kabat-Zinn . . . fuck kinda name is that . . . so fuckin' wired . . . patrol . . . miss something . . . shit storm on everybody behind me . . ."

"I don't think I should be listening to this. Too private."

"Up to you, Cousin."

"I mean, doesn't it sound kinda private to you?"

"Well, yeah, but, uh, most of it I already heard. A lot of this sounds like him talking to Jimmy. You know, don't you? Jimmy was there too. He did the whole tour, he didn't get a—whatta you guys call it? A golden wound the first day? Get shipped home after you fall off a truck or something. Least that's the way he and Rugs talk about it. Jimmy was in some bad stuff. Rugs told me one time, if Jimmy'd had the wrong commanding officer, he could've wound up doing life, you know, in Leavenworth."

"Jesus, I never heard that, what'd he do?"

"When they'd start talking about that, they were always talking around me, over me. All I'm saying is what Rugs kept telling me, Jimmy was there, he didn't see it on the six o'clock news. So when he's telling Rugs what he has to do to calm himself down, it's 'cause he did it first—for himself."

"Well I was in 'Nam, too, you know, did my whole tour, I didn't get no golden wound. And just 'cause I was in logistics and supply, that didn't mean I was some candy-ass R-E-M."

"R-E-what? What's that?"

"Rear Echelon, uh, you know—starts with mother?" Nowicki said. "You could be doing your job, but all the hot-shit grunts, they'd come in from wherever, look at us like we were some kinda candy-asses. Didn't think shit about the enemy in the tunnels right under us."

"C'mon, Wick, don't start that again."

"You hear that? I heard him—he's talking."

"Don't get excited, he does that every once in a while."

"But you heard him, right?"

"Yes, I heard him, I'm sitting right here."

". . . c'mon, Wick, don't start that again," said Rugs.

"There he goes again! Don't tell me you didn't hear that."

"Cousin, I think maybe you should go back to work."

"Okay, okay. Anything changes, you know? Call me. I'm telling you, Fran, I couldn't believe the beating he took. That guy was six one, two hundred easy, thirty-five years younger than him! Rugs put him down. Put his ass down. This is legendary, Franny. I'm telling you, legendary."

"Well, Cousin, I'm sure he'll just be thrilled to hear that."

"Why you being sarcastic? I been meaning to tell you, lately you been more and more sarcastic—you still pissed at him? Why, what'd he do was so bad?"

"Like I'm gonna tell you."

"So you *are* still pissed at him? What the hell, Franny, he needs your support now, he don't need you being all pissy 'cause of something he did, uh, whenever."

"Go to work, Cousin, a counselor you aren't."

"I mean it, Franny, he needs your support, he don't need you all hissy-pissy—when did this happen—oh, I know when this happened. This is when you got popped in your group, ain't it? Yeah, exactly, that was the night I sent him up deal with the Virgin."

"Oh, well, good for you, Cousin. Maybe you should call Reseta, tell him he can retire and open up a Burger King, 'cause you got the counseling covered."

"See, that's exactly what I'm talking about, right there, that sarcasm."

"Oh, Jesus Christ, like I need one more person analyzing me—go to work!"

". . . no . . . don't let my mother out . . . please, somebody, don't let my mother out. . . ."

"I ain't touching that one. See you around, Cousin."

"Yeah. See you around."

She stood and edged close to the bed. Put her hand on Carlucci's right hand. All the IVs fed into one arm just short of the crook of his left elbow. She petted his hand.

"Have to go, Rugs. Got a group in twenty minutes. My mother's praying for you. They're not telling me when they're gonna wake you up. Want your body to heal as much as it can on its own—I don't know what I'm talking about. Just go with it—well, what else you gonna do? My cousin's having a hard time believing what you did. It's all over the courthouse, too. Skinny old Rugs put the hurt on that big kid."

". . . everybody's talking . . . rumors . . . rumors of rumors . . ."

"Detective? Detective Carlucci?" a nurse said, checking IVs. "Are you singing? Detective? Are you awake? Can you hear me?"

"Can't hear . . . can't hear . . . can't hear no mo', no mo'. . . ."

"Oh, you're not awake, that's just the haloperidol."

". . . I'm singing . . . in the rain . . . used to wanna sing that song . . . never could."

"Let it work, Detective, your body needs the rest."

". . . leeches telling me get outta here . . . fucking Americans . . . go home . . ."

———

Councilman Egidio Figulli stuck his head into Carlucci's room. "You awake?"

"They tell me I'm awake. So what's up, Councilman, you visiting the sick, or you just in the neighborhood?"

"My sister's down on the second floor. I thought, you know, long as I'm here, might as well check, see how you're doing."

"Your sister? What's her problem? Which sister?"

"Female stuff, some problem with the pipes, you know, down there. Marie. My oldest sister. One never got married. So how you doing?"

"Okay, I guess."

"You don't know?"

"Still mostly fogged up on some kinda dope. Forget what it's called."

"They say when they're gonna let you go home?"

"Wish it was yesterday."

"Uh-huh. Well, uh, listen, Carlucci. I know, uh, you know, everybody's talking how you're the big hero for taking that nut-case down all by yourself, but, uh, I just wanna tell you, in case you forgot, we still got some business to take care of, you know, you and the Safety Committee? You don't remember? Shooting off your gun up in Norwood?"

"Oh, yeah, sure, me putting three in the dirt up there, I remember."

"Yeah, exactly. I didn't want you thinking, you know, just 'cause everybody's singing your praises now, I don't want you getting any idea we're gonna forget about that because we're still gonna hold a full inquiry, that's what I'm saying."

"And you stopped in just to tell me that? Up here checking on your sister, and you decide to show me your memory's still working, right?"

"Well yeah—not exactly, but that's about right."

"Tell me, what else have you been checking up on?"

"Uh, I'm not sure I know what you're talking about."

"Not sure? You aren't working behind the scenes to find something to force me into retirement?"

"Jesus Christ. I'm offended you even ask."

"Well, Councilman, I can't tell you how thrilled I am to know that. Just make sure you send me a written notice for the inquiry. And then you can ask me whatever you want, and if there's something I don't understand, I'm sure my attorney'll explain it to me so I can you give the answer that'll satisfy you. Hey, I don't wanna be rude, but I'm feeling kinda woozy, I need to get some rest, if that's okay with you."

"Oh, yeah. For sure. Absolutely. Uh, your back really broken? I mean that's what I heard, you know, people saying your back's busted."

"I don't know if, uh, compression fractures qualify."

"So what're they gonna do about that, anything?"

"Nothing, far as I know. Not unless a nerve gets pinched and I can't stand the pain. So far, I'm just real, real sore. For now all they're doing is keeping me asleep and putting cold and heat on me when I'm awake."

"They say how long you, uh, you might be outta action, you know, off duty?"

"No. Tell you the truth, I'm kinda enjoying it, this laying around not doing nothing. It's a new thing for me."

"It'd drive me nuts. Can't stand not having something to do."

"Well I guess that's why you're always doing something, Councilman. Pretty well known for that."

"I guess I am." Figulli's mouth curved in a tight smile. "Not a bad thing to be known for, right?" He gave a quick wave and disappeared into the hall.

Carlucci waited a couple minutes to make sure Figulli wasn't coming back. He picked up the phone and dialed 0. "Operator, would you connect me to Miss Figulli, please? On the second floor?"

"One moment please." A pause. "Uh, there's nobody registered by that name."

"You mind checking again? She's supposed to be on the second floor."

"No, not on any other floor either."

"My mistake. Thank you."

A surprise visit to check up on me? What else is he doing?

Jagoff. Hope you trip on the curb, break your fucking ankle.

———

A week later, Carlucci, with a tight brace around his lower back, was driven to his house on Norwood Hill by Patrolman Robert

Canoza. Chief Nowicki followed in Carlucci's car. With them on each side, Carlucci made it up the steps to his front porch, unlocked the door, started inside. Some of his neighbors cheered and applauded, followed him into his house carrying food, a pan of meatballs and marinara, a strawberry pie, a sponge cake, and many plates of cookies and quick breads. They fussed and gushed over him till he said he was tired and needed to rest. Nowicki thanked them all and shooed them out, while Canoza hovered near the food they'd brought, especially the strawberry pie.

"Take that pie, Robert. I'm not gonna eat it."

"Why not? Looks really good."

"If who made that is who I think made it, she uses too much sugar. Nice lady, but . . . I know you got a sweet tooth, man, take it, really, I'm never gonna eat it."

"How 'bout these meat balls?" Nowicki said. "You giving them away too?"

"Aw no, those I'm gonna eat."

"Look at the size of them. Each one's like a little meat loaf."

"Look, Wick, no touch. With them I won't have to cook for a coupla weeks."

"You thinking you're gonna be out for two or three weeks?"

"Weeks? What's cooking got to do with that? Docs told me I'd be wearing this brace for at least two more months. But so what? August is over, everybody's back from vacation."

"You just can't leave that alone, can you?"

"Sooner or later, Wick, you're gonna have to straighten out the mess you made—"

"The mess I made?"

"Okay, the mess you allowed to happen—"

"Made? Allowed? Go lie down, take a chill pill—"

"I'm just saying—"

"Don't say it! I'm gonna have enough trouble filling your slot. And your docs, they didn't tell me two months. What they told me was, wait and see, that's all they said, wait and see."

"I heard specifically two months with this brace, and I've only had it on for two weeks."

"According to what they told me, they could be waiting and seeing for maybe a month. Meanwhile, we're nine bodies short now."

"Hey, Wick, that bastard slammed me into the wall, remember him? He didn't ask me if that was gonna fuck up your table of organization—"

"Aw stop it, Jesus, get some rest. If that's what's gonna heal you, better get started now. What do you want—you want ice or heat first?"

"I'll take care of it—go on, get outta here. And take that pie, Robert."

"I don't know if I should," Canoza said, shooting a look at Nowicki. "Supposed to be losing some weight. Last physical everybody made a big deal out of it . . ."

"Just eat a little bit every night, you don't have to eat it all at one time."

"Don't tempt him."

"Then you take the pie."

"I don't want the pie. Didn't you hear me?"

"Then get outta here, both of you. I need to get flat."

"Fine. Go to bed. C'mon, Boo-Boo, let's go."

"Don't call me that, I asked you at least a hunnert times. You know my name."

"Exactly right, Patrolman. Robert. Now lose the pie, c'mon, let's go."

Carlucci locked the door behind them, didn't want anybody else coming in—with or without food. What he really didn't want was the whole rigmarole of telling them how he got hurt, how bad it was, what they could do for him. It would just make every pain worse.

On his way out of the kitchen, he saw a message blinking on his machine. He stabbed the play button. A hang up. Didn't he have another hang up recently? And there was that no message—message at the station. Who was trying to track him down? Jesus, were the pain meds making him paranoid? It's not like he had a lot of people wanting to talk to him and it wasn't uncommon for a fair number of the calls coming his way to be wrong numbers.

He was tired. Getting in and out of the car, climbing the steps, dealing with the neighbors, most of them women only too familiar with the problems he had with his mother. Some used to be her friend but over the years grew so wary of her, they didn't even ask where she was or how she was doing, which was fine with him.

He crept gingerly into what had once been their dining room and then his mother's bedroom. She'd demanded that it become her bedroom after she tripped going up the stairs to what had been their bedroom before his father was killed.

As weeks of her incarceration at Mamont stretched into months, Carlucci, little by little, had moved her things to the cellar and replaced them with his, and with every piece of her furniture he moved, he felt an almost physical wrench of guilt, which became the subject of another session with Jim Reseta.

Franny Perfetti was herself going through a nearly identical fracture in her life: her mother was now spending all her time on the first floor of their house, restricted to what had been their dining room, and to the bathroom built on what had been their back porch. Though Rugs and Franny were lapsed Catholics, in spite of themselves they held on to most of the feelings of maternal respect drilled into them by the Sisters of Mercy over twelve years of school.

While their situations were similar in many ways, Franny's was different because she'd promised to never put her mother in a nursing home. Franny had made it with her whole heart, but as months passed into years it felt less and less a promise and more and more a sentence. Once she tried to joke that it came with no possibility for parole, but her laughter abruptly ended in tears.

Now while Franny was at work, she had to pay a neighbor to sit with her mother, one more ball added to her juggling house bills while also paying for her mother's prescription drugs. Mrs. Perfetti's small Social Security benefit was spent almost entirely on health insurance, both Medicare and Plan B Supplemental. Her prescription-drug costs hit the so-called donut hole around the end of July, so, like everyone else in the same prescription boat, from the end of July to about the end of the year, she—or rather Franny—paid full price for her drugs. One of them cost more than $500 for a three-month supply, necessitating many consultations with her doctor and the mail-order pharmacy. When Mrs. Perfetti finally accepted the truth about the price, she fainted. After waking, she cried off and on for hours that stretched into days but said not a word about the nursing home promise.

———

A couple weeks later, as Franny talked to Jim Reseta about this, bitterness clearly crept into her tone and expression, surprising Carlucci because he'd never heard Franny speak of her mother with anything other than respect and devotion. Exhaustion, frustration, yes, Carlucci had heard and seen them in Franny's words and expressions, but in all the sessions with Reseta that alternated between Franny and Rugs, depending on which was feeling more guilt and conflict, Carlucci had never heard Franny complain specifically about the promise her mother had demanded.

Reseta said, "I know we've all heard this before, you know, if parents can't pick their children, children can't pick their parents. We all get what we get. Sometimes everybody's happy with what fate gave them, but that only happens about once every two hundred gazillion births. The rest of the time, we're stuck. Parents, kids; kids, parents, it's a crap shoot—and the whole game's legit.

"Your mother makes you promise you're never gonna put her in a nursing home. You made that promise, great, she's happy. But now, in addition to everything else, you gotta pay for somebody to watch her. I'm not gonna ask if you're withholding all the taxes you're supposed to, turning them over to the state, the feds, I don't wanna know about the income taxes, Social Security, never mind the state unemployment insurance—all of which you're supposed to be paying—"

"Oh God, I never even thought about that! Jesus, I could be arrested! I'd lose my job! Rugs! Why didn't you tell me?"

"C'mon, Franny, before they get around to you, they're gonna have to arrest half the people over fifty, everybody's taking care of somebody, mother, father, old aunt."

"See, that's why I hesitated to bring it up before, but Rugs is right. Don't know if it's half exactly, but let's get back to your mother. This promise you made, what your mother doesn't understand is that making her happy puts you in a financial and bureaucratic bind. On top of which, you're a good Catholic girl, you say you don't go to church except on Christmas and Easter, and I believe you, but I also know what the sisters did to you for twelve years. Same stuff they did to Rugs and me. They took our brains out, sent them to the car wash, had them detailed with Clorox, and now, you can't get through a week without breaking out in guilt-sweats so bad sometimes you wish—I'm gonna say it now and I know it's gonna upset you, but I know it's eating you up—sometimes you wish your mother would just die already."

"Oh my God, don't say that! Jesus, I never never never wish that! How can you say that?"

"Okay, Fran, then you tell me, okay? Why do you come in here every week? Is it 'cause you're so satisfied with your life? So pleased? So fulfilled?"

"No, Jesus, no, but—do I hope she dies? Do I wish she would die? How can you say that to me?"

"I repeat, why do you come in here every week? You and the master of silence over there, the great warrior. Whatta you say, Rugs, when was the last time you wished, probably even prayed, your mother never gets out of Mamont—oh, I forgot you don't pray, right?"

"Aw c'mon, Jimmy."

"Truth time, Rugs. Stop lying to yourself. You been lying to me for months; I tried every way I could think to call you on it. Now I'm just saying it straight out. Are you gonna sit there, look me straight in the face, and tell me and Franny and yourself you're praying and hoping your mother comes home? You can't wait to see your mother walk back into your house, huh? The woman who cracked Fishetti's skull—put him onto disability retirement? Is that what you want me to believe? C'mon, Rugs, say it out loud, so we can all hear it: 'I want my mother to get out of Mamont so she can come back home to her house on Norwood Hill and move back in with me?' Say it, c'mon. Lemme hear you."

"Aw, Jimmy, Jesus, man, cut it out."

"No no, you're not gonna get away with that."

"You want me to say it? Huh? Okay. Here it is, here goes, I don't want my mother to ever get out of Mamont, never, ever! But you know what? The state's getting ready to shut that place down. No money, too much to maintain, that's all you hear outta Harrisburg. Gonna put everybody in group homes, I know you know what I'm talking about.

"You know what I think of that, Jimmy? Huh? It's a fucking murder waiting to happen, that's what it is. Twice in the last eight months, my mother's attacked people—no, three times. One of them, poor bastard, he works there, on the grounds. My mother said he was putting ideas in her head when he cut the grass, she'd walk out there, pick up the grass on her slippers, they'd work their way up her legs into her head. She got so pissed, she went outside, found a clay pot somewhere, ER report said he'd been hit at least three times—do I want her out? Hell no! But I'm telling you, as sure as I'm sitting here, she goes into one of those group homes, she'll kill somebody for sure. You think I got guilt now? Over Fish? What kinda guilt am I gonna have then?"

Carlucci broke down, put his face in his hands, and sobbed. Franny hugged him. Reseta patted his knee. He waved them both off, still in pain from his war with Ronald Reagan Kipple, but this guilt he'd just admitted hurt far worse, in ways no ice or heat or brace could ease. He didn't know the pain from an idea could pierce him as deeply as sharp steel, but he felt like his whole body had just been rolled over a bed of Berettas.

If that wasn't enough, Councilman Figulli, citing the police training manual, was now chirping to a reporter from the *Rocksburg Gazette* that Carlucci violated procedure by not calling for backup when he was trying to handcuff Kipple. Figulli said Carlucci had his chief's radio and his own chief and another chief from another department were both ready and willing to back him up, but Carlucci didn't call them, meaning his so-called heroics not only were not heroic, but just one more reason it was past time for Carlucci to retire. And Figulli told the reporter it was his job as a ranking member of the Safety Committee to get exactly that outcome.

John "Radio" Radoycich hooted at the next Safety Committee meeting: "We don't have no rankings on this committee, Figulli, the hell you talking about?"

"I been on this committee longer than either one of youns two, that's all I know."

"So that's what you told the reporter? Huh? What did you say? You been on this committee longer than either Bellotti or me, or did you say you was 'the ranking member,' c'mon, I gotta hear this. What'd you say?"

"Whatta you care what I said?"

143

"I care 'cause you're pumping yourself up with some fancy bull-crap like you're down in Congress, like we got two parties here, and each party got ranking members. What? You forget we're all Democrats, huh? What'd you say?"

"Get off my back, Radio."

"I ain't on your back. You're the one busting balls here, and I'm calling you on it."

Mayor Angelo Bellotti strode quickly into the council meeting room and said, "I see the meeting's started without me."

"Yeah, Figulli's trying to blame this on the reporter—you see what he said in the paper here? He's the ranking member of the Safety Committee, woo hoo! Now he's trying to say he didn't say it."

"I didn't say it!"

"Yeah, right, the older you get, Egidio, the more you bullshit—"

"All right, all right, that's enough," Bellotti said. "Listen, I don't have much time, so how 'bout we pass on all the procedural stuff and get right to it. So, Egidio, you're the one wanted this meeting, regular meeting's not for two weeks, what is it this time?"

"We just got unfinished business from when Nowicki come busting in here and pulled Carlucci out 'cause that kid shot his roommate—"

"Oh, for Chrissake, Carlucci's still on sick leave and you wanna haul him in here and make him sit in a chair? He got two broken bones in his back."

"Compression fractures is what I hear, and that ain't nearly as bad as like if the bones shifted around where they broke. Anyway, far as that goes, I ain't seen no medical report—"

"Wait a minute, Jesus, wait a minute here," Bellotti said. "I can't believe you, Egidio, why you got such a hair up your butt about

Carlucci? He's a goddarn hero. I thought you were calling this meeting to say we should give him the Mayor's Medal for what he did."

"What? For what he did? What he did was violate procedure, for Chrissake! He was supposed to call for backup before he even tried to cuff that guy—but no, not him, he gotta do it his way—which is the way he's been doing crap as long as I can remember—"

"No shit, Figulli, swear to God, what is your problem with him, you sound like you got some kinda blood vendetta going—"

"Will you stop it! This is strictly about procedures and regulations, this guy loses equipment, his radio, his pepper spray, he's shooting his gun for no reason—what're you talking about, vendetta? Trying to make me sound like it's some kinda personal thing going on here? Starting to make me mad, Radio—"

"Will you two cut it out! I mean this is starting to get ridiculous, the way you two are acting. C'mon, is it too much to ask? Can we be professional here?"

"Tell him; he's the one can't keep his relatives in line."

"You leave my relatives outta this or I'm gonna smack you one."

"Meeting's adjourned. When you two wanna act right, let me know, we'll reconvene. Otherwise, regular meeting's in two weeks."

"There, Egidio. Satisfied now?"

"Don't talk to me, Radio. I don't want you talking to me no more."

———

"So what's the word, Doc?" Carlucci said.

"Well, the radiologist thinks that you're knitting very well. How's the pain?"

"Still pretty much sore all over, 'specially my right side, where it got all tore up. They took the sutures out like six weeks ago, but it still hurts down deep. And my right leg, my shin, man, that still hurts."

"I'm not surprised. But how about your back now, how's that been? Any pain in your arms? Chest? Legs? Down the back of your legs? Either one?"

"No. The pain's mostly where it's still all black and blue. And green. And yellow. Least that's what my girlfriend's telling me. I can't turn enough to see it in a mirror, have to take her word for it."

"Well, if you're not feeling referred pain, that's good. You keeping up with the exercises? How much are you trying to walk?"

"Well just lying around by itself, that's a pain. I don't care how comfortable you get, you can't stay there for, like more than ten minutes, things start getting numb, they start going to sleep, all pins and needles."

"Yes. Happens to everybody."

"I'm sure it does, I'm just saying, that's all."

"What do you think, Miss Perfetti? Fran? Seeing much improvement or not?"

"Really? You want to know what I think?"

"That's why I asked."

"Well, considering how bad his back looks, I think he's doing amazingly well. After he's been up for a while, he moves around pretty good. I mean, when I think he's got two bones cracked back there, compression fractures or whatever, I'm amazed he can move at all. And the color of his back, wow. First time I pulled his shirt off, I almost threw up."

"Uh-huh. Well, what's important is no referred pain. That's good. The stiffness and general pain, you're just going to have to be patient, Ruggiero, that's all there is to it. Uh, I've been meaning to talk to you about this. I suppose I should tell you I went to see your, uh, what do you call them? Actors? Perps? Subjects?"

"I know who you mean. You went to see him? When?"

"It was after his surgeries. More likely maybe three, four days after. I was surprised by the size of him. He was much bigger than I'd heard. I mean, I'd seen you, examined you. But given his size, his age? I have to ask you—how did you beat him?"

Carlucci hung his head for a moment, then looked up. Anybody else asking him, he wouldn't have answered, but he thought his doctor deserved an answer.

"Look, Doc, he already killed one guy. I knew if I didn't beat him, he was gonna kill me, what else did he have to lose? I just kept going, that's all, kept fighting, kicking, biting, clawing, gouging, anything I could think of to hurt him I did. When he stood up and I was hanging on him, he picked me up like I didn't weigh nothing, then he ran backward, slammed me into the wall, I thought . . . oh shit. But it turned out, where I bit him, I hurt him a lot worse than I thought . . . something, maybe, 'cause he couldn't use his hand to grab with. Tried to pick his shotgun up, but he couldn't get it level, the barrel kept drooping. And then he pulled the trigger and, uh, we both found out it was empty. I finally got my piece out and I shot him. Twice. Coulda killed him. But I didn't want to do that. That stays with you. Don't know why. It just does."

"That's remarkable."

"Nah, no, it isn't . . . it's just that over the years I read a lot of stories and articles by guys who teach self-defense, and they all make a really big point out of not giving up, not quitting. Plus, no question, if I quit, he would've killed me. And I didn't want some jagoff singing the theme song from *Cops*, you know? That TV show? 'What you gonna do when they come for you?' I wasn't gonna let him kill me, that's all there was to it."

"As I said, remarkable. But you make it sound like just another day at the office."

"Another day at the office? You think that's what I sound like?"

"Oh no, I'm sorry. Just trying to, uh, never mind. How are the drugs holding out? You need new script?"

"If you mean the pain pills, the, uh, whatever they are, no, I'm not taking them."

"You're not? Why not? You need to manage your pain."

"I'm managing it."

"No, really, Ruggiero, pain management is a very significant part of recovery. Inseparable, really."

"Yeah? Well those pills? They make me not able to, uh, to move my bowels. And that's a part of pain management I really don't like. 'Cause not being able to do that makes my back hurt way worse."

"Ruggiero, I can't feel your pain, but I've been a doctor long enough to know that when pain is close to unbearable, there's no reason to endure that when there are meds that can help."

"Doc, you can quit talking 'cause there's no way I'm taking those pills. They don't make the pain stop, they just make me woozy. On top of which, they make me paranoid, and worst of all they stop me up, so I'm telling you, quit talking, I'm not taking them."

"All right, all right, then keep working with the physical therapists. My PA will give you script for X-rays. So, I'll see you in a month."

"When can I start driving again?"

"Ah, let's see how it goes."

"That's what you said last time."

"Patience, Ruggiero. It's only been two months now."

"Yeah, I know, patience, but this doesn't just affect me. Franny here, this turns her into a taxi, and she already got a job and she has her mother to look out for, and every time I need to go somewhere and can't get a ride with anybody else, I have to call her."

"What? You got something against taxis?"

"Hey, Doc, you're a little outta touch here. There hasn't been a taxi company in this town for, like, four years now. Who you think hauls old people around when they have to go shopping, or see a doc or a dentist? Retired cops. And nobody's paying for their gas either, and the ones I know? It's been old for them for a couple years now."

"You serious?"

"Well, I'm not joking. Why don't you, and a bunch of your doc buddies, check with your accountants, start up a Chapter S cab company, you know? Write your losses off against your doc business? I know you docs are always looking for ways to lose money, and this town, especially the old people—you'd be doing a real public service."

"Well, I just might look into that. Bankrupting restaurants isn't as much fun as it used to be."

"There you go, Doc. Call it—what's that symbol you docs have? Caducey taxi?"

"I think you can go now, Ruggiero. Keep an eye on him, Fran."

———

Carlucci took his brace off and stretched out on the floor in the living room.

"Hey, I didn't hear him say you could take that off."

"I been taking it off a little bit longer every day for, like, a couple weeks now."

"Really? A couple weeks? You think you should be doing that? Without talking to your doctor?"

"Physical therapist, he said it was okay."

"He's not your doctor."

"I'm taking it easy, you heard him say my bones were knitting real good."

"Yeah I did. But why didn't you tell him what the therapist said—ask him what he thinks. I'd trust my neurosurgeon a lot more than I'd trust a physical therapist."

"Okay, look, I started out, you know, a half hour. The therapist said, get up, move around, see how it feels, don't do anything stupid, take it easy. If it don't cause you any discomfort, any pain, keep it off a little bit more the next day, which is what I been doing. And I'm not having any more pain than I been having. And if the doc would've said, you know, the bones ain't knitting right, that would've been a different story, for sure I would've talked to him about it. But he didn't say that—"

"You should've talked to him, Rugs. Really."

"Okay, Jesus, you want me to talk to him, I'll talk to him. Next time."

"Why you getting mad? All I'm saying is you should've talked to him."

"I'm not getting mad—"

"Could've fooled me. Your voice goes up, your mouth goes down, you won't look at me, it's been that way ever since . . . ever since that night."

"What night?"

"What night? Come on, Rugs, you know what night I'm talking about. *The* night. The night you had the problem with what's-her-face. The Virgin. And Sitko."

"Oh."

"That's it? Oh?"

"I guess what you really mean is the night I had the big problem with you."

"Well what it is now, four months? Jeez, let me think, that was August, September, October—"

"Okay, okay, I get the point, it's November."

"Yes. November. Does that mean we're gonna finally talk about it?"

"I thought we talked about it enough in Jimmy's office."

"We didn't talk about it in Jimmy's office—I talked about it in Jimmy's office, you sat there, didn't say ten words. I was doing all the talking—I'm always doing all the talking."

"Well, you're good at that—"

"Aw come on, Rugs, Jesus—you're still so pissed off about that night, you're so pissed at me, at Jimmy, you didn't wanna go back to Jimmy's after he told you what he told you, which he told you I don't know how many times before—"

"Okay, okay, I get the picture—"

"You don't. That's exactly the problem, you don't get the picture, you keep saying you do, but Jesus, you won't even look at me—right now you're not looking at me—look at me, Rugs. Please, look at me."

Carlucci inhaled deeply, then sighed and turned to face her. "There. Am I looking at you now?"

"Do you think you could look with a little less hostility?"

"I'm not looking at you that way, what're you talking about?"

"Oh, God, I gotta start taking pictures so you could see what I'm talking about. I don't know how you're ever gonna believe me—"

"I believe you. You don't need to take no pictures with your phone, I believe you."

She stood up, went into the kitchen, poured a glass of water, and drank it before returning. She looked at him for a long moment.

"What?"

"I think . . . I think maybe we shouldn't see each other for a while."

"What? We shouldn't see each—so when is it you think we see each other? You take me to physical therapy and my appointments with the doc, you come in here for five, ten minutes, then you gotta leave 'cause your mom's alone—so when exactly you think we're seeing each other?"

"I just think we both need a break. I know I do. And I think you know you do even if you won't admit it."

"Well then, hey, I guess, you know, you've done all the thinking, right? I don't need to bother my pretty little head about it—"

"Cut it out, Rugs. Don't be a smart ass. I hate it when you're like that."

"What can I say, Fran? Lately, you pretty much hate it no matter what I say or where I look."

"Where's my coat? I'm going."

152

"It's right where you put it, on the chair behind you."

She shrugged into her parka and zipped up. "Guess it's good bye, for a while."

"I guess it is. Guess I should tell you I made up my mind, I'm retiring. I know we didn't talk about that either—"

"What? When did you decide that? God, Rugs, you don't tell me anything anymore—"

"I thought I just did."

"Oh Rugs, Jesus, why're you doing this? You wait till I put my coat on to lay this on me? You think I don't deserve better than that?"

"What're you talking about, deserve better?"

"Yes, deserve better! Jesus, don't you think I rate a little more consideration? Rugs, you think you retiring isn't gonna be a huge change? In all our lives? I thought you were gonna try to work as long as you could to build up your pension—"

"I was, yeah, that's right, but I don't think I'm gonna need that much anymore. I just . . . I just don't think they're gonna let my mother out. She's back in the Binger Building again, another 'visit'—"

"Since when? What happened?"

"Since day before yesterday. Wouldn't clean her room, the aid came in, she jabbed him in the eye with a broom handle, really messed up his eye. They called the state cops, they came in, arrested her, gonna take her in front of a DJ, which means I'll have to get a shyster, and if she's found guilty, which I don't see how she can't be, means they'll have to put her in with the other cons in there. Probably leave her there—' course that all depends whether they're gonna close that place, but if they do, I don't know what's gonna happen to her."

"Oh, Jeez, Rugs, I'm sorry."

"What're you sorry for? Why you saying that?"

"I'm sorry for you. Every time she does something like that, I think how you must be feeling."

"Well, you can save your sorry, 'cause I'm not feeling much about her."

"You say that but I don't believe you."

"Believe it! Lying around here all day, what else do I have to think about? All the shit she put me through? Everybody around here, they think she started losing it when my dad got killed. Believe me, whatever everybody thought she had, she was losing it long before then. Man, when I said I wasn't gonna be a cook, she flipped out. And when I told her I was gonna join the army, she started looking around for something to hit me with. I couldn't get outta here fast enough. Can still hear her screaming at me. 'Idiot, there's a war going on, you wanna go to war? Instead of be a chef? What kinda son do I have? Gotta good life and throwing it away? How can you be so stupid? I'm not stupid, your father wasn't stupid, why're you so stupid?'"

"And here's what I said back, yeah I said this, I said, 'You say my father isn't stupid, how come he married you?' Which would've been really chickenshit for me to say, 'cause my old man, he wasn't that bad. But I don't know why I say that, couple weeks ago, I did what Jimmy told me to do a long time ago, I started writing, whatever comes into my head, and the next thing I knew I was writing down every reason I could think of for why I liked my old man. And all I wrote were a bunch of nevers: he never hit me, never yelled at me, never took me anywhere except shopping, for groceries, or clothes, that was it, that was all I could write about him, he never did this, he never did that. What he did do, he backed her up, everything she said. Some story, ain't it? Oh, wait! Wait! I'm wrong.

"There was one time he stood up for me. She'd been on me for I don't know how long, trying to get me to go to confession. She went to church every day, man, I forgot that, yeah, she was dragging me to church with her, every fucking day. Then she started up with the confession thing. Said the same thing to him, and he said I go once a year, that's enough. Let him alone. He ain't done nothing he gotta confess to. He's only eleven years old for Chrissake. You know what she said? I'll never forget this—she said you think he's only eleven? You think kids that old never do nothing bad? That's how much you know. Kids eleven, twelve, they can do stuff you never thought of. I forgot about that. I forgot about him doing that. And her saying that. Thinking that about a kid. Her kid."

"I'm sorry, Rugs."

"You keep saying that, why you sorry now?"

"'Cause my parents weren't like that and I feel bad for you, my mother never gave me a hard time until, you know, well, till now, the last couple years, and that's only because—well, you know why. But my father, Jeez, he was a prince. Everything I did, he thought it was wonderful, he thought I was the prettiest, the smartest, the best, whatever I did. And I just feel bad you had to grow up like that and never heard your parents say that kind of stuff to you, praise you or compliment you."

"I had a parent who praised me."

"Who? Balzic? Yeah, right, sure, but Balzic wasn't your real father."

"Didn't make any difference to me. Whatever my father didn't give me, I got from him. He was my Training Officer when I started, and for the rest of the time he was there, he was always looking over my shoulder. Nobody could've been more of a father to me. I saw one of the fitness reports he wrote on me. I read that, I cried. I still remember what he wrote. I memorized it. 'Detective Carlucci is not fearless. Only fools and crazy people are fearless. But when Detective Carlucci is on a scene that calls for crisis entry, he's always the first officer through the door.' Those three sentences right there, they more than made up for all the stuff my father didn't say.

"I never told you this—the whole time I was in 'Nam, I had a letter from her, carried it right here," he said, tapping his left shirt pocket. "First letter she wrote after I enlisted. I was in basic for two months before she answered any of my letters—' course in my mind I was writing them mostly to my dad—even though, you know, he was dead. And she still thinks I was in the car when that happened. Anyway, this letter, she told me what a huge disappointment I was to her, how she couldn't believe I could turn down this huge, great opportunity to go to the community college, learn how to be a chef instead of doing what I was doing now, or then, you know, being in the army, learning how to be a soldier.

"In 'Nam, every time I got back from being point on a patrol, I'd take that letter out and read it, and I'd hold it up, you know, toward the sky, and I'd shake it, and I'd say, 'Hey, Ma, what do you think of your boy now? I got another patrol out and back and I was on point both ways. How you like me now?'

"So, I guess why I'm telling you this, Fran, is so you can stop feeling sorry for me. I survived my whole tour over there, I survived my father's dying, and I survived Ronald Reagan Kipple. Told you, didn't I? That was his whole name? And I survived Sister Mary Michael. Remember her? She still there when you were in school?"

"Oh yeah, was she. Jesus, how could anybody forget her?"

"She's who told me I could work at Kmart, they were always hiring. I could get a job stocking shelves, and some day maybe, if I applied myself, I might even get to manage the garden department. Joke is, after I got discharged, I did work there for almost a year—you know all this, I don't know why I'm repeating it now."

"Probably because you want me to know you'll survive without me."

Carlucci shook his head. "That can't be why. I don't wanna survive without you."

"You don't? Well you could've fooled me."

"No, I mean I know we got a problem now, and I know I'm a big part of the problem. But you gotta take a little part of this too. I mean, you talking about we need a break from each other? How could we be seeing each other less than we are now? I mean, since I got hurt, when was the last time we had sex?"

"Oh, Rugs, for God's sake, we've never had sex. Masturbating while we're talking on the phone? I mean, Jesus, really, who calls that sex? You maybe, not me."

"Yeah? Well the way we both been living, what other kind was there? Is there?"

"You must have a lot better imagination than I do—we've never even seen each other naked—that's not true, I've seen more of you since your fight with that, uh, you know who."

"I'll take mine off if you take yours off."

"Oh Jesus, Rugs, don't joke about this—I have to go—"

"See? There's the problem right there. You say we have to stop seeing each other, but the fact is, we don't see each other. For a long time the big obstacle was my mother, but the last coupla years—"

"I know, I know, you don't have to say it."

"Well, Fran, Jesus, how long we supposed to be 'cuffed to our mothers? Ain't we allowed to have a life? I'm fifty-seven, you're fifty, I mean, Jesus, how much time we got left?"

"Well I can't retire for another twelve years—and that's only if they don't change the rules."

"So there you are. You're gonna spend the rest of your mother's life working to pay for her meds and for somebody to watch her. How 'bout this? How 'bout I watch her, and you can fire that woman you're paying, what? Eight bucks an hour?"

"Well how much would I have to pay you?"

"Fran, for Chrissake, you wouldn't have to pay me nothing, I'm trying to make your life easier."

"Are you serious? My God, you're serious."

"'Course I'm serious. She likes me. Sort of. I think. Least she used to."

"Yeah, but Rugs, watching her, you know, it's not just watching her. She can't get up off the toilet without help. And sometimes, you know, she messes herself—"

"So? So it'll be a little bit awkward at first, so what? She'll get over it. We'll work it out, she'll get used to me; she'll see I'm not gonna invade her space—or her; she'll know I'm there to be helping her, not just her but you."

"You're making it sound way too easy. It's not that easy—"

"No, I'm not. I know this is no picnic for anybody, Fran, everybody'll be walking on eggshells for a while. But you know as well as I do, I saw people at their absolute fucking worst in 'Nam. And they haven't exactly been a bunch of cuddly puppies since then. Your mother can't do anything I haven't seen before—or cleaned up after."

"She's very shy, Rugs. Very modest. Old school all the way. I don't know—"

"I know she is—you've told me. But when you need help, and you know you need it, you get over that shy stuff pretty quick."

"You're still making it sound too easy."

"Fran, listen to me, the only thing I didn't do for my mother, when she was living here? That I'd have to do for your mother? I didn't have to take her to the bathroom, help her out there, or give her a bath, or anything like that. But everything else—everything—cooking for her, cleaning up the kitchen, the dishes, the pans, washing the clothes, cleaning the house, man, all that stuff, I did—she didn't do nothing around here. Like she had a vendetta against picking up one goddamn thing. When I got discharged, got back here, this place, Fran, Jesus Christ, this place looked like a junk yard. Every night I got here after all day at Kmart, all I did was jam crap into garbage bags, took them out on the sidewalk, hoped the garbage guys would pick them up.

"And then, couple or three years later, can't remember when exactly but it was after I got on the job, she goes and busts Fischetti's head. Next day she's in Mental Health. So how am I making it sound too easy? Uh-uh, no way. There ain't nothing easy about taking care of somebody always bitching, always complaining about every fucking thing I did or did not do for her, hating the two women I hired to look out for her, Jesus Christ, how they took her shit for all those years, I'll never know. And we all could've got in a world of heat, you know, if anybody dropped a dime on me for not paying their taxes, Jesus, I don't even wanna think about that.

"Now, wait, Fran, before you say it, yeah, I had those two women to help me, that's for sure. But they were here to watch her—they couldn't be cleaning up or cooking, they had to be watching her all the time, 'cause she was always trying to make a break for it. I'm just saying, the rest of the stuff around here, I did, I had to do it—everything. And I'm not painting it pretty, believe me."

"God, Rugs, I don't know. Little while ago you were being such a wise ass, but now . . . you sound like you've given this a lot of thought, but how do I know you aren't just, you know, how do I say this? You sure this isn't 'cause you suddenly find out we're gonna break up and you had to come up with some way, you know, to keep on the way we were? Or are? Are you sure you aren't forgetting the way we've been since that . . . that goddamn night I got smacked and you wanted to tell me what to do? How do I know for sure you aren't reaching for a life jacket here?"

"Okay, okay, that's fair. I don't know how you're gonna know that for sure, but I'm not. I love you, Fran. I loved you from the first time you talked to me. I know I don't tell you that nearly enough—"

"Nearly enough? Jesus, Rugs, when did you ever tell me that? Believe me, if you'd've told me that, I'd remember. In high school, when everybody was trying to get in my pants, it was, oh Franny, I love you, Franny, please let me get your pants off, Franny, oh, you know I love you, blah, blah, blah. Takes a while for us girls to separate the bull from the bullshit, you know? But when we hear it from a serious guy, believe me, we don't forget it—and this! This is the first time I'm hearing it from you. First time ever!"

"What can I say, Fran? I'm a dumb shit—"

"Oh I'll drink to that. About some things you really are."

"—I can't believe I never said that before—"

"Well now that you said it, you wanna say it again?"

"Sure, absolutely. I love you, Fran. I do. I love you."

"Okay, okay, I'm starting to believe you."

"Well?"

"Well what?"

"Is that all you're gonna say—you're starting to believe me?"

"No. I love you too, Rugs. But I never thought you felt the same—especially the last couple months. Jesus, I thought you were just waiting to get better so you could dump me."

"Dump you? Jesus Christ, you're who said we need a break, not me."

"And you're not just saying it 'cause you're scared? Please, Rugs, don't do that to me, I couldn't stand it if I thought the only reason you loved me was 'cause you were scared to be alone."

"Scared to be alone? Aw, man, when did I ever tell you I was scared to be alone?"

"Rugs, I've just watched my mother go from a really strong woman, emotionally now, not physically, she was never strong that way, but emotionally, she was always a rock. But in the last couple years, Jeez, she's just become this needy, clingy, demanding person who's terrified I'm going to hand her over to a bunch of strangers, and, believe me, all the physical demands she makes? Those are easy. What I don't know is how to deal with this woman who makes all these emotional demands."

"Just keep telling her, that's all you can do, keep telling her she can stop thinking about that. Can't you do that? Just keep telling her you ain't gonna walk away."

"Yes, but that's what I'm talking about, no matter how many times I tell her I would never do that to her, she keeps asking me. And now you're talking about coming into her life and as much as we both think she likes you, you know, she could change—"

"Well, hell, Fran, who can't change? Or couldn't—talking like a numb nuts here. What I'm trying to say is either we change or we all stay the same. All we can do, Fran, is give it a shot. How's this? I could take her on patrol, lead her around the first floor, get her back safely."

"God, Rugs! Jesus, it's not a joke!"

"Who's joking? I'm good at leading patrols. She'll see. I'll lead her out, I'll get her back. Never have to leave the first floor. It'll give her something to do instead of lying around worrying if you're gonna toss her under the bus."

"God, Rugs, oh Jesus, why am I thinking you don't know what you're doing—do you know what you're doing? I don't think you do."

"Fran, nobody knows what they're doing. Everybody's guessing. And hoping. And praying—even when we don't know who we're praying to. And whatever comes up, hey, you deal with it, that's all. I don't care how much you train, how much you prepare, how good your equipment is, Murphy's Law, man, whatever can go wrong, can and will go wrong. You cannot prepare for every little thing that's gonna happen, I don't give a rat's ass what anybody says, you can't. You just try to do your best, that's all. Just keep telling her you love her. Just like I'm gonna keep telling you. 'Cause I do."

"I got to go, Rugs. I been gone way too long. She'll be calling the cops—if she hasn't called them already."

"Who you talking to? Remember me? I'm the cops—ain't I?"

She started for the front door. "I don't think it's a good idea for you to come with me."

"Why not? We get there, we'll do a dry run, I'll take her on a patrol, she'll see I'm okay."

"It just doesn't—I don't know—it just doesn't feel right."

"Doesn't feel right? Didn't we just tell each other I love you? Huh? Now it doesn't feel right? What just happened? What the fuck just happened?"

"I have to go, Rugs. This is all too, I don't know, this is all too goddamn sudden."

Before he could respond, she was out the door.

He turned around and there was his new lounge chair, his five-position massaging lounge chair, just delivered yesterday. He hadn't sat in it yet. Hadn't even read the brochures that came with it. He dropped onto it. Leaned back, leaned back a little harder, and the chair moved smoothly into a vee. His body settled in. It felt like no chair he'd ever sat in. It felt smooth, firm, like an envelope would feel if it was a chair. He wondered—could he mail himself somewhere? *What? Could I mail myself somewhere? Fuck did that come from? Jees-us, could I mail myself somewhere?*

———

"Safety Committee meeting of the Rocksburg City Council will now come to order. All members present, me, Angelo Bellotti, Councilman Egidio Figulli, and Councilman John Radoycich. I move the reading of the minutes from the last meeting be waived. Second?"

"Second," Radoycich said.

"Old business?"

"Yes, right, here we go," Figulli said, reading from notecards. "Old business, right. This committee was trying to find out what happened at approximately 2210 hours on August 6, 2011, on Norwood Hill, involving Rocksburg resident Virginia Carpilotti, uh, responding was Rocksburg PD Detective Sargeant Ruggiero Carlucci who was working patrol. Also responding was Fire Chief Edward Sitko whose assistance had been requested by Sergeant Carlucci."

"Objection," said Panagios Valcanas, Carlucci's attorney.

"What? I ain't even got through my whole statement here—"

"I'm objecting to your characterization that my client asked for the assistance specifically of Fire Chief Edward Sitko. My client asked a 911 dispatcher to send volunteer firemen with portable ladders to assist him. He never requested the fire chief specifically by name."

"Oh, what? You gonna start picking nits with me already?"

"I'm here to represent my client, Councilman. If that means picking nits with you, then picking nits with you is exactly what I'll do."

"Aw, Jesus Christ," Figulli grumbled.

"Object to the profanity. I was hoping this inquiry would be conducted in a professional manner."

"Point taken, Counselor," Bellotti said. "Egidio, watch your mouth."

Figulli cleared his throat. "Where was I? Uh, here. That inquiry was interrupted by Police Chief Fred Nowicki, who reported an unusual incident on Popper Street, Rocksburg, at approximately

1005 hours that an unidentified male had been shot, and the shooter, he kept on shooting at cars parked on the street. Chief Nowicki told Detective Carlucci to respond with him to the incident, and so the inquiry was adjourned. So now we're gonna pick up where we left off. Present, in addition to the members of the Safety Committee is Detective Sergeant Carlucci and his legal counsel, Panagios Valcanas."

"Point of order," Bellotti said.

"What point of order?"

"A majority of this committee wishes to suspend this inquiry."

"Huh? What for? What majority?"

"What for is nobody cares about this crap but you," Radoycich said. "And we're the majority, so we're saying forget about this, 'cause this is all crap, that's all it is, and it's all your crap."

"You can't say that—when a cop shoots his gun it's standard procedure, the Safety Committee gotta find out why, that's the regulations. And youns guys both know it and don't try to tell me youns don't! Besides it's a city ordinance, anybody shoots off a gun in the city gotta come in here and say why they did it—what're youns two trying to pull here, huh?"

"What we're trying to pull here, Egidio, we're trying to save everybody a lot of time and money. The city's been sued by Virginia Carpilotti for excessive force, damages, medical expenses, pain and suffering, God knows what else, I don't even know if the solicitor's read the whole suit—"

"What're you talking about? That woman, she can't sue nobody, she's in Mental Health. Been in there for three months now—"

"How do you know that?" the mayor said. "I haven't heard anything about that."

"How do I know that? I asked, that's how. She been in there since the night Carlucci shot off his gun to get her and Sitko to stop fighting. The EMTs put her in there on a 302, danger to herself or others, and every time she has a new hearing, she's screaming she wantsa kill Sitko and Carlucci, plus her husband, so they just keep holding her for I don't know how many days, I forget, twenty, thirty days, whatever the law says, so how's she gonna sue anybody?"

"Well, there you go, Egidio, you just said yourself why Carlucci fired his gun, so even you gotta know this inquiry's a lotta hooey."

"I wasn't testifying, that was off the record—"

"So this civil suit," Bellotti said, "this is bogus then? Well, who filed it?"

"Who cares who filed it if it's bogus?" said Radio. "Wanna know who filed it, go down the courthouse, they'll tell you, take them five minutes."

Bellotti said, "Where's the solicitor? Why isn't he here? This woman, honest to God, she's caused us more trouble—"

"Yeah, absolutely," Figulli said. "And the guy sitting right there, he's who vouched for her, told us she was okay, so the city hired her on his word! Remember that? Remember she took her shirt off, tossed dirt on her boss. That's another reason he oughta be suspended!"

Radio threw up his hands. "Aw, man, how long you gonna keep harping on that? That was old news, uh, I don't when it happened, for Chrissake, come on."

"Mister Chairman," Valcanas said, "this is a farce. Councilman Figulli is sailing accusations around this room like paper airplanes. Most of the conversation here has had little or nothing to do with the subject of this so-called inquiry, and I'm appealing to your common sense, please, you have the power to end this, let's everybody go home, let's get on with our lives."

"Couldn't agree more," Radio said. "Let's go home."

"This is bullshit—baloney!" Figulli said. "Youns guys took a vote before it started and I wasn't here, I don't care what youns say now, it don't have nothing to do with what the regulations says, which is we're supposed to hold an inquiry any time a police officer shoots his gun, we're supposed to find out why he did it and if he was okay doing it. There's nothing in the regulations says youns two can vote to stop this before we reach a decision, or a ruling, or whatever."

"Well," Radio said, "everybody knows what happened—you talked to Sitko about it enough—and I know you talked to the EMTs about it, I was with you a coupla times when you was talking to them, and you just said it yourself why Rugs shot his gun. I mean, there ain't no mystery about it. Anyway, the whole council's getting ready to give him a commendation and the Mayor's Medal for—"

"The Mayor's Medal? You gotta be shitting me! For capturing that Kipple guy?"

"Once again, I object to the profanity—"

"He broke regulations there too! He shoulda waited for back up, which if he'da done that, he'da been back to work right after it happened, instead of being on sick leave like he is now! For three months for Chris sake—"

"Objection—"

"Aw shuddup, Mo—"

"Objection to the nickname, the disrespect. Councilman is fully aware of my name."

"Egidio," Radoycich said, "if he was suspended for losing his pepper spray and radio like you said he shoulda been, he wouldn't even have been on duty that day—to capture anybody, so what're you talking about here?"

The mayor said, "He found his radio, for crying out loud—the next day. That wasn't even an issue three months ago, so why're we still talking about it? And why is anybody talking about anything here, a majority already said we shouldn't even be having this inquiry. This inquiry's over, period, end of story."

"Oh no, nothing doing. Any vote youns took on stopping this, youns took it before we even got started here, and if the whole committee wasn't here—which I wasn't—that ain't a legal vote. Where's the solicitor? I wanna hear him tell me this ain't legal, where the hell is he? This whole thing here, this ain't legal!"

"Amen," said Valcanas. Turning to Carlucci, he sang, "Pack up your troubles in your old kit bag, and smile, smile, smile."

"Is that a song?"

"You couldn't tell?"

"Sounded kinda like you were growling."

"Well it was long before your time, Rugs. From World War One. Before my time. I'm going to Muscotti's, you better be going there too."

"Why?"

"'Cause you owe me a drink. Or eight. Or nine. You haven't paid your bill from the first time these clowns wanted your shield."

"You never sent me a bill."

"I'm not talking about the last meeting. I'm talking about three years ago."

"Oh. Well, I don't think I got a bill for that one either."

"I see I'm gonna have to find a new office manager. Can't blame everything on the Republicans."

———

"Okay, Fran, so what's up, what's wrong—oh, man, you look terrible."

"Never mind how I look."

"So, just start talking. Best way I ever found. That's all, whatever you wanna say, you start talking, you'll get to it. Eventually."

"It's not that easy. You make it sound easy."

"I didn't say it was easy, I said it was the best way, best don't guarantee easy."

"Okay okay—this is really hard, Rugs. I never thought in my life I'd ever even be thinking I was gonna talk about this." She took a deep breath. "And you gotta promise me, please, Rugs, please don't interrupt me."

"Okay, Fran, I won't. Promise."

She turned her hands into fists and pounded her thighs.

"Just do it, Fran, just start that's—"

"You promised you wouldn't interrupt!"

Ruggiero splayed his hands. Shrugged. Shook his head.

"Okay. I'm starting, I'm starting—Jesus, this is so hard. You know I love Mom. You know I do. I know I do. But I can't keep doing this! Every morning, every day, I get up, I make her breakfast, I make sure Mrs. Sancotti's here, don't leave till she's in the kitchen. Then I leave. On my way out I kiss Mom on the head. Last week she started telling me—no, not telling me, yelling at me, 'Don't kiss me on the head, I keep telling you don't kiss me on the head and you keep doing it.'

"So I say Mom, I didn't know that bothered you, this is first time you ever said anything. If I knew it bothered you, do you think I would've kept doing it? And she gives me this look—Jesus, this look I never saw before . . . this look says I don't know, you used to be so smart . . . and she shakes her head at me. And when she said that yesterday, it was in a tone I never heard before . . . and when she said that, Rugs, it really hurt. All of a sudden it felt like she was trying to make me feel dumb. I was suddenly trying to remember if she'd ever made me feel like that. And I turned around and I practically ran out of there. Then I got to work. You know, where I get paid? But lately, every day, for the last week maybe, aw, crap, for I don't know how long, it's starting to feel, I don't know, same old, same old. I never felt this way before.

"You know, checking the roster gets faxed down from the judge's clerk, putting a face with the name, making sure everybody who's supposed to be there is there, and every day it's the same. Somebody from the day before who's supposed to be there isn't there, and somebody I've never seen before is. And of course, the ones that I've never seen before, they have no idea why they're on my list. And I call the office and I get screwed around for a while, happens every morning. I mean it, you know, finally, it gets straightened out, but right away I'm playing catch up. And it happens every day. Every fucking day."

She held up her index finger. She coughed and struggled to hold back a sob.

Rugs reached out to pat her hand. She jerked it away.

"You promised, Rugs! You promised!"

"What? All I was gonna do was touch your hand—Jesus, that's an interruption?"

"Well if it isn't why am I talking about it?"

"Aw, Fran, come on."

"You promised!"

Rugs threw up his hands. "Okay, okay, Jesus, no talking, no touching, I get it."

"Promise."

"Aw no, come on. I'm . . . I'm not promising again. I just did that."

"Okay then."

He started to shake his head, caught himself, stopped in mid-shake. *What the fuck. This is starting to sound . . . weird. No. Not weird. Wrong. Starting to sound wrong.*

He leaned forward, but not too far. Looked into her eyes. Didn't know what he was seeing.

"Yesterday. I got so frustrated, work was just one damn thing after another. And then I come home. And Mrs. Sancotti, soon as I come in the door, she starts giving me these looks, and she's shaking her head. And Mom, she's, uh, she was uh, just not right. And I'm thinking, Jesus, did she have a stroke? So I'm looking at her face, you know, seeing if both sides of her face were the same, you know, symmetrical. But I couldn't tell. And then she starts yelling at me. 'Where were you today? I didn't see you all day.' 'At work,' I tell her. 'Where I go every day.' And she says, 'Oh no you don't. You don't go to work every day. Every coupla days, you're right here, you stay with me.' And Mrs. Sancotti's still giving me these looks . . . and you know what? You're not gonna believe this, and I'm so ashamed of myself, honest to god, Rugs, I wanted . . . I wanted to hit her! Right then, I'm telling you, Rugs, no, I didn't just wanna hit her, I wanted to hurt her. Honest to God, Rugs,

I was looking for something, I don't know what, her rolling pin, something, and the next thing I know, I'm on the floor, on my knees, and Mrs. Sancotti, she's down there with me, she got her arms around me, she's trying to tell me, 'It's okay, honey, it's all right,' and I'm telling her, 'No no no it isn't all right, something's wrong with her, something's wrong with me.' I was still mad. Furious! Honest to God, Rugs, I was . . . terrified, I thought I did it. I thought I hurt her! I thought, Jesus, I killed Mom—oh shit, oh shit, I need a Paxil. Where'd I put them? Help me, Rugs! Help me find them, they're in my purse!"

"Where's that?"

"It's right there." She looked where she thought it was, but shook her head, grabbed her head, gasped. "Oh, Jesus, don't tell me—did I leave it at work? No, uh-uh, I never did that, I never do that. Must've put it someplace else—look, Rugs, okay?"

"Okay—where you want me to start?" Rugs said, thinking this is really getting wrong. "How do you come in? The front door? Or through the kitchen?"

"Rugs, you know I don't park on the street. You know where I park—in the alley!"

"Okay, so you came in through the kitchen." He went there. Looked around, every flat surface, starting with the floor. No purse. Headed back through the dining room, checking all the flat surfaces there, including the bed and her mother in it and the chair seats. Nothing. Checked every place he thought she might've hung it by the strap. Still nothing.

"Not in the kitchen," he said. "Dining room neither. Not on the bed. Ever put it in the closet?" Pointed with a nod.

"Why? Why would I put it in there? I never put it in there."

"Just checking, that's all. I'm looking all around, I don't see it, gotta be here someplace."

"Didn't feel like you were gone very long."

"Didn't feel like I was gone very long? How do you—never mind."

"How do I do what?"

"Hey, bad question, shouldn't've said it, shouldn't even have thought it."

"You patronizing me? I'm starting to feel like you're patronizing me here."

"Maybe you should go."

"What? Go? You mean leave? Aw no, no way I'm leaving you here, not like this, not when you're like this."

Rugs turned for the front door. "C'mon, get your coat, I'm taking you to see Reseta."

She hugged herself, stood, shaking her head. "You're not taking me anywhere."

"Franny, don't make me do something you know I can do. Something I have every right, every duty to do and you know what I'm talking about. I'm not gonna leave you here, not the way you are."

"Well you're not taking me anywhere—not the way you are!"

"Never seen you like this, Fran. All the years I've known you, I've never seen you like this before—"

"Well maybe you weren't really looking, huh? You think?"

"Aw, Fran, Franny, man, what's with you? You're scaring me."

"Scaring you? You wanna be scared? I'll tell you scared—the other night I woke up, I thought I was I dreaming. I ran into her room, there she is . . . she's snoring. Jesus Christ, I thought, what am I doing? Am I dreaming or what? And then, you know what, Rugs? Honest to God . . . I wish . . . I wish I'd killed her!"

"Aw, Fran, c'mon, you're trying to make something outta nothing—"

"Something out of nothing! That's what you think? Really? I'm opening myself up to you, Rugs, and that's what you think?"

"C'mon, Fran, you need to sit down, take a coupla deep breaths—"

"Oh God, Rugs, Rugs, who're you talking to here? I'm the queen of deep breaths, Jesus, every hour at work I say that ten times—"

"Then you know that's what you should be doing now."

"Goddammit it, Rugs, you're gonna give me shoulds! You?"

"Right now? Yeah, that's exactly what I'm giving you. You need to hold up, Fran, I mean it!"

"You wanna hear shoulds? You should go! You! You should leave! Now!"

"Aw, Franny, Jesus."

"Don't Jesus me, get outta here, go!"

"Okay okay, I'm going." He shuffled through the front door, shaking his head with every step. On the first step off the porch, he turned around. Went back inside.

"Franny, listen to me—"

"Listen to you? I told you to leave and yet here you are! Back!"

"Fran, I know what you told me—"

"Then why're you still here?"

"Goddammit, Fran, listen to me, just listen—everything you just told me, you were thinking about offing your mother for Chrissake, you think I'm not supposed to do something about that?"

"Rugs, get outta here! I mean it! Get out!"

"I know you mean it. That's exactly why I should do what I just said. You're talking about hurting yourself! You're talking about hurting your mother! Or somebody else! You know I can't walk away from that."

"What I know is you should leave."

"Can't do that, Fran. Like it or not I'm still a cop. What you been saying? I gotta take you up to Mental Health. I love you, but love you or not, I been a cop—I can't just sit on what you just told me."

"Aw, this is perfect. You're gonna stand on your badge now—"

"Fran, listen to me, I walk out that front door and you ain't with me? I'm gonna get in my car, call the station, tell them to get two patrolmen up here with a bus. You don't go with me you're going with them, that's where I am, that's where we are, and that's your choice."

"And oh, Jesus, I used to think the thing I loved about you most was how loyal you were to all your friends. I thought, well, you can't be anything but the same to me. And here you are, telling me what? You're gonna sic your buddies on me?"

"I'm not siccing anybody on you—you coming or not?"

"No I'm not coming! Jesus Christ, Rugs, just because I was telling you how I feel about my mother . . . oh, God, I don't believe you! How'd I think you would ever—you!"

"I'm gonna go do what I said, Fran. You ain't coming, you give me no choice."

"Here's my choice." She thrust both middle fingers up at him.

He couldn't believe his eyes. That was it. Jesus fuck! He turned toward the front door, and this time he didn't turn back. This time he walked, head up, eyes front, to his car, to his radio. Made the call.

Then he sat. Waiting. And started to cry. Tears sliding down his cheeks, mucous dripping on the steering wheel. A sob, then gagging, trying to choke off his sobs.

The fuck am I doing, calling a bus? Taking her to Mental Health? Tell somebody there what she said and how she said it, what she looked like, what she sounded like? What the fuck?

Audio came back on. "Rugs? You copy? Rugs, Nowicki here, you copy? Rugs, where you at?"

"I'm in my car, in front of my girlfriend's house, you know who I'm talking about?"

"Course I know who—d'you just call for a bus?"

"Yes."

"The hell you want a bus for?"

"Your cousin was saying shit I never thought I'd hear coming out of her mouth—not in a million years."

"Like what?"

"I want a bus, you hear me? Two males, one female and I fucking want it now!"

"Okay, okay, it's on the way. Rugs—oh Rugs, Jesus, I almost forgot. Your mother's social worker said call her. Urgent."

"Urgent? She said urgent? Aw fuck me, what now?"

—

"Sergeant, is this you?"

"It's me, Miss Thigpen, I'm scared to ask, what's urgent?"

"Well I'm scared to tell you, Sergeant, but, uh, we've, uh, we've lost your mother."

"Whoa, what? Lost her how? You don't mean lost her dead, you don't mean that, right?"

"No no, no, it's a lot worse than that."

"Worse? Jesus, tell me, she ain't dead—what's worse?"

"We don't know how she did it because the aide's in pretty bad shape. All we can think is she must've got behind him when he went in to help her after she pulled the string, you know, the help string from the toilet. She had to've smashed his nose on the shelf under the mirror, blood all over the shelf, the mirror, he was out when we found him. He didn't have his wallet, his car keys, we went looking for his car, his car's gone."

"Car keys and car? Gone? Jesus Christ."

"Pittsburgh and state police have been alerted, but we haven't heard anything so far."

"She smashed his nose—how the fuck—how'd she do that?"

"Sergeant, I just told you, you know what I know, okay?"

"Well it ain't okay, Miss Thigpen. Jesus Christ, this ain't okay!"

"Sergeant, if I were you, and the Good Lord knows I'm not, as angry as she is with you, I would, uh, I would be preparing for anything. There's no doubt about it, your mother has been holding a heavy grudge against you, but she fooled us all, every one of us, got us thinking she was honestly sincere, honestly saying she had forgiven you, she was ready to reconcile with you. Six weeks ago, half the team, and I'm not overstating this, half were fully prepared—right then—to sign her discharge papers. Other half was nowhere near that certain, and I have to tell you, Sergeant, I was with them—I was not ready to sign her discharge papers."

"Miss Thigpen, I warned you, I told you when she put her mind to it, she could sweet-talk anybody, and believe me, I don't get any warm fuzzies saying that, 'cause I would rather be wrong, and I hope you know that. Only other thing I wanna say is I hope nobody takes any heat for this, and I hope that mostly for you. But I gotta go now. I got my own problem right here."

Carlucci put his phone away as the EMS bus pulled in behind his car. Two males and one female got out. Waving his badge and ID wallet, he called out to them. Didn't recognize any of them. Up close they all wanted a better look at his badge and ID.

"I'm Detective Sergeant Carlucci, Rocksburg PD, the person you're looking for is in the house, top of the steps, a woman, five six, slender build, brown hair, brown eyes, fifty, mad as hell right now, she's not gonna wanna go. Right now she's seriously pissed at me, thinking I way overreacted, but she plainly threatened to hurt her mother, who is also in there, in bed in the dining room. I'm not gonna to tell you how to do your job, I'm just warning you she's not going easy—but she has to go to Mental Health. I'll handle the paper when we get there. Get going! See you up there."

Minutes later he parked in the lot opposite the ER door of the Mental Health building and walked, slowly, back and forth, trying to guess what his mother was going to do when she found out all the doors to the house are locked. He threw up his hands, said, "Shit!" and punched the palm of his left hand.

Just remembered he forgot to call the woman who watches Franny's mother when she's at work.

Before he could punch one button, his phone rang. Nowicki said, "Forget something, Rugs?"

"Yeah, just remembered."

"Well somebody better be real nice to my cousin or somebody's gonna have to babysit my aunt."

"Ain't gonna be me, Wick. My mother's loose."

"Your mother's what?"

"You heard me, loose, escaped, got out."

"You're joking. You're not?"

"Wick, knowing what you know about me and her, why the fuck would I be joking—call Mutual Aid, ask them if they got another female EMT there—she should get to Franny's house, stay with her mother. Sirens and lights! And if they don't have anybody up there, man, then it's on you!"

"Me?"

"Yeah you—she's your aunt! Be good if you were waiting on the front porch for the bus!"

Carlucci clicked off before Nowicki could come back at him.

———

The bus pulled into the discharge space in front of the Mental Health ER just as Carlucci quit his call with Nowicki.

He could see her struggling, trying to squirm away from the EMTs. When the door opened, he heard her screaming, "Take this thing off me; I'm not crazy what do you think I'm gonna do?"

Oh, fuck, no wonder she's screaming, they got her in a jacket, Jesus!

Carlucci felt a surge of wanting to help her, but he knew if he tried he would make everything worse. He forced himself to go near the bus door as she was being led out, but quickly stepped aside as soon as she saw him and started cursing.

"Jesus Christ! You ordered this jacket—don't even try to say you didn't 'cause I know you did! Course you did, who else would?"

Carlucci shook his head no, no, he didn't order it.

"Anybody as crazy as I am, yeah right, because you, Carlucci, you have to protect everybody from crazy me, right? Your ex-girl-friend? Your masturbation lover? Right? That's you, goddamn right it's you, fantastic lover, really good at jerking off, all those times,

Rugs, why'd you never ask me what I was doing, huh? Why'd you never say anything about this to Reseta?"

Carlucci didn't know whether to speak or run. Opened his mouth to speak. Couldn't. Couldn't close it either.

All this time—as his mother's son, as a kid in Sister Mary Michael's school, as a patrolman, a detective, a sergeant, as chief—Jesus fuck, every one of the patrols in 'Nam—none of it blistered his mind more than hearing Fran Perfetti screaming what she was screaming, where she was screaming, who she was screaming at.

And still to do were all the questions to answer, all the papers to sign, everything she was going to scream as she was led away from the office.

Driving home, crying, trying to breathe away her screams.

———

Across the street from his house, he shut off the engine, closed his eyes, let his head drop forward, inhaled for a count of four, held it for four, exhaled it for four, grinding to wrap himself in fours until the pulses in his temples—were they slowing? Were they? What the fuck?

How much time till his mother showed up? 'Cause she was going to show up—where else would she go? What would she look like? What would she say? How would she be? That's a fucking laugh, Carlucci. There ain't words for how she's gonna be.

He felt his presence slip from Mother to Fran, how she was thinking now, how she was feeling now, how furious she was . . . he felt a sharp hard cringe in his gut, Jesus fuck! Coming off the bus

at Mental Health, Fran . . . looked . . . sounded—like his mother!
What? No! No! Stop! The fuck you mean? Not that! No! That is not
what I meant—I did not mean that!

Am I here? Am I now?

Pounding on the window, his mother screaming, "You got the
goddamn house all locked up, how am I s'posed to get in?"

Jesus Christ, if I lost it like this in 'Nam, I would've come back in a
box. Half of everybody behind me would have! Half? Shit! All of them!

"Hey, you gonna sit out here the whole goddamn day? I'm
hungry! Thirsty too!"

Inhaled for four, held it for four, exhaled for four. Wasn't
working. Temple pulses ramping up.

She pounded on the window again, this time with keys.

He unbuckled his seat belt, turned to look at her full face, saw
eyes harder than he'd ever seen. From her.

"Back away from the car!"

"Oh, listen to you, getting all tough-guy cop on me, huh? Never
worked before, Ruggiero! Think it's gonna work now? Maybe you
think I'm all better. Ha ha, oh God, that's so funny. Think they
gave me some magic pills, huh? Made me better? Better than what,
I guess you wanna know, huh?"

"Back away from the door, Ma. Do it now!"

She bent farther over, put her face closer to the window.

"Not gonna tell you again, Ma. I don't wanna hurt you—"

"Oh boy oh boy oh boy, you think you could hurt me now?
More than you already did? Must be something wrong with you
upstairs, something really wrong, you know, in your head? Trying
to pretend you don't remember how you hurt me? Jesus Christ,
I can hear you now, I can see you now, I can see you then and I

can hear you then. But you? You don't remember? All the times you didn't wanna go to church? All the times you didn't wanna go to confession?"

She wasn't backing away. She was leaning in. She know what she's doing? Does she know the only way I'm getting—oh Jesus Christ, Ma!

Who's looking at me—anybody looking at me? Nobody got a cell phone around here, all too old. Could've got one from their kids, grandkids.

"Ma, last time, please back up! Please? Ma?"

"Oh, listen to you now, please, Ma, back up, please, Ma."

"I have to get outta the car, Ma, close as you're standing, I open the door, you're gonna go down!"

"You wanna get outta the car, huh? Okay, okay, but first you gotta promise me you're gonna open the front door, you're gonna let me go in first."

"I promise, Ma, I'll open the front door for you."

"Aw no, no, no, I ain't falling for that. I go in first, you smack me in the head, put your handcuffs on me—nothing doing, you're going in first."

"C'mon, Ma, make up your mind—who's going in first?"

"Woo boy, make up my mind—all of a sudden I got a mind! Put me in a place fulla people can't remember their name, but all of a sudden I got a mind!"

As twisted in the seat as he was, the only choice he had was to use his forearm, put everything he could get from his body into it. No other way. Fuckit! Do it!

Down she went! Backward !

He scrambled out, stumbled on her foot, turned her over, cuffed her, stood up, saw the red, saw the blood in her hair.

Words spilled out of his mouth, "Hail Mary, fulla grace, pray for us sinners, at the hour of our death . . ." Christ that ain't right, could never memorize it, fucking rapping me on the knuckles every time for messing it up, hair Mary fulla grace. What? Hair Mary? Forget hail Mary, get a bus!

"Sergeant Carlucci, Rocksburg PD, I need a bus, person down, not conscious, bleeding from the back of her head, eyes closed, breathing—she's still breathing!"

"Sergeant," came a woman's even, unhurried voice, "what's your location?"

"One five one, Oriolo Street, Norword Hill, Rocksburg. Oh man, Norword? Norword? I mean Norwood."

"I knew what you meant," she said.

"You know—who is this?"

"Sergeant, you of all people should know I can't tell you that . . . but I heard what you said . . . and that was funny."

"Funny, huh? Listen the fuck up, I just knocked my mother down, you hear what I just said? Slammed my car door into her, knocked her down, my own mother, goddammit! Get me a bus up here!"

Back on the street, kneeling beside her. "Aw, Jesus Ma, don't die, don't die, told you back away! You didn't listen—you never listen, please, please, Jesus Christ, Ma, don't die!"

He was sobbing when the bus arrived. Stood up, recognized the driver from one of the nights with the Virgin. Held out his ID wallet and badge for the EMTs he didn't know. Scurried out of their way.

They stabilized his mother's head, strapped her onto a body board, strapped it to the gurney, then put the gurney into the bus. Driver said, "Wanna ride along?"

Wiping his nose and mouth with the back of his hands, he said, "No, no, get her up there, Jesus, don't be waiting on me, go, go!"

———

Carlucci, swearing, sobbing, smearing her blood between his thumb and index finger, sweating, pulses pounding, scared in a way he'd never been. *How scared can you be? And still do what—think? Oh fucking yeah, try that, try thinking, go ahead motherfucker, try that—Motherfucker? Motherkiller? Oh shit . . . Hail Mary, full of grace, the Lord is with me—thee. With thee, not with me, never with me, never asked him to be with me, fuck no! Sister of Hitler Mary Michael coming at me with that triangle of wood . . . Goddamn that hurt. Why would I ask Jesus's mother? Never asked him—or her—when she was coming at me with that ruler, coming at us, boys, just us, not the girls, they never got the ruler, never got that fucking pain. Fuck am I thinking this? Now? That's what I'm thinking? Now? What did I do? Fuck did I do? Put Franny in Mental Health . . . she threatened to hurt her mother . . . had to, no choice . . . that's it right there . . . she got to go, 302 . . . no choice, not after she says what she said!*

"Oh no, Jesus fuck, Ma, why wouldn't you back away?"

Carlucci pressed the heels of his palms onto his forehead. *Say stop! Shout it! Try to make the thinking stop . . . stop!*

Shifting from foot to foot, Balzic tapped a passing doctor on the shoulder, "You know anything about him?"

"Him who? Oh you mean the patient was just here?"

"Yeah. Like, uh, how long you think before he wakes up?"

"Hard to say, some come out of it in one, two hours. Some three, four, I've had a few didn't wake up for a lot longer than that—you a relative?"

"No, used to be chief of police here. He was on the job."

"Who? What job? He was on the job—what's that mean?"

"Him, the guy was just lying here. On the job means he was—is—a police officer. Good detective, smart, gutsy. My daughters used to moan he was the son I never had, uh, weren't always happy saying it, sometimes weren't too quiet about it—but, uh, that's not important. When he was brought in today, anybody saying he threatened anybody? Himself or anybody else?"

"I just heard what the EMTs were saying when they brought him in, something about him sitting on the curb, crying and swearing, but not loud. They gave him a shot to calm him down. Think that's what they were saying. Could've heard it wrong."

"So unless you hear otherwise, you can't hold him—I mean I know you can't, right?"

"Not unless he wakes up flailing, hurts somebody in here, no."

"Well, here, let me give you my cell number. When he comes around, call me, I'll come get him, okay?"

"No relatives?"

"No. Years ago he had a couple uncles, but they're all dead. His father was the youngest, he died in a traffic accident, way back, thirty, thirty-five years ago, not exactly sure."

Balzic thanked the doc for talking to him, said he had to go check on something. Went to the ER admissions clerk, asked if there was any problem admitting Carlucci or his mother.

"There was no problem with the male, he's in our system, he had insurance. If you're talking about the woman, she wasn't conscious, straight up to radiology, no reason for me to hear any more about her."

"Well, you mind checking to see if she's in the system? Same last name as his."

The clerk typed for a few moments, then squinted at the screen. "Doesn't look like it. No."

"Okay, thank you," Balzic said and walked out the ER door to the ambulance parking lot. Out there, he thought, *What am I trying to do here getting involved? Am I trying to make something out of this? This me being bored? This me trying to figure out how bored I am? Wish Ma was here. Goddamn I miss her. Hear that, Ma? Still missing you. Oh shit, got to stop this. Gotta stop or I'm gonna start bawling. Whoa, what the hell am I doing here?*

"What'd they give me? How long I been out?"

"Nurse said you been out at least four hours," said Balzic.

"How long you been here?"

"Doesn't matter, I didn't have anything else to do. Just wandering around thinking, all kindsa crap. I don't know why, just curious, when you were in the army, who paid the taxes, the utilities, on your house, was that you?"

"Uh, not at first I didn't, no. But it sure as hell wasn't her, she didn't know anybody was supposed to."

"She didn't pay the bills? The taxes? How'd they get paid?"

"Well, my best friend in high school was a kid named Jackie Morano. And he told me one of his mother's relatives did the taxes for a lot of people in their family. His parents threw him a graduation party, man, house was jammed, all their relatives were there, that was the night my mother picked to tell me I was gonna go to the community college, learn how to be a chef. And, man, we got into it that night, real bad, you know? That's when she starts giving me all this crap about what Sister Mary Michael told her about me, how somebody always had to be telling me what to do, had to have somebody pushing me, or I was never gonna amount to nothing. She springs this pile of brochures on me, from the college, tells me I was gonna sit there and read them, and I said uh-uh, nothing doing, I'm not reading them, I'm going to Jackie's party. And I did, and while I was there, he introduced me to his uncle, and one thing led to another and I asked him, you know, I said maybe someday I'll have some money, who knows, and if I had a problem about it, could I ask him and he said yeah. Gave me his card. That was the first card like that anybody ever gave me, first business card, you know? And I'm really glad I hung onto it too.

"Next day I enlisted. Jackie and his dad, they drove me into Pittsburgh, left me off at the recruiters' office. First time we got paid, in basic, they asked us if we wanted to send any money home. I didn't even think about it, until this sergeant started talking about who bought the groceries, what kind of stove we had, what kind of heat we had, whether we had indoor toilets, whether somebody had a car, who paid for the gas, oil, tires, that kinda stuff. There was actually three guys didn't have indoor toilets. Sounds stupid now, but I didn't know who paid for any of that, I must've just thought that's what my dad did, but he never talked about it to me. Never heard him talking about it to my mother either."

"So you wrote to her, right? About it?"

"Oh yeah, sure. But she never answered anything I wrote. She just wrote how I was such a goddamn disappointment to her. I kept writing to her, I don't know why, at least once a week, the whole time I was in basic, but she never said anything about that, just kept telling me shit like I was my father's son and all the rest of his brothers were just like him and on and on and on, just pissing and moaning about how lousy her life was—uh, you heard anybody say how she's doing?"

"Nope. Nothing."

"Jesus, if she dies, man, oh fucking Christ. Man, I never thought I would ever say this, uh, I wish I could pray. Wish I knew how. No shit, Mario, I never, uh, never since I got rapped on the knuckles by this sister—we used to call her Hitler's daughter—no way was I ever gonna pray to anybody she prayed to. Never prayed in 'Nam. Not even there. Got the shit scared outta me, and I mean that exactly, didn't even know the first time where the stink was coming from. And that wasn't the only time."

Balzic rubbed his cheeks, blew out a sigh, said, "You forget I was at Iwo Jima? I was in the third wave—how many times you think I shit my pants there? On the beach the first time. Japs waited till the whole goddamn beach was just jammed full of us and all our gear and trying to get up and get off the beach was, hell, you couldn't do it 'cause every step you tried you sank in up to your ankles. Or deeper. And wherever they were, man, they were dug in deep, machine guns, artillery, Jesus Christ, boats were blowing up behind us, whole lotta guys got wounded, killed, from the parts of those LCPs blowing up behind us . . . listen to me, Jesus, listen to us, talking about how many times we shit ourselves. I remember one guy, from deep in the South, he said, honest to God, he said this on the beach, we oughta get a PUC for shitting ourselves—with oak leaf clusters for every time we did. Said nobody could tell what those things looked like, might as well've been clusters of turds. The shit we remember. So, uh, getting back to this relative of your best friend."

"Oh yeah, well I still had that card he gave me, so I wrote him, asked him what I should do, you know, told him my mother thinks everything's free, and he wrote me back real quick, he said he'd set up some kinda account in his bank, escrow account. I didn't know what that was. Gave me the bank's address, said I had to write them a letter, tell them he was gonna pay my mother's bills out of the money he got from me. Later on he told me what escrow meant, or was.

"And then, Jackie, he said when his uncle opened the account, he put in three hundred bucks of his own money in there. Before taxes, my first pay wasn't much, ninety, hundred bucks, something like that. And then he, the uncle, told me write to the post office and tell them what he was doing for me and he'd pick up our mail, and that's what he did. I met that guy just that one time, at Jackie's party, and he did all that stuff for me. Went to see him after I got discharged, you know, ask him why he did all that, and he said Jackie told him I was the only reason he made it through high school. He said that was all he needed to hear. Said he wished Jackie was his son."

A nurse carrying a clipboard came in and asked Carlucci for his name, birthday, and address.

"Rugs, need anything, give me a call."

Carlucci nodded, waved, turned back to the nurse and said, "Hope you're here to tell me you got my discharge papers."

"You have to show me you can stand, walk, and not fall down."

Carlucci swung his legs off the bed, stepped down, touched the floor with his left foot, then his right, smiled at the nurse, and the room started to whirl.

She grabbed his arm, said, "Thought so. I'll be back later. There's a doctor here to see you anyway."

A man in surgical scrubs knocked on the door frame and said, "You Mr. Carlucci?"

"Yes."

"I'm Doctor Jarwal, I'm a neurosurgeon."

The doctor came close to Carlucci's bed, lowered his voice, and said, "Uh, Mr. Carlucci, there's never a good time to say this, never a good place to say it, and the words are never good enough. I am truly sorry to have to say them. We lost your mother."

Carlucci closed his eyes, felt pain blazing down the back of both legs. He said, "Whatta you mean lost her? Lost her how? You telling me she died?"

"I'm afraid so—"

"You're afraid so? You know what you're telling me? No you fucking don't, you don't know what you're telling me, you got no idea what you're telling me, so lemme tell you, I'll tell you what you just said, you just said I killed my mother, that's what you just said, I just fucking killed my mother—"

"Mr. Carlucci, wait, I didn't say anything like that. I know it's hard for anybody to hear, anybody who loses their mother—"

"Doc, Doc, you don't know what you're talking about, okay? You don't know nothing about me or my mother—"

"Well, I may not know that, but I'm trying to tell you, as clearly as I can, we did everything we could, and I do mean everything. Every one of us in the OR, including the Code Blue team, we tried everything we knew. Her heart just quit. But there was no reason for it to quit. I'd just closed up her scalp, there was absolutely no reason for her to die, the fracture would've healed by itself, six, eight weeks, she would've been fine, there was no depression, no pressure on her brain, very little bleeding, just a very thin crack—"

"Hey, Doc, you sound like you're talking to a lawyer. I ain't a lawyer, okay? I'm a cop, you get that? I'm a cop!"

"Uh, yes, I think so, I think I get that."

"Well, the next thing for you to get is to go the fuck away, you get that?"

"I want you to know I'm really sorry for your loss, it—"

"Yeah yeah yeah—just go away leave me the fuck alone. Having a stupid fucking day! I'm hoping I can get through it without hurting anybody—anybody! Mostly me! And right now, I don't know if I got it in me to do what I think it's gonna take.

"You happy, Ma? Huh? You fucking happy now? You wouldn't back away from the door, typical you, and now I got your blood all over me, fuck me! All over my mind. And I got the woman I thought just a little while ago I might ask her to marry me, and today, Ma, today she freaked me the fuck out. One time when she was hollering? Got-damn if she didn't sound just like you! A whole lot! And now all I can think is why did I never hear her sound like that before? Sound like you!

"What the fuck? Holy fuck!"

——

Nowicki's voice, loud even through the front door, startled Carlucci.

"Hey, Rugs, somebody here to see you."

"You don't say. Is it one of those fucking reporters? If not come on in."

"Yeah, well they're making a nuisance of themselves on the sidewalk and I'm sure they'd love to talk with you, but that's not who I'm talking about. It's this lady right here. Go on, go on, he's okay, he won't bite ya. You have to introduce yourself, 'cause I'm sorry, I already I forgot your name."

The woman, head bent slightly forward, grayish from her hair to the tops of her cheeks to the crepey skin of her neck, asked if he was Ruggeiro Carlucci, asked so softly he barely heard her.

"Yeah, that's me, but I don't know you, do I?"

"Oh we've never met. Your mother's first name, was it Renata?"

"Yeah, that's her name. Was her name. Why you asking? Who are you?"

"My birth name was Mary Tomchak. I heard about your mother and I am so sorry for your loss. I'd been looking for her for a while, sad to hear I got here too late."

"Pretty sure I don't know you—we ever met?"

"No. But there is a story I have wanting to tell and it's a tough one, I owe Renata that. I need you to please just listen. Don't think I could dwell on it too long or tell it twice. "

Carlucci shrugged, shot a what-the-hell look at Nowicki, then said to the woman, "Okay. Come on in. Get her a chair, Wick."

Took her a few moments to sit.

"This all—everything I'm gonna tell you, this all happened forty-six years ago. Started in Lyndora, Butler County. That's where we're both from. Your mother was orphaned about the same time I was. I was a year older than her, but we didn't know each other in school. Her father was a really bad drunk. Mean. Get drunk every payday, come home, beat her mother first and then her. Finally beat her mother so bad, she went in the hospital, never came out. Later on, Renata told me she was terrified he was gonna do her the same way.

"People today, most of them forget, if they ever knew, most men at one time, and not so long ago either, they thought their wives belonged to them. Kids too. Anyway, about a year after her mother died, her father got killed in a mine. So, just like me, she sorta became owned by the state. I was already in the foster thing, that's what I mean. Her family was sort've a copy of mine.

"Anyway, I was already in that place when she got there, and that place might as well've been a jail. Every couple weeks, we'd have to get all showered up and shampooed, we'd sit around and people looking for kids they could pretend was theirs, they'd come in and look us over, like we was a buncha animals. Felt like that anyway. After one of those times I met her, Renata. She was crying, and I asked her what she was crying about, she said there was this man and woman, they looked at her for a long time and then looked at each other and they just started laughing, and she said that made her feel worse than anything. Getting beat up by her drunk father didn't hurt as bad as those people laughing at her."

"Jesus Christ!"

"Oh, that wasn't the worst. Anyway, we got to be sorta friendly, then later on, we got told there was somebody wanted to talk to us, maybe wanting to take us in. Always wondered why they picked us. We met them, everybody was okay with it, or they said they was, next thing, don't ask me how long it was, can't remember, they came and picked us up. But it wasn't long till we found out they weren't nothing like they were first time we met them.

"They were all lovey dovey for a while. Then one day we're sitting at the kitchen table, there's this thing looks like a long metal pipe, copper I think, with two pointy things sticking out on one end, never seen anything like it, and the guy tells me take off my top and I look at him, you know, like what's going on, and he reached over, jerked my shirt up with one hand, picks up this tube thing in the other and presses the end with the prongs into my belly. I felt the jolt of pain unlike anything I'd felt before and I thought I might pass out, it hurt so bad I couldn't even scream. It was a cattle prod, though I didn't know that at the time. Tried to pull away and as I fought I could see him grinning. He was enjoying this.

"Renata, she tried to run out of the kitchen but the woman grabbed her and slapped her, couple times, and Renata, she just started bawling and the woman kept slapping her and telling her shut up. I thought he was gonna kill me, but he stopped. Still grinning, he asked me how did I like that and I couldn't talk and he said, 'From now on I tell you to do something and you don't do it I'm gonna get my little pal here out and what just happened? That's gonna happen again. You just put that in your head and you keep it there, okay?' I can hear him saying that like it was yesterday.

"I froze up. Couldn't move. Couldn't talk. Looked down, I was all wet, peed all over myself. That was the first time, 'cause every day from then on, he'd give me this look and crook his finger at me and when I'd get there, he would do things to me. Things I can't bare to say out loud.

"That was my life. Him abusing me and enjoying it whether I took it or fought it. And he preferred me fighting back 'cause what he really loved was inflicting pain and he knew he was gonna get his way in the end either way.

"That happened every day. And after he'd be grinning at me, and he'd say, 'Boy, that felt really good. How'd that feel for you, honey? You like that as much as I did? Bet you can't hardly wait till tomorrow, can you?'

"About the fourth or fifth time it happened, I said to myself, *This ain't gonna happen to me no more. I don't know who it's gonna happen to, but it ain't gonna be me.* From then on, I just told myself, *It ain't me, I'm not here, I'm somewhere else,* and from then on I never felt him touching me or me touching him. All that did was made him madder. He said hearing me cry was almost as much fun as the rest of it was. No, here's what he said. He said hearing me crying was almost as much fun as the best of it was. The day he said that, I promised myself, I said it ain't gonna matter how long it takes or how it was gonna happen or how I was gonna do it, but I was gonna kill him. I didn't care if I got sent to prison the rest of my life, it couldn't be any worse than it was right then and there, 'cause we were already in jail and I knew we were in hell 'cause he was the devil."

Carlucci had heard about cases of orphans being abused by the people who adopted them, just as he'd heard it about kids in the foster system, but he'd never heard anything as outrageous, as horrible as what he was hearing.

"Okay if I interrupt you for a minute?"

She nodded.

"While this was happening to you, what was happening to my mother?"

"Okay, I'm gonna tell you. She was catching hell from his wife—if they was ever really married. I'll just keep calling her the woman. She was every way just as bad as he was. It's bad. You sure you wanna hear it?"

"Well, I'm not sure I want to, but I think maybe I have to. Might explain a lot. About who she was and how she got the way she was, so yeah, just go ahead and tell me, you don't have to ask me, just say it."

"Well, you put it that way, here goes. The woman had her doing all the house work, the laundry, the ironing, the cleaning, washing the dishes, all that kinda stuff, except the woman, she did the cooking. But the woman told her do everything exactly the way she said to do it, and if she didn't, the woman would make Renata strip and lock her in a cupboard. Renata could be left in there for days, freezing and starving. Sitting in her own filth, begging to be let out. And if the woman was really mad, she'd tell your mother if she didn't do her work the way she wanted, she'd tell me to go get his little friend and she was just as happy to use it on Renata as her husband was to use it on me. And I had to do that. A lot."

"Well, Jesus Christ, was there any way, I mean, did you ever call somebody, try to report them? How'd you get out of there?"

"Can I drink some of your water?"

"Sure, yeah."

Out of nowhere, he saw Fischetti reaching for a glass beside the sink, a vision gone as fast as it had come.

She drank a full glass, filled it again, drank it. "That helped a lot. Thanks. Okay, one day, starting to be summer, can't remember exactly, don't even know what year it was, just remember it was real hot, and he was out in the backyard, sitting in a kind of a lawn chair, his shirt off, there was a cooler, four empty cans on the grass I could see. Budweiser. His eyes were closed, his belly was going up and down. I was pretty sure he was asleep. Then I heard the water turn on upstairs, and I tiptoed up there, bathroom door was open, there she was, naked, getting ready to step into the tub. And I thought, okay, okay, he's asleep, she's getting a bath, it was gonna be then or never.

"Went in their bedroom, went through all the drawers, looking for I didn't know what, whatever I could find. Under all his underwear, I found money, fives, tens, twenties, grabbed them all, stuck them all down in my panties. Two closets in there, first one was just fulla woman stuff, dresses, coats, nothing I wanted, so the other one had the usual man stuff, except for a couple shoe boxes up on a shelf. Pile of shoes on the floor, made me wonder what was in those boxes.

"Got a chair, climbed up careful as I could, didn't want to fall down, make a bunch of noise, bring them both running, so I grabbed the bottom box, all of them came down. Corner of one hit me right under my eye, damn near made me scream. But that one, after it hit me, fell down on the floor, and there was a gun in it and a couple little boxes. Boxes said period twenty-two LR. Didn't know what that was, but I saw right on the gun, printed right on it was a period twenty-two LR. Got so excited, had to bite my lip to keep from hollering.

"I never shot a gun, but I seen some cowboys and Indians movies they showed us, where I met Renata, and I started remembering what all those guys did to make those guns shoot. They'd pull the little thing that was on the back top, they'd pull it back and then they'd pull something underneath, and it'd make noise and a little bit of smoke. Gun wasn't very big. Had a round part in the middle. I tiptoed downstairs, didn't look for Renata, just sat down in the kitchen so I could watch him through the window, started turning that gun every which way, trying to figure it out.

"It was plain which part was the handle, so I turned it upside down, looked at it from the long end, and I saw these roundish gray things on both sides of that middle round part. Then I opened one of the boxes, and they looked like bullets to me, and the short part of each one, it looked the same color as the things on both sides of the round part. Kept messing with it, and the round part in the middle fell out to one side, kept fiddling with it and heard something hit the floor around my feet. I looked down and there was six of the same things that was in the box. So I picked up what was around my feet, and I thought if they fell out, I could put them back in and that's what I did, there was only one way they'd fit. Got them all in, kept fiddling around, finally got the round part back in. Didn't know how I did it, I was just hoping I could do what those cowboys did. Said to myself, right then, I said, 'Okay, you miserable son of a bitch, this is for every time you cranked up that handle.'

"I tiptoed out of the kitchen, there he was, still there, mouth open, snoring. On the way out, I figured if I pulled the thing in the top, back far as it could go, all I had to do was pull the thing my finger just naturally fit around, that had to be how it worked. I walked right up to him, put the end I wasn't holding right up under his nose.

"His eyes opened up, he tried to wave away the part up against his nose, I pulled it away and he got wide awake real quick. Put it back under his nose, and all of a sudden I heard the noise and him scream at the same time. Didn't know what happened, I didn't think I did anything, but I was real happy 'cause the front of his nose was just a mess of blood. I said to him, as smart-assy as I could, I said, 'Was that as much fun for you as it was for me?' And he started to cry, the son of a bitch, started whimpering like a little baby, and I said it again. He just kept on whimpering, and I put the front part of the gun over in front of his left eye, real close. I said, 'Can you see that?' He just kept on whimpering and I said, 'Take a good look, I think you're gonna see this thing go right into your eyeball.' Oh, right then, I was having a good time with him. And then I heard the noise again, just like before, I didn't think I did nothing, but his head just dropped back a little bit. He didn't make no sound, and I tried to hear if he was breathing. Watched his belly for a while see if it was going up and down. It wasn't. Last thing I said to him was, 'How does it feel in there in hell? Meet the devil yet? Won't have no trouble recognizing him 'cause it'll be just like you looking in a mirror.'

"So then I went right up to the bathroom. She was standing up, just holding a towel, didn't know if she heard the noises or if she was anyway just getting out of the tub. Pointed the thing right at her face and told her sit down right where she was in the tub. Didn't make no speech, just waited till she sat down, she started crying too just like him. Whimpering. Pointed the thing right up close to her left eyeball. Pulled the top back thing, and then the I pulled the other thing, underneath, I actually pulled the thing that time that made the noise, but she didn't make any noise. Just slid down the tub, her head sorta fell back a little bit, off to one side, slightly. Watched her belly, see if it was going up and down. It wasn't."

"What did you do then?"

"Well, first thing I had to do was get Renata calmed down. She was sobbing so hard her whole body was shaking. All she would say was I shouldn't have done that. I didn't even know she seen me. Must've come up behind me on the stairs. I said, 'If I didn't do it, you know, don't you? Tomorrow would be the same as yesterday, and yesterday would be the same as the day before that, so you telling me now that's what you want? To keep on like we was? Like every time you did something she didn't like, or you were doing it wrong, you forget what the next thing she said was? Forget all the nights you couldn't get closer to me, huh? How many times you said, tell me how to do what you do, you know, how to say it wasn't happening to you, it was happening to somebody else.' Didn't matter what I said, she wasn't gonna be nobody but Renata."

"Well, Jesus, how'd you get outta there?"

"Gonna sound crazy, but I don't remember much of anything happened after that. Got his wallet and keys outta his pants. They had a car, but only one of them would take it at a time, for groceries and that, usually her. My father, times when he was only half-drunk, he let us kids ride along when he was teaching our oldest brother how to drive, and their car looked a lot like ours, a little bit shinier, but I figured it out, mostly 'cause I talked to my brother a lot. Told Renata, I said, 'Write a note saying we had their permission to drive the car, sign both their names on it.' She wouldn't do it. Would not. So I did it. Wrote the woman's name with my right hand, wrote his name with my left hand.

"Well, I got it running, got it out onto the first road was paved, but pretty soon it just quit, just kinda rolled to a stop, I didn't know why. Then here comes this cop, he was on a motorcycle, asked us if we needed help. I must've said yeah, but I don't remember saying it, or what I said, but he made me get out, he tried to start it, wouldn't start, then he says didn't you look at the gas gauge, no wonder it wouldn't start. Had to show me the gas gauge, then he asked me for my driver's license, and that was something neither one of us thought of. I just thought that note I wrote would be enough. Those cops locked us up for more than a week, till they found out nobody was asking where their car was, and that was that."

"So they found out whose car it was, right? And after they found out whose car it was, how long before you got charged?"

"Not long. Didn't matter. All his money I thought was gonna be enough to get us somewhere, it wasn't even enough—it was a pitiful joke when we heard the judge say how much was the bail bond."

"Well, I don't wanna guess now, but how long was it before my mother said it was all your idea?"

"Well, yes, that's what she did, but I don't hold it against her. Never did. They bullied her, same as they tried to do me. But she was just her, she couldn't stand up to them like I did."

"Jesus," Carlucci said, "that tells me almost more than I thought I would ever wanna know about how she got to be the way she turned out to be—if that even makes any sense. I guess the only thing left to ask is how long did you get and how much of it did you do?"

"They gave me twenty-five to life, no parole till I was sixty."

"Even after you told them what those two did? And you told everybody who asked, right?"

"Well, yeah, sure, told everybody, but that didn't make no difference."

"What, so the public defender you got—he graduate last in his class?"

"Yeah, you could say that, he wasn't real smart. But I forgave him a long time ago. Because, I'll never forget it, Fourth of July, right in the middle of year thirty, this lady lawyer showed up, said she'd been studying my case for a while, and she said, to her mind, I'd been screwed worse than anybody she'd ever heard of. She said, I'll have you outta here within a year, and three years after that, I'll have the state begging for mercy. She said I promise you, we're gonna be rich, you and me, beyond our wildest dreams. I told her I never ever had a wild dream like she said, but she did it. Did everything she said she was gonna do."

Carlucci cleared his throat. "If you don't mind telling me, how much did she get? For you, I mean."

"Every time I say how much, it chokes me up. Almost a half-million dollars. That's what the jury said. And all she took outta that was one hundred thousand dollars. I told her, Jesus, take half, I don't know what to do with this money. Most money I ever saw was what I took outta that sonsabitch's drawer, in there with his underwear.

"But that woman, boy, bad as that sonofabitch was, that's how good she was. Let me come live with her, gave me my own room, took me everywhere she went, let me watch her do what she did, watched TV in the living room with her, hugging me tight every time a thought of him just took over my mind. That alone would've been more than enough, but then she took me to see this man, called him her money guy. And they took me to some kind of salesman, called him a broker or something, and when all three of them were talking, I didn't have no idea what they were talking about, but when they got done, had me to sign a buncha papers, giving him and her power over something, me I think, and after this whole big to-do, the guy told me that for as long as I was satisfied, I'd be getting a check every month for two thousand dollars, but that could be increased at any time. And a couple days later, she took me to her bank, got them to give me a whole buncha checkbooks and registers, she taught me how to write a check and how to write the registers, gave me a little thingamajig so I could do the arithmetic right. Had to show me how to use that, I didn't even know there was such a thing. Shitty as my life had been, boy, I can't tell you how much she turned it all around and upside down."

"So, then, uh, why'd you come looking for my mother?"

"Well, here's the thing. Somebody in the joint tried to tell me, for the longest time, you can't keep hating on people. They said that's like you drinking poison and thinking the person you were hating on was gonna die. The only person gets sick from that is you. And there was way more than one person told me that. Finally, I guess it just sorta sank in. That's what I come to tell her, got the private detective to find her for."

"Wait, you hired a private detective?"

"Yes, well you don't think I would be able to find her on my own? Renata is not that common a first name but I didn't even know what her married name might be. The detective thought he figured it out and thought you might be the best way of reaching her."

"So he checked up on me? Maybe even followed me around?"

"Yes, I didn't think there was anything wrong with that. That's what detectives do. I wasn't trying to intrude but I needed to be sure this was the right Renata. My apologies if you feel I overstepped."

"No, no apologies needed, just a few things clicking into place."

"Like I said, I was trying to make things right, I come to tell Renata I wasn't holding nothing against her, and in fact I was gonna give her a lot of the money I got.

"Being inside was hard for Renata. Real hard. She pretends she's tough, but she ain't. When she was saying I shouldn't have murdered those two, she couldn't stop crying and kept saying God was gonna get us for that, he was gonna send us both to hell. I told her if God sends me to hell for that, then God can go to hell himself. Those two, I'm not gonna call them people, whatever they was, they didn't deserve life. They took our life from us and we never did nothing to them. But Renata, she just couldn't get over that. So I was hoping this time when I talked to her, maybe she'd believe me. And maybe me giving her the money would've helped too. And now it's too late."

———

Carlucci stared into space trying to get his head straight from the conversation with Mary Tomchak. It had been hours ago, and while it explained much from his childhood, it raised more questions still. What kind of mother would she have been if she had been raised in a normal home? Three sharp bangs on the front door forced Carlucci to stop torturing himself.

Franny stood on his front porch with her arms crossed.

He eyed the TV vans and onlookers on the street and sidewalk, they hadn't missed he had a visitor. Fucking vultures.

"I had to find out where we stood. I know it's a lousy time for you but it's been a lousy time for me. You called those EMTs to take me to Mental Health—in a straitjacket! No matter what is happening with you. With your guilt about your mother. It can't be worse than what you've put me through. I need to know where we stand or I am walking and you're never gonna see me again."

"Fran . . ."

"Don't fucking Fran me. Don't try to calm me down or tell me what to do. All I need is for you to tell me where we stand."

"Have you talked to Reseta? "

"You two. Jesus Christ. Forget the both of you. You know what? It's none of your business. Not anymore."

The reporters, sensing an opening, made their move toward them, mics out, as Franny turned, and burned a path through the crowd.

———

"Rugs? Bad news, man."

"Nowicki? Man, for a while now I been thinking bad news is my middle name."

"No, uh-uh, man, no joke. Bad news. My aunt died. You know? Franny's mother?"

"Oh shit. When? Does she know?"

"Not yet. Have to figure out how to tell her. Gonna be bad, no matter what I say."

———

"C'mon in, Rugs," Reseta said. "Have a seat. Wondering how long it was gonna take you to get in here."

"Couldn't have been wondering too much, all the shit in the papers, on TV, fucking word buzzards, they just won't let it alone. One day I don't know when it was—that's another thing, my sense of time, it's all fucked up. So I don't know how long ago this was, I opened the door, reached for the mail, across the street there's two fucking camera trucks over there. I grab the mail, turn around, before I can get back inside, there's people coming at me, two of them got mics in their hands, they're already on the steps, and there's two more behind them, they got cameras. The ones with the mics, they're trying to put theirs in front of my mouth, I get smacked in the mouth, and I said, 'That's it, get the fuck outta here or I'm gonna go get my Beretta'—which was bullshit because it wasn't my gun anymore. It was the department's gun. Had to turn it in. Anyway, they finally figured out I wasn't gonna say anything they wanted hear, so I go inside, ten minutes later who you think is knocking on my door?"

"Franny."

"Whoa! Whoa, man, hold up! How'd you know that?"

"'Cause she said that's what she's gonna do. I said Fran, right now, there's nothing you could do that'd be any worse than that. Knowing what you know about him and his mother, can't you imagine what he's going through? Now?

"So that's how I knew she would show up at your place, I just didn't know when exactly. I shouldn't be telling you this, but just so you know, Rugs, I'd been telling her, repeatedly, emphatically I couldn't help her anymore. She needs meds. She's suffering severe anxiety and depression, and talk therapy was not working for her, at least not with me.

"I told her I already made her an appointment with a psychiatrist I know, told her he'd prescribe the meds she needed and he would also take over her case—I'd had a long talk with him about her. But she said nope, nope, nothing doing, that wasn't what she needed. Okay, I said, I asked her so what is it you think you need?

"Know what she said? It was none of my business. I said, 'Fran, if you don't agree to see the psychiatrist, I've set you up with, I'ma have to call the police and tell them you need to be 302ed as soon as possible.' At which point she said—shouted—'You and Rugs, you're two of a goddamn kind, you think you know everything and nobody else, nobody, could possibly know what you two know and that's bullshit.' She walked out, I called 911. So right now, she's on the third day of a 302—might be a 303. So, Rugs, you look like hell, how you doing?"

"How am I doing? You're joking, right? Except for one little ugly fucking detail, I'm doing just like everybody else, how about you?"

"C'mon, Rugs, you know what I mean."

"Okay, okay, you wanna know? I'll tell you what I think. I think I got post-traumatic stress syndrome, or disorder, or whatever it's called. I got it, 'cause those are just another bunch of words for regret and grief and guilt. But lemme finish with this fiasco on my porch. So, while I'm trying to get those people gone, here comes this priest, looks like he just graduated from junior high school."

"Wait a minute, what about Fran? She still there?"

"Hey, man, I was surrounded by these word vultures, they backed down off my porch but they were still there, still on the sidewalk. She was there, then she wasn't. Anyway, here comes this priest. And he starts talking over the word vultures, tells them be quiet, he wants to talk to me, and they look at him, and that's what they do. They stop yakking at me, they start listening to him—"

"Probably all Protestants, right?"

"Some other time, Jim, maybe that would be funny. Who knows? But Jim, listen, here's what he says to me, this priest. He says I can come talk to him anytime I want, his office door will be open to me no matter what I have to say. Anything that's bothering me, anything at all. I said, yeah? That's really good to know, padre, but I told him, I said, I know a little something about you priests. For example, you happen to hear anything about that grand jury report, the one just came out a little while ago? The one that said all over the state, all over Pennsylvania, there were more than three hundred of you priests, you been messing with kids. Messing with them in a really crappy way, you know, sexually? And even worse than that, turns out there were all these bishops, all their bosses, all those fuckers knew that shit was going on and you remember what their solution was? Their solution was just move those pervs around, just transfer them from one parish to another, and the only people they were telling were the priests that were still there, in their new church. But that didn't matter, 'cause they were all in on it.

"His eyes, Jim, man they started getting big, and I said, you know how I know about this? I'm gonna tell you how. I know about this because when I was eleven, my mother decided not only was I gonna go to church with her every day, which she'd been dragging me to since first grade, but I should also start going to confession—and you know which church I'm talking about, right? It's the same church you just got what? Promoted into? The one you just came out of, right there down there on the next block? Yeah that one. She'd been going there every day, every goddamn day, and then she starts going to confession—every week. You understand, I didn't know what any of that was about. But she did.

"So she's going to confession at least once a week, and then one day, not only was she dragging me to church, she gets me in there and instead of telling me to stay with her, she starts pointing at this door, right inside the church there, she's telling me go get in that little room right there, go on, get in there and kneel down, pretty soon, there's kinda like a little window in there, on one side, and that'll slide open, and somebody will be talking to you. That's the priest. He's gonna ask you some questions, and you better not try to tell him any lies, 'cause he'll know right away if you're trying to lie. Whatever he asks you, you tell him the truth. And when he gets done listening to all your answers, he'll tell what you have to do after you get outta that room. Probably won't be too much, probably just be a couple Hail Marys and Our Fathers, that's all.

"And right there's when it got bent, 'cause I told my mother I didn't know what those were. And she grabbed me by the shoulders and started shaking me real hard and bent over and got her face real close to mine, she started screaming 'They're the prayers we're all supposed to know by heart and you're supposed to be learning them in school and don't you dare try to tell me you don't know them.' And all I could say was ain't I supposed to always tell you the truth? And she said I was a smart-mouth little shit, and I didn't see it coming, but she slapped me so hard, I fell down sideways, fell on my hip and elbow. I was something—I didn't know what I was, shocked is what I'd say now. Shocked and so mad I couldn't catch my breath. And then, there I was, looking at that priest, and Jim, something just told me I left out the whole point of why I was telling you what I'd been telling him.

"Oh, got it. Anyway by that time he was trying to leave and he got all tangled up in his own feet, falls backward, and damn if he doesn't hit his head. And I'm thinking oh shit, not again. I start shouting, get up, get the fuck up, and he does, gets up, he's holding his head, turns around, starts walking, then he's running, and I'm thinking, what the hell's this priest think I have to talk to him about? What's he gonna say? After he hears the rest of what I got to say? Gonna tell me go to Mass? Light some candles? Go to confession? Pray the Rosary? I been hearing that shit from every old lady around here—including my mother for Chrissake—for I don't know how long. Pray the Rosary?

"That stopped me, right there, I said, nah, no fucking way I'm gonna pray the Rosary. That's what always started the shit with Hitler's daughter. Sister Mary Michael. The Rosary."

Reseta held up his hand. "Before I get into what you were saying about that priest your mother wanted you to confess to, what about the priest you were just talking about? He make it back to Mother of Sorrows?"

"Oh yeah, when he went down, the word vultures, what they saw was, you know, hey, here's a fresh body, so they chased him down there. He just barely beat them inside. Don't know what kept them from going in after him, but they didn't."

"Uh huh. Rugs, whoa, hold up, wait a minute. Why'd you say what you said to him? You've never said anything at all about any of this before—not in all the time you been talking to me. You never said anything like this about your mother. Of all the things you could've said to that priest, that's what you said? Why?"

"Why? 'Cause he was a priest, that's why. A fucking priest!"

"A fucking priest? Man, Rugs, I'm confused. Where's this coming from?" Carlucci looked at the floor. Then up at Reseta. Looked at him for a long moment.

"Man, I hope I'm not wrong about you."

"Hope you're not wrong? About me? What's that mean?"

"I wanna tell you something, but I'm not sure. I don't know. Never told this to anybody, and I mean nobody. Never."

"It's that bad?"

"I'm taking a big chance here, man."

"Well, Rugs, whatever it is, you know I'm never gonna repeat it—"

"Okay, okay, okay, here it is. Sixth grade, my mother, she's been taking me to church, every day after school since I was in the third grade. Soon as I'd get home from school, she was waiting, c'mon, let's go, we have to go, hurry up. And off we'd go, to Mother of Sorrows, we'd get in there, there's this priest waiting. He's sitting on one of the benches in the front. My mother, she takes me up there where he is, says something to him, and soon as she stops talking, he starts talking, and smiling and talking, asking me about school, how do I like it, what am I learning, who's my favorite teacher, am I learning about all the sins, and all the, uh, what's the opposite of sins? Virtues, right?

"Same dumb questions every day. One day, after we get down where the priest is, my mother picks me up, sits me down beside him, then she walks away. I turn around, she goes and sits down, way in the back by the front door. Right away, he starts telling me, 'It's okay, she's okay where she is, don't worry, Jesus, he'll be watching out for her, you don't have to be afraid, you know Jesus is watching out for you too, don't you?'

"I remember looking at him, and I'm thinking, I'm pretty sure at that time, all I knew about Jesus was when it was his birthday, everybody would be giving each other presents, except in our house—but that's another story—and I couldn't figure out why if it was his birthday, why wasn't he getting the presents, you know? And the rest of the time people would be talking about him, they would be talking about how he was dead, and couple days later, he wasn't dead anymore. Completely mixed me the fuck up.

"But this priest, he just keeps going on and on like that every day. Then one day, I turn around and I don't see my mother. And he starts right up with the don't worry, nothing to be afraid of, she's all right, don't forget, you know, Jesus is right there beside her, nothing bad can happen to her, just like he won't let nothing bad happen to you.

"Jim, man, I gotta stop for a while. This crap, too much of it's coming back at me, too fast. And anyway I gotta piss." When Carlucci came back from the bathroom, Reseta was on the front half of his chair.

"Still okay with this? Still feeling okay with telling me?"

"Yeah, I think. So far, anyway."

"You sure?"

"Sure I don't know, but at least I won't have to piss for a while."

"You're good enough to keep at it?"

"Yeah, except I forgot where I was."

"The priest was telling you your mother was gonna be all right—"

"Yeah, right, next thing I know, he just picked me up and plopped me down on his lap and he starts in with what flavor popsicle I like, he couldn't remember, was it strawberry or cherry or banana. And then, the next thing he does, he's tickling me and not easy either. And I really didn't like that, 'cause even though it hurts you can't stop yourself from laughing, and people see you laughing they think it's okay, 'cause one of my uncles used to do that to me till my dad told him knock it off. That was the only time my dad stood up for me.

"Then, and when he got into it with her 'cause he wanted to know why she was taking me to church every day, and I remember him saying, bad enough you're doing that and then he finds out—and I never did find out how he found out—she's trying to get me to go to confession. I remember him yelling at her I was eleven years old, what did I do was so bad I had to confess to a priest? They really got into it over that. She was telling him that's how smart you are, you think just 'cause he's eleven he can't do nothing bad, you don't even know how smart-alecky he talks to me, and besides that, you're like a lotta people, you don't know what kinda stuff kids eleven years old can do, terrible stuff. You're never around to hear him, and he said, 'Yeah, I'm not around 'cause I'm working all the time, trying to get all the overtime I can get to pay for everything we have to have around here.' And she said, 'Oh yeah, right, I guess you think I'm the queen of Norwood.' Oh man, they were going at it for I can't remember how long, a long time. That was the first time—the only time—I ever saw him, you know, not back down from her. About me."

"So, uh, Rugs, this is, man, I almost don't know what to say. I had no idea about, uh, you know, you and the priest. Makes me think for sure you should be seeing the psychiatrist, not me. I know him, Rugs, he's good."

"No, no, man, no, I gotta stick with you. Go with a shrink, a new guy? Uh-uh, I don't wanna have to talk that much. With you, we got all this history, here, Rocksburg, on the job, the army, you in 'Nam, me in 'Nam. With a new guy, you know, just catching him up? It'd take forever. We just need some time, that's all, you and me. I'm okay sticking with you, really."

"If you say so, but, Rugs, you can't let this slide. This stuff with you? And the priest? You gotta deal with this."

"Yeah, okay, okay, I hear you. But I only told you a small part of it. There's a lot more. And it's a lot worse. And most of it—I'm gonna tell you right now, I'm not gonna talk about it, not with you, not with anybody, ever again. Whatever I say now, this is all I'm gonna say, you hear me? You ready?"

"I hear you, Rugs, I do. Go on, I'm ready."

"Okay. That priest is why I joined the army. That priest is why I wanted to kill somebody. And now this next thing I'm gonna say, this is really confusing. It's still confusing. 'Cause I have asked myself over and over, how the hell could I have known at that time, as young as I was, that I couldn't kill that priest. How did I know at that time, if I did that, how'd I absolutely know I couldn't get away with it? And how did I know I had to go someplace, find some place I could go and do that and get away with it? Sometimes I think I could not have known where that was, you hear me? But if I didn't, then why did I enlist? In the army, why?"

"I hear you, Rugs. I'm listening."

"Okay, okay. Where was I? Oh. I knew there had to be a place where I could kill somebody and get away with it. I know now no way I didn't find out where that was till I was in high school. That I know for sure. There was only one place, one way I could do that and not go to jail. And that was in the army, in a war. That's why I joined the army, man. Okay, fast forward, I got over there, 'Nam, and one day I was in a hootch, in there with half my squad, they're doing what I was supposed to be doing, you know, looking for weapons, ammo, intel, whatever, and the worst part is my guys got four of their guys, all VCs, on their knees in the dirt with their hands behind their heads, but I got this one guy looking at me, square in the eyes, hard, like what you gonna do, big bad American guy, wanna kill me, maybe?

"He didn't even have a weapon. He had a 47 in front of him, but it didn't have a magazine in it, and there I was, had my weapon in my hands, loaded not locked—means ready to fire, and I leveled—"

"Rugs, Jesus, I know what it means. Opposite of locked and loaded. I was there too, remember?"

"No, I know you were there, I'd never forget that. I was just saying, you know, I had it leveled on his forehead, just because of the way he was looking at me, and I was thinking, you know, this is why you're here, Carlucci, this is why you're here instead of doing life. For killing that priest! Here's this grubby enemy of America, he's sitting here staring at me, and no doubt I know what he is. He's a sub, a stand-in, second teamer, for the priest! Kill him! Press the trigger back! Four pounds of pressure, maybe four and a half, practically nothing at all, and he's gonna learn the hard way, if there really is a heaven—or wherever those Buddhists go, I don't know, I remember thinking that. Exactly that.

"And the next thing I'm thinking? The very next thing? I couldn't do it. Could not press the trigger back. I started to laugh. Started to cry. Both. 'Cause right then, bigger than shit, I knew how fucked up I was. How fucked up my thinking was. How in the fuck could I have let that priest fuck me up like that? And bigger than shit, man, bam—it wasn't that priest! It was you! You let him! No, not you, Jim—me! I mean me! I let him get in my head! And I couldn't believe it! Could not believe I let him get in my head so fucking deep, I, me, I'm sitting there, looking at this grungy fuck, getting ready to kill him! Because there we were, Jim, all three of us, me, him, and the priest, all of us, same time, same place. And then we weren't. And don't ask me how I got out of there, 'cause I have no idea. The whole the rest of the time I was in the army, the whole rest of the time I was in 'Nam, it was nothing but a big bunch of muddy fuzz. I don't remember when I got out, where I got out, all I knew was one day, I was working at Kmart. In the fucking garden department. Where Hitler's daughter told my mother that was gonna be the best I could ever do. Or be.

"Ah, forgot where I was again. Oh, yeah, I didn't tell you what that fucking priest did to me, right? About my mother taking me to church every day?"

"Yes, you did."

"Did I tell you about her making me go to confession?"

"No, I think you started to, but then you had to take a leak."

"Okay, okay, here goes. Took me to church every day, then when I get in sixth grade that's when she decides I gotta start going to confession. Finally she quit dragging me there every day, but then after the first time I got in the cubicle with that priest and found out what that shit was all about, she had to start dragging me again, and one day she opens that little door and she pushes me in there, tells me I gotta go tell him all my sins. And I'm saying what are you talking about, what sins?"

"You went to catechism, Rugs, right? You didn't know?"

"Sure I went, same as you, same as everybody, who paid attention to that shit?"

"Sorry, shouldn't have interrupted."

"No, the sins she was talking about was how I talked back to her, how I didn't put my clothes away right. But forget that, let me get back to the priest. I don't remember exactly when he started talking about popsicles, but pretty soon that's all he was talking about, do I like them, what flavor do I like, you know, strawberry, cherry, banana. Next thing I know I'm on his side of the closet, I'm on his lap, and he's tickling me. I hate being tickled. Already told you that, right? Anyway that's what he was doing, and he was saying, you like that, don't you? Feels good, don't it? He did that tickling shit for about a week, then the real shit started. Next time I go around to his side, he pulls me in, he got his pee thing out, you know, the thing he pees through. That's what I called it then, I know, sounds stupid now but it don't matter when I heard all the other words for it, 'cause right then that's what I was looking at, and he's asking

216

me what flavor do I think it looks like. And I remember thinking there's something wrong with that, I mean, what flavor does it look like? And next thing I know he's holding my hand and he's using his hand to rub my hand all over the end of what he pees through.

"And the next thing he's moaning and his middle starts going up and down and all of a sudden there's this slimy white stuff all over my hand, and he starts smiling at me, and then he tries to put his arms around me and, man, I just squirmed, squirmed as hard as I could, I got away from him, and ran home and I was crying the whole way.

"And when I get there, there's my mother, and she's grinning at me and asking me did I feel better confessing my sins. And I said no, no I don't. All I feel is icky. I don't know where I heard that word icky, but it sounded exactly like that was the way I felt. And I'm not gonna tell you any more than that, Jim. Uh-uh, nothing doing, no more. 'Cause it just got worse from there. And I'm pretty sure you know what I'm talking about."

"Jesus, Rugs, I almost don't know what to say. Except, you have got to see the guy I told you about. You really got to see him, 'cause what you just told me, man, this is way over my pay grade. You need help, Rugs, 'cause it's eating you up, but I'm not good enough."

"I get it, Jim, I'll go see him, I will. But my mother, man, down in my gut, I just got this real bad feeling I'm never ever gonna get over her. That scares me, man. Really scares me. When that woman showed up and she told me what they went through, what those pervs did to them, Jesus, man, I tried to think, you know, did I ever hear her say anything about that? Nothing. Never anything remotely about that. Some things about her make more sense now but it don't make anything easier. All she ever did was boss everybody around, my dad, me. Man, I used to think, why'd he ever marry her?"

"You remember them ever celebrating their anniversary?"

"Huh? Their anniversary? Hell, we barely celebrated Christmas. I'd hear kids talking about what they got for their birthday, I'd say why'd you get something for your birthday, I never got nothing. They'd look at me, they'd laugh, tell me I got the worst mom and dad they ever heard of—and far as that goes, I never heard my dad say anything about anybody in his family ever doing anything like that."

"Well, Rugs, I hesitate to say this, but it might be a good idea, and I emphasize might, before you start with the doc I want you to see, it might be helpful for you to find out when they got married and how long after that you were born."

"What? What're you saying? You saying what I think you're saying? You saying he knocked her up? Had to marry her? That's what you're saying, ain't it? And that's what you tell me? Before I start with this new guy?"

"Hold up, Rugs, wait, wait, I'm just suggesting, that's all, because I think it never hurts to, uh, separate what we're convinced we know about who got us here and then find out, you know, we have to have some evidence, that's all I'm saying. You know, Rugs, how when you were sure you made a case and then you had to lay it out in the DA's office, what'd they say, huh? Let's see what you got, you know, the evidence, that's all, I'm saying the same thing."

"Oh, yeah, sure, that's what you say you're saying, but that ain't what I'm hearing. What I hear you saying, Jesus Christ, you're saying I'm gonna be working this case the rest of my life."

Reseta hung his head for a moment, cleared his throat, then shrugged. "Yeah, Rugs, it doesn't make me happy saying it, not in the least, but I think that's what I am saying. And I can't believe what I'm gonna say now because I don't think I have ever said this to anybody before, but . . . I sincerely wish you luck."

"Wish me luck? Huh? That's the best you got? Wish me fucking luck? Well, at least you didn't say what a lotta people would say, you know, that *vaya con salud, vaya con dios* bullshit."

"Oh, Rugs, man, no, I would never say that. Not to you." Reseta held out his right hand. Carlucci took it, shook it, covered it with his left hand. His eyes filled up, tears streamed down his cheeks.

"Jim, man, can't tell you how much I appreciate what you just said. I will go see your guy. Promise. But, man, let me say this, okay? Your pay grade, it's higher than you think. Way higher."

———

"C'mon in, Rugs. What's up?"

"Remember you told me to see when my parents got married, remember that? And then you said see when I was born, find out how long after they got married?"

"Sure I remember, what—oh man, you look like hell. What's up?"

"You're not gonna believe this. You're not. 'Cause I don't believe it."

"Okay, okay, sit down, man, sit sit sit, you're looking worse by the minute."

"Nah, I don't wanna sit. Worse? Okay, wanna hear worse? So where do I start looking—here, right? Wrong. No record of their marriage, no record of me being born, not in this county. My mother must have had a copy of my birth certificate at some point, probably a marriage certificate, but I sure as shit can't find them. They tell me I got to talk to the people at the Division of Vital Records. It's up in New Castle, they give me their number, I call them up, give them what I want, they said, you know, okay, gonna take a while, blah blah. I wait a couple days, call them, I listen. Can't believe what they're telling me. No record of anybody named Angelo Carlucci getting married—they went back eighty years, which is what I told them, go back at least that far. Nothing. They tell me it would help if I knew my mother's maiden name, no guarantee, but that would help. I said, I'm sure it would help, but I got no clue. I never heard either one of them, him or her, ever say what her name was before they got married, so I'm thinking, that's okay, the woman who came after my last visit to the ER, told me the shitstorm they went through, all I gotta do is call her, right? She told me her birth name, Tomchak, yeah. But she never told me and I never asked her what her name is now.

"I don't know if I ever told you, every time my mother wanted to get on my case, you know, her way of busting my balls, here's what she'd say. 'Some detective you are. What smart guys hired you?'

"So I remember the woman told me they both came from Butler County, some small town, small mining town named, uh, Lyndora, I think. So I call Butler County Courthouse, rings one time, I hang up, 'cause what are they gonna say, right? Call Vital Records, right? So there I am, thinking the hell they went through with those pervs, and I can hear my mother, like she's standing right next to me, 'Some detective you are. Who's the smart guys hired you?'"

Reseta got up, started walking toward Carlucci with his arms out.

"Stop! Stop right there! You look like you're getting ready to give me a hug, don't you try to hug me! Don't you fucking dare! If there was ever anybody, anybody! Who didn't deserve a hug, it's me!"

Reseta turned quickly back to his desk, grabbed a Post-it pad off it, wrote something on it, held it toward Carlucci's chest and pressed it onto his shirt. "Rugs, listen to me, please listen. That's the number of the guy I want you to see. Call him, promise me you'll call him, okay? Promise!"

"Yeah. Yeah yeah yeah, I'll call him."

Carlucci went home, drank two glasses of water, dropped onto his recliner, immediately felt all cramped up. He scrambled back up, went looking for his Beretta. Shook his head as though shaking it would clear up whatever was in there. Was there something in there? Was it his mind or something clogging up his mind? Whatever it was, he couldn't say it. What he did remember was his Beretta wasn't his anymore. It belonged to the department. He'd turned it in. He remembered handing it to Nowicki.

He wondered if he had really retired. Did I really do that? Retire? Who did I retire to? I don't remember retiring to somebody. Just filled out some forms. Tried to remember who he gave them to. Couldn't remember giving them to anybody. He wondered what he would do tomorrow. He wondered, if he did something, would it be something worth doing or would he be doing it because it was the only thing he could think of to do. He felt something on his shirt. He pulled it off and looked at it. It was a small square piece of yellow paper. Had a telephone number on it. He remembered Reseta gave it to him, pasted it on his shirt. He looked around, wasn't sure what he was looking for, but then saw his phone on the table just inside the front door. Yeah. This is the number for the guy he wanted me to talk to.

He touched the numbers slowly, carefully, he heard ringing, then after a moment, a woman's voice announced that he had reached the office of a doctor whose name he was sure he'd heard from someone. Reseta. Yes. The woman was saying that she was sorry but no one was available to take his call, but his call was very important to them, and at the sound of a tone he could leave a message saying his name, his age, his phone number, and the reason for his call, and a member of the doctor's staff would get back to him as soon as possible.

A tone sounded, like tones he had been hearing for many years. When it stopped, he said, "This is Ruggiero Carlucci." He spelled both names slowly and distinctly. Then he said, "A clinical psychologist wrote your number on a little piece of sticky paper and stuck it on my shirt. He made me promise to call you. He said you were good. I hope you are 'cause a little while ago, I went looking for a gun I returned to the police department of the city of Rocksburg, where I used to be on the job, which I'm not anymore, which means I didn't find the gun. I think I'm glad I didn't find it. I hope you are as good as Jim Reseta says you are. Please return my call."

Then he said his phone number, slowly and distinctly, and pushed the button he thought would end his call.

It did. He went back to his recliner, sat in it, leaned back, pushing it into a kind of bed, and then he waited, hoping he wouldn't have to wait too long. Hitler's daughter and the priest, whose name Carlucci vowed to never say to anyone, had ended any belief he might have had in God, the Pope, the Roman Catholic Church, and in all of Christianity for that matter, but he still hoped. He wondered where and when he had found hope. He felt certain he'd found it the moment he learned in 'Nam he could not press the trigger of his M16, could not murder a sub, a stand-in, a second stringer, an enemy of America any more than he could murder a priest.

Hope, Carlucci thought, was good no matter what anybody else might say. Hope was good because it was always there, always willing, able, and ready to help. No need to bow, kneel, cross yourself a certain way, or put money in a collection basket. Hope was good just 'cause it was free.

2012

"Rugs, any change in the way you've been feeling?"

"No. The same. Shitty."

"What are you thinking about?"

"What else? My mother."

"Any more thoughts about the mail? Last session you'd just found it."

"Yeah. The mail. Three drawers full. Three fucking drawers."

"Anything other than the solicitations?"

"Oh yeah. Thank you bullshit, thanks for your last gift, see if you can find it in your heart to send more. Use the enclosed envelope blah blah blah."

"Anything other than religious ones?"

"Oh sure. They sell your address, make a little more that way, you know how it goes. The missions this, the missions that, the brothers, the sisters, feed the starving, make the poor rich, make the fat thin, and every fuckin' one of them's a 501(c)(3). Tax-dodging motherfuckers."

"That really bothers you, doesn't it? Charitable organizations."

"Question is why doesn't it bother you?"

"I think the question might be why do you think you never found the mail before?"

"I told you, I wanna sell the house. It's fucking haunted."

"That's not what I asked you. It's haunted?"

"Okay okay okay, I'm haunted. Fact is, who wants to buy a house, first thing you gotta do is rent a dumpster soon as you move in. Who wants to do that? I don't wanna do it and I been doing it for it feels like forever to clean it up. And then I gotta find this goddamn dresser? And if finding it's not bad enough, I don't ever remember seeing it before, how can that be?"

"You're asking me?"

"No I'm not asking you. It's just . . . what I don't get is, uh, all the postmarks, most recent one I found is 2007, which means she was using my money, which means she was going through my pants while I was asleep, and the thank you notes, they were thanking her for a dollar, dollar and a half, Christ, one was for a quarter. She puts a quarter in an envelope, sticks a forever stamp on it and puts it in the box, mails it to these fuckin' pervs."

"And you, Rugs, you're still feeling guilt for what you've managed to convince yourself was murder because of what—"

"I know I know I know I know I know all the shit you're gonna say about how fucked up I am because I can't forget or forgive myself for knocking her down with the door—and worse, how

I can't forget or forgive her for thinking she set me up with that perv priest."

"Couldn't have said it more accurately."

"What? We're talking accuracy now? Hold up now, wait! Jim Reseta sent me to you 'cause he said you were good and 'cause he thought trying to straighten me out was way over his pay grade."

"So you've said."

"Yeah? Well, we been at this for a year now, more, not sure when we started, but far as I can tell we're still talking the same shit we were talking when I got here."

"Can't disagree."

"Aw fuck your can't disagree—when's anything gonna change?"

"Rugs, I say again what I've said before, I am who I am and I am what I do, nothing more. The change you want, the change you insist you want, is not something I can put in a syringe and inject into your arm. Any change to be made here is not going to be made by anybody but you. I've prescribed the meds for your anxiety and your depression. Unless you're not being truthful, you're still taking them, right?"

"Yeah, I am."

"Then what do you think we're doing here?"

"Beats the shit outta me."

"Yes, I'm certain it does. And it will continue to do that until and unless you recognize that you are not a murderer, that you did not cause your mother's death by an act of violence, and that she did not cause that priest to molest you. Tell me, do you think for even a moment that your mother knew what that priest was going to do to you? And further that she made it possible for him to do that, and indeed, encouraged him to do that? Do you believe in your mind and heart that your mother intended to do that? And did in fact do that? Tell me, Rugs, I want to hear—"

"Fuck no!" He burst into sobs, covered his face with his hands, and squeezed.

"Of course you don't. Listen to me, are you listening?"

Rugs nodded, still hiding his face, still sobbing. Stopped squeezing.

"I want to see you in two days. Don't want you to wait a week to come back here, do you understand? Same time of day, same hour, but two days, Rugs. Don't forget, okay? You can stay here as long as you like, as long as you think you have to; my next appointment cancelled. But, Rugs, listen to me. You're braver than you believe, you're stronger than you seem, you're smarter than you think. Right now you think you're everything but those qualities. But it will get better, Rugs. It will. I can help you. I know I can. And I will."

"Hey, wait a minute. You know what? You're telling me a kid story. I heard that stuff before, that braver than you believe, that stronger than you're something. I can't remember what, can't remember where but I heard that before, but I know I did."

"I'm sure you did, Rugs. It is from a kid's story. Lots of people have heard those words. They're very famous words, from a very famous book. Winnie the Pooh."

"Well why're you telling me that now? Winnie the what?"

"The pooh."

"The fuck we in here? Story time, at the, uh, at the library?"

"No. We're here, we're here now, but you're also way deep in the there and then, and now, while we're here, suddenly you wanna know why we are because you want with everything in you to get to the there and then."

"How much you getting paid for this—whatever this is you're doing right now?"

"That matters to you? Now?"

"Yeah it matters. You starting this kid shit, I'm starting to wonder what I'm doing here."

"I'll tell you now, Rugs, what I tell everybody else who asks me the same question, the one you just asked. I say that those words are some of the kindest words ever written, because Christopher Robin is talking to his friend who's down, down really really low, and he's trying to tell him how brave he is, how strong he is, how smart he is, all the things his friend thinks he isn't, and what amazes me is how many people I see day in, day out, week in, week out, year after year, people who have never heard those words, not from anybody, not in their whole lives, has anybody ever said those words to them, and they react almost exactly the way you did. They get indignant, why am I using words from a kid's book? Do I look like a kid to you? Is that what you think I am, really? Because I have to spend the next two, or three, or four sessions explaining that words don't mean less just because they're plain old everyday words, words we all use. They were written by a father to his son, a child. Does that make those words childish? Does it, Rugs? I had a patient once told me he didn't want to hear childish words, he was an adult and he had adultish problems, and goddammit he was only gonna pay for adultish therapy."

"Yeah, well, it's not easy listening to your shrink telling you what somebody says in a kid's book."

"Fair enough, Rugs. I hear you just like I heard him. But just so we're both on the same page, I won't spend any time next session explaining those words to you, understand? Because I know you know what they mean."

Rugs shrugged. "Maybe I do. Yeah, I think so, yeah."

"Good. Oh, I almost forgot, I finally got around to calling Jim Reseta, thanked him for recommending you to me. Don't know why it took me so long. Here's what I want you to know. He's your friend, Rugs. Stay friendly. With him, with all the friends you can make. You can't do this by yourself, Rugs, no matter how much people who think they mean well think you ought to be able to. The grief, the guilt, most people I see think you have to be in a war to get PTSD. When I tell them war is here now, it was there then, it's anywhere and everywhere, they start to get the fidgets, and then when I say most of the time guns are seldom required, they look like for sure they picked the wrong doctor, like I should be sitting where they are. But, uh, that just goes with the territory. Remember now, two days, don't forget."

"I won't. Two days, I'll be here. I'll be here then. Probably still trying to figure out how to get from then to wherever the hell it is I think I'm going. Or wanna go. Or think anything's gonna be changed just 'cause I got there."

"As I said—"

"Yeah yeah yeah it's up to me."

"As I said, Rugs, stay as long as you think you have to. And if by some chance you find yourself praying, or even wanting to, do it. It won't hurt. But whatever you do, try not to bring your mother into it, okay? That will be hard, I know, but try."

"Okay, Doc, I'll try, but I remember telling Jim Reseta once, when he said I had to look at this thing with my mother like it was a case I was trying to make to a DA, I told him I get that, but it felt like I was gonna be working it the rest of my life, and I think, no matter how much we talk here, I'm still gonna have to look at it like it's the coldest case I'm ever gonna work."

"Rugs, it might sound strange, but that's the most optimistic thing I've heard you say. We might finally be getting somewhere. Oh, when you leave, don't pull the door shut too tight. For some goofy reason it locks when I do that. Two days. Don't forget."

"Yeah, yeah, I won't."

Rugs stayed for almost a half hour, struggling to think of something he might be able to say was praying, but every struggle brought more struggles with his mother, with Sister Mary Michael, with the priest he couldn't murder.

He started to leave. Got as far as the doorway. Stood in the middle there, running his hands over the wood and metal on both sides. It started to feel like a door that belonged in a jail. When he told Jim Reseta about standing there, Reseta asked how long he'd stood there. Carlucci said he couldn't remember. "Why'd you wanna know that?"

"'Cause it's you."

"'Cause it's me? C'mon, man. Ain't you gonna ask me if I pulled the door shut?"

"Did you?"

"Who's the psychologist here, you or me?"

Reseta smiled, shook his head, said, "I know that what I'm gonna say is probably the most unprofessional words I've ever said, but you are one crazy fucker, Rugs. If I knew how to write, I'd write a book about you."

"Yeah? You wanna know crazy, Jim? It's you wanting to do that, that's what's fucking crazy. I'm going to Muscotti's. You coming?"

"Can't. Got somebody coming. First session. Said he knows you. Anthony Carpilotti. Bringing his daughters."

"Aw man, finally. Good for him. What I'm gonna say next, don't tell him, okay? Figure out some way to, you know, give him a good price."

"A good price? What? You think I'm selling used cars here? No, I'm not gonna say you even suggested that—this is my business, Rugs, not yours. See you next week, same time."

———

Dear Rugs,

I didn't put a return address on the envelope, and I don't live where I mailed it from because I don't want to be found. I wish I knew a softer way to say that. I don't want to hurt you, but I don't want any confusion, or any more than there already is. I wish I could still say it was all on you, but after thinking about this for three years and talking to a really good, really smart friend, I had to accept what she said, which is I was just as much a part of the problem as you were. It's really hard for me to write that. Even now.

When the cops you called knocked on my door, I was stunned, I couldn't believe you had called them, and even worse that you ordered them to take me to Mental Health. When those cops walked in, it felt like you kicked me in the stomach. I don't have any words for how much that hurt. And then when we got up there and the door opened and there you were, I felt so betrayed, and I couldn't believe it was you who betrayed me.

The first couple years after Mamont got shut down, those were hard, really hard, the hardest of my life. I got sent to three different group homes, the second one was worse than the first one. The third one was different, not much better but different. That's where I met the woman who is the mother of my really smart friend.

The only way I could get through the first two homes was to just think of you and the anger and the blame just poured out of me. My friend said how could I miss, the target on your back was as big as the side of a building. But then, crazy as this is going to sound, she started asking what kind of weapon I was using. Was it a rifle? What kind? Turned out she knows a lot about rifles. Her whole family does. Her father, mother, sister, they all shoot rifles, but only just at paper. They're not hunters, they don't kill anything.

My friend started out with a BB gun, a Red Ryder she called it, but she quit using that one because it was only accurate out to about ten yards. And she wanted to shoot the rifles like her parents and her sister shot. Her sister was on the high school rifle team and they used rimfire .22s. Her parents belong to the Civilian Marksmanship Program. All the rifles they shoot have been used by members of the US military. Her parents shoot in competitions all over the Northeast USA and so do she and her sister. She said every weekend is like a vacation. And this is really going to surprise you. I have a rifle, my own rifle. It's an M16. When I told her father you were in Vietnam he said mine was probably just like the one you carried when you were there. Once I actually wondered if maybe it had been yours. No, I didn't wonder that for very long.

They also own part of a gun store, they sell rifles, pistols, shotguns, all kinds, ammo too. I work in their office part-time. Also work twenty-four hours a week at a CVS pharmacy. I'm not getting rich but I'm a long way from starving. Mostly I'm okay because of the money I got for the house.

I'm guessing my cousin didn't say anything about the house, did he? He found me, I don't know how but he did. He asked me if he could tell you, and I said no. Period. He never said another thing about that. He told me he knew two people wanted to buy the house, a woman and her boyfriend. He told them it wasn't his it was mine, and he didn't want to get so involved I might think he was trying to get something out of it, so he vouched for a salesman he said wouldn't rip me off, and that's who sold it to the woman and her boyfriend.

The woman who's the mother of my good friend was in charge of the last group home I was in. She couldn't wait to retire, the job was just eating her up, that's how we got friendly, I told her how my job was doing the same to me. I didn't say anything much to her about you. It's her daughter who I talk to about you. She's my friend, and she really is smart. We can talk about anything, and she's not even thirty .

I don't know if I'm ever gonna be able to forgive you, Rugs, but I'm trying, I really am. I hope some day you can do the same for me. We sure screwed up, didn't we? My friend said to make sure I put that sentence in, more for me than for you.

The hardest part of all was the only way I was allowed to leave Mamont to be at Mom's funeral was a policeman had to be holding my arm. That's how bad things got in there, how bad I got in there. I'm still thanking God that cop wasn't from Rocksburg. Some of my relatives asked me who he was and I said he was my newest special friend. And yes, that's what I used to say about you. More than once. That's one more thing you have to forgive me for. Please try. Even if you don't or can't, just try.

Yours truly,

Fran